# The Dancing Girl and the Turtle

## Karen Kao

Published by Linen Press, London 2017
8 Maltings Lodge
Corney Reach Way
London
W4 2TT
www.linen-press.com

A CIP catalogue record for this book is available from the British Library.

Cover photograph: © www.arcangel.com
Cover design: Louise Santa Ana / Zebedee Design, Edinburgh
Typeset in Sabon by Zebedee Design, Edinburgh
Printed and bound by Lightening Source

ISBN 9780993599705

# About the Author

© Maurits Bos

Karen Kao is the child of Chinese immigrants who settled in the United States in the 1950s. After a long, fulfilling career as a corporate lawyer in the United States and the Netherlands, Karen returned to her first love of writing and the stories she heard as a child of Old Shanghai. *The Dancing Girl and the Turtle* is the result. Karen is a poet, short story writer and essayist whose work can be found in *Jabberwock Review*, *Cha: An Asian Literary Journal* and her blog at www.inkstonepress.com.

For Gina
A long lost buddy
Karen

For my father, a storyteller

# Prologue

I shot the horse four days ago.

Its foreleg was broken and the horse screamed for release. A farmer and his wife heard the cries.

He said, 'You can use my gun. I'll bury the horse too, but you'll have to give me your wagon in payment.'

What else could I do?

His wife took pity on me and fetched a handcart her son had once used. I put all I could into that child's cart and walked away. When I turned back, the farmer's wife was fingering the books and scrolls I had left behind, as stunned as if she had just been anointed Empress of all China.

The road had looked honest and straight. A journey of two weeks, I thought. But here in the mountains the mist rises from the river and the road turns milk-white and the way forward is lost.

Soon, I'll be out of this hinterland, back in the city where there are people and bowls of soup and a dry place to sleep. Soon, my Uncle and Auntie will find me on their doorstep and how surprised they'll be! They'll praise me for having found my way all alone from Soochow to Shanghai. They'll welcome me into their home and my new life will begin.

I walk on. The cart squeals with every step I take. I close my ears to its agony. I only want to look and smell.

The sea! Its silver threads lace the air, weaving themselves into the trees. The road curves just ahead, a path of seashells made to mark the land or maybe just to please a child. The afternoon sun spreads from the path and warms my knees.

The wheels of my cart slow and finally stop. It was only a matter of time before I would have to jettison a little more of my past. What do I leave on the road this time?

The sky is still clear, the promise of a radiant night. Now that the wheels have stopped, I can hear the birds.

They sing to me, 'Don't cry, Song Anyi, daughter of the most famous silk weaver in Soochow. You cannot fail now, so close to Shanghai.'

I turn. The two boys are ragged and dirty, no older than I. They wear the ill-fitting uniforms of privates in the Chinese army. There's a man, too, whose boot presses the wheels of my cart into the soft earth. He doesn't speak as he approaches. He takes my long braid in his hand as if it were a strand of pearls. He smiles at me but I cannot smile back. He hits me and I fall to the ground.

The birds wheel away, cawing for help. The man tears my garments, scraping each layer away until I am a fish with no scales, flailing on the chopping board. The boys know what to do. They each take an arm. The man takes my legs.

'Cover her face,' he growls and the boys obey. Dead leaves fill my mouth, strangely sweet.

I count faces, fingers, teeth and toes. I was good at counting. It was the one thing I did that earned my father's praise. Fourteen yuan for a roll of washed silk, thirty-five yuan for a heavy brocade. I sat behind the screen at Baba's workshop and counted. There was a time when the great and the good would come and beg Baba to weave something special, just for them. So many rolls of silk left, the mould creeping from thread to thread, all because Baba wouldn't sell to the Japanese.

What would you say now, Baba? Do you and Mama look down from the heavens and weep?

I will not cry.

I smell the earth, damp and fecund with the seed of these men. They rest for a while, lounging bare-bottomed on a fallen tree. The boys smear mud on my face while the man throws stones at my bleeding hole. They laugh and the trees laugh back.

'Shame!' the birds cry.

They sit in black rows. Their red eyes glow in the night.

'Shame on you, Song Anyi. You were too proud to marry any local boy. You were too good to live in Soochow. Ambition has brought you to this end.'

Death?

The birds deliberate. The trees shiver in the wind. A leaf drops, delicate in the air. A perfect specimen adrift on the forest floor, so close I can see its veins.

'Is she dead?' one of the boys asks.

'Who cares,' the man says.

'Should we bury her?' the other boy wants to know.

The man pulls on his pants. He spits into his hands, wipes the grime off his shirt.

'Leave her for the dogs,' he says. 'They'll come soon enough.'

I wait.

# Part One: Yin, Asleep

# Chapter One

# The Girl Upstairs

*Cho*

The singsong girls cling to me. They chime, 'Don't go yet, Song Cho. Let's watch the sun rise together.'

But the driver has already come inside. He helps me into my coat then heaves me to standing, his hands hard under my armpits. He walks me to the front door.

'How about another pipe of opium?' I ask, turning back.

'Young Master, it's time to go home,' Driver Zhang mutters. 'Please watch the step.'

The girls cluster in the doorway. They shiver in their thin silk sheaths. The long red banner that covers the front of this house, announcing the nature of its residents, snaps in the wind.

'Come back soon,' they call. 'You're welcome anytime, Master Song!'

The rickshaw weaves across the road, through the vegetable carts and the congee vendors and the factory workers. The entire city of Shanghai is on the move. Thank all the gods I'm headed for bed. There's a plump feather mattress and plenty of quilts and maybe the maid, Blossom, her hair loose and her skin warm, waiting for me at home.

When I arrive, Mama is already awake and at the breakfast table. She tries to eat cake but the crumbs spill from her trembling fork. 'Something terrible has happened,' she says. 'Anyi is here.'

'Who?'

'Your cousin, Kang's sister,' Mama answers.

'Is she good-looking?'

I lean against the mirrored wall of our dining room. I pull a gold inlaid case out of my breast pocket and light an American cigarette. Mama talks about carts and leaves and girls who disobey their elders. I try to concentrate. Mama never could tell a story in one straight line.

'Send her away if she's going to be a nuisance,' I say.

Mama's nails click-clack on the table. Why is she so nervous?

'She's family, Cho. Family is everything.'

Mama's pudgy hand reaches for mine but I pull it away before her fingers of jade and gold can grip me. I hate this family nonsense. Baba talks about it all the time, especially when he wants to remind me of my duties. Why should I work when we have so much money? And what do I care how others think of me?

'Cho, listen to me. I want you to be kind to Anyi.'

'Why?'

'I don't think she'll survive otherwise. Come with me now and see for yourself.'

I follow Mama upstairs. I've never had a living thing of my own to love. The dogs belong to Baba and he won't allow any other animal in the house.

The bedroom is dark. The wooden shutters are closed though one slat of light touches the bed. The smell of camphor is heavy in the air.

'Look at her,' Mama whispers. 'Isn't she beautiful?'

She is. Her eyebrows are delicate birds in flight and beneath them lie her dark lashes and their shadows. Her skin could be porcelain but for the two spots of red high on her cheeks.

One foot peeks out from under the mound of quilts, small and white and cold to the touch. I hold it in my hand for a moment before tucking the quilt carefully around it.

'What's wrong with her, Mama?' I whisper.

'She's broken inside.'

'Will she live?'

'The doctor swears it.'

'Can she hear what we're saying?' I ask in a low voice.

'No one knows,' Mama replies. 'She hasn't spoken yet.'

I look at my cousin, so small and frail. I could be kind to someone like that. I could take care of her for a little while.

'I'll help you, Mama. I'll take care of Anyi. I'll sit with her for as long as she needs me.'

*Anyi*

Sometimes it's the moon I see in my dreams, an old one with pockmarks in its face. Sometimes it's the taste of dry leaves that wakes me, my body covered in sweat.

The doctor comes. He doesn't like Auntie Song hovering so he sends her away. He holds my wrist and counts my pulse under his breath. He questions the amah who sleeps at the foot of my bed and misses nothing.

The doctor leaves and I sleep once more, if sleep is what I can call it. Maybe this is how Mama felt during those last long days. She lay on the brick bed that was heated like a furnace to warm her shrivelled body. The quilts were piled so high I could barely find her face. She never spoke to me, never acknowledged my presence. On the day she died, I saw a shudder and heard a long sigh. Then, it was over.

I went to the study and told my father that she was dead.

'Leave me,' he said.

The next morning he was still at his desk, his hand clutching my mother's fan. It was made of sandalwood and once smelled sweet. I pried it out of his hand, each finger as heavy as a dead body. I took the fan with me and left him with his tears.

My father and I were the only mourners. We watched as the smoke from my mother's pyre melted into the grey autumn air. We took her ashes to the river where we scattered them into the water at our feet. When we were done, our fingertips were stained grey.

Baba soon followed Mama to the grave. I wrote letters, so many of them, to announce his death to the world. I sold the house and his studio and all those beautiful bolts of silk. Uncle promised to fetch me as soon as his work allowed. But he didn't come, not to Baba's funeral or for weeks after that. I had done all that could be done so I left Soochow on my own.

I've waited so long to be in this city, to sleep in this very room where Kang slept too when he first came to Shanghai. He sent me letters every week. *Come to Shanghai*, he wrote. *Anything's possible here.*

He wrote about the two sisters who came to Shanghai and founded a bank. I thought I could be like them and find my own door to freedom, to a place where a girl could be more than a wife.

Now I'm bed-bound, unable to feed or clothe or even relieve myself without pain. I have bandages on my feet and hands and legs. A great gaping wound pulses inside me.

How did this happen? Does the young man in the chair know? He sits by my bed and stares. I pretend to sleep and he leans down to brush the hair from my forehead, as if I were a child. If I asked him what's wrong with me, would he say?

The amah doesn't talk to me. She's sewing today. Her needle is large and sharp and she uses it to pierce the thick layers of canvas. She's making a shoe, I think. Her name is Nian.

I hear footsteps in the hallway and the heavy breathing that belongs to Auntie Song. Nian moves to the centre of the room so that she can bow deeply to her mistress the minute the door opens but Auntie ignores the amah. She ignores me too. All her attention is fixed on the handsome young man seated at my side. She strokes his cheek and I understand.

This must be Cho, the only child of Auntie and Uncle Song, the cousin Kang wrote to me about, a gambler and a playboy and a blemish on the Song family name. My parents never wanted us to meet. 'No good girl is safe in his company,' they had said.

Yet he straightens the quilt so that it comes up to my chin. He touches my hair so softly I wonder if he's a dream. My eyes trace the line of his arm and the neat shoulders. I do not dare to look into his eyes, not yet.

## Nian

It was time to clean the room, time to rid the air of the bilious fumes of sickness. Nian washed the windows first, opening the wooden shutters for the first time since the girl's arrival. A robin landed on the windowsill and tapped its yellow beak against the glass. Its black eyes gazed quizzically at Nian, its head cocked first on one side and then the other.

She couldn't whistle like the broken girl. Her chirrups and trills beckoned birds from all over Shanghai. When she stood at the window, the birds sang. Now that Nian stood there, the birds waited in groups of twos and threes until it became clear their friend wasn't coming. Then the birds rose as one and flapped away.

Nian turned her attention to the floor. Long sinuous trails followed her damp mop. She dusted the heavy rosewood cabinet that contained on a single shelf all of the girl's belongings. Nian even got down on her hands and knees to scrub the dark skirting boards. Once the room was sparkling with water and elbow grease, Nian left it all to dry.

She was entitled to a rest. Mistress Song was out and no one in the household would know where Nian was so she curled up in the chair the doctor had placed ready by the window.

The commotion downstairs woke her: the bells of the rickshaw and the shouts of Mistress Song. How could she have slept so long? It was already dark outside and Nian rubbed the sleep from her eyes before hurrying down the back stairs to prepare the broken girl's evening meal. When she returned with a bowl of congee, Driver Zhang was lowering the girl on to the chair by the window. Outside, the moon hung low and yellow, a swollen orb heavy with intent.

The girl looked spent. Her head drooped from the stem of her neck and her eyes were closed. Nian pulled a low stool close to the chair.

'Here,' she said, offering the bowl.

The girl didn't even raise her head. Nian cast a questioning glance at the driver who shrugged and said, 'Look at the moon, Young Mistress. Isn't it beautiful tonight?'

As if in reply, the girl fell to the floor and began to crawl like a beast. Driver Zhang bent down to lift her on to the bed but the girl's body went rigid and her eyes turned to glass. Her body jerked and her knees drew up in spasms. A low animal noise came from her throat.

'Let me try,' Nian said, pushing the driver aside. 'It's me,' she whispered to the girl.

The moan rose in volume and pitch. The girl's eyes rolled into the back of her head. She was shrieking now and a thin stream of white foam seeped out of one side of her mouth.

Nian ran. She bounded down the back stairs two at a time, her bare feet as sure as any cat's. She sped toward the kitchen, the only safe haven. The place was empty, all the other servants hurrying up the main stairs to see what was the matter, Mistress Song heaving slowly in their wake.

Nian wedged herself among the tall stone jars that stood in one corner of the kitchen but she could still hear the screams, wave after wave. The agony-filled cries were sharp enough to pierce any soul. Nian clapped her hands over her ears and jabbered nonsense, children's songs, the names of all her family, anything to block out the sounds of the broken girl.

The housekeeper found her. 'What kind of an amah are you?' she shouted.

'There are ghosts in that room!'

'I know that. Go get the oil lamps from the garage and all the candles from the dining room! Bring everything upstairs to the Young Mistress's bedroom.'

The room was ablaze with light, as bright and garish as the

17

Great World amusement centre. The doctor had removed his coat and his jacket. His forehead was bright with sweat.

'I don't know what's wrong with her,' he told Mistress Song. 'I'll give her a sleeping draught.'

Nian poured the black potion into the girl's mouth. The girl gagged and the potion streamed out, staining the red poppies on her quilt a loathsome green. For a blessed moment, the only sound was the girl catching her breath. Then the screaming began again.

A rickshaw entered the courtyard, its bells clattering loudly through the open window. Mistress Song leaned out.

'Cho!' she cried.

Feet pounded up the stairs and into the hallway. He stood for only a moment in the doorway to take a deep breath before the plunge. He put his arms around the girl and murmured into her ear. She turned to look at him, still screaming, but her eyes grew less wild as he held her.

'I'm going to pick you up now,' he said, 'so you can lie down on your bed.'

She clung to him, weighing him down, so he pulled her up until they were both on the bed with their backs against the wall. Finally her screaming turned to tears that ran down the front of the Young Master's fine woollen suit. Not once did he complain or try to move away. He sat and held her, his mouth close to the crown of her head, murmuring words only the girl could hear.

They fell asleep that way, the Young Master propped up in the corner and the Young Mistress peaceful in his arms. Nian turned down the wick of the oil lamps, one by one, until a quiet hissing filled the room. Only the candle at the Young Mistress's bedside still burned. Nian was reaching out to snuff the flame between her fingers when the broken girl spoke.

'Leave it alone,' the Young Mistress said. 'Don't make it dark in here.'

18

After that, Mistress Song decreed that Nian must stay with the broken girl at all times. The girl slept most of the day so Nian did too. The amah liked the feel of the sun on her face and the muffled sound of the grandfather clock downstairs eating away the hours.

But as the moon waned, Nian knew the calm could not last. She listened as the broken girl talked in her sleep: to her parents, to the soldiers, to other ghosts Nian had not yet met and had no desire to know. She lit the candle every night and hoped for the best.

*Cho*

I wake as soon as the sun peeks over the rooftops of Shanghai. Blossom is here already, kneeling by the side of the copper bathtub.

'Please, Young Master,' she says. 'Let me get into your bed and help you ready your body for the day.'

I brush the maid aside. I've no more time to tumble with a servant. 'Fetch the hot water,' I say. 'I must shave and dress and eat so that when Anyi opens her eyes, mine will be the first face she sees.'

Blossom leaves in tears. I stand before the window and look out on Shanghai. I can still hear the city's siren song but for now I ignore it. Anyi needs me and that's all that matters.

The blue brocade curtains are heavy. I'd never noticed the embroidery before. I finger the silver strands, as smooth and taut as Anyi's skin. My touch is all that's needed to stop her tears, my smile all it takes to lift her spirits. She depends on me now for everything: the sun streaming into her room, the flowers at her bedside, the lychees I peel with my own hands and drop into her waiting mouth.

I want her to get better. I want her to become as strong as she must have been before. We walk every day along the perimeter of her room, each time just a little farther.

This morning when I arrive, Anyi laughs for the first time.

The sound escapes her throat, musical and bird-like and blessed with life. The sound startles us both and we laugh.

'Tell me about yourself,' I say. 'What was your life like before you came here?'

'It was quiet,' she says. 'Each morning, my father and I would go to the silk looms. The studio was close to the Grand Canal where the water is clean enough to wash the raw silk. He made beautiful things, Cho, from silk that felt alive in your hand and like a whisper on your skin. My father was an artist, maybe the greatest of his time.'

'And you? Did you weave, too?'

'I don't have that gift.'

'What did you do then?'

The corners of her mouth droop and a note of aspersion colours her voice. 'My father had no head for business. I kept the books for him, paid his creditors, collected the bills.'

'But you're just a girl!' I exclaim.

'I'm eighteen,' she says. 'How old are you?'

'Ten years older. You should be more respectful to your elders,' I say gravely.

'We're cousins. I don't have to bow to you,' she says and for the first time I see a spark in her eyes.

'That's good, Anyi,' I whisper. 'Fight back. Stand up for yourself.'

Her eyes drop. Her fingers pluck convulsively at the quilt. She grows so pale I'm afraid she might be bleeding again. My nightmare is that a leak springs from her broken body that no doctor can repair.

I lean forward and grasp both of her hands in mine. I bring them to my lips and blow on them softly. 'So cold,' I murmur.

She gets out of bed on her own this time. She stands inside the curve of my arms. I take one step backward and she takes one step forward. We glide together like a pair of ice skaters over a pond glistening with rime.

# Chapter Two

# The Sketchbook

*Anyi*

'We found your sketchbook,' Auntie Song says. 'Your father told us how well you could draw. Maybe it will help you pass the time.'

She places the notebook on my bedside table with a pencil by its side. She touches the cover of the book so tenderly I want to weep. Her thickly painted lips smile at me.

'What's wrong with me, Auntie?'

'What do you mean?' she asks. Lies print themselves all over her mouth. 'You've had a long journey. You just need some rest.'

'I have dreams, Auntie, about men who take me into the woods. They hurt me, Auntie. Is it true?'

Auntie Song fumbles with her thumbs. She picks at the braids of my hair, rough and tangled from lying in bed.

'Your hair should be oiled,' she says. 'I'll have my hairdresser come by tomorrow. You should rest now.'

Once Auntie Song leaves, other visitors arrive. The dead come first. My mother's hair is loose and long. It drapes over the arm of the chair and falls to the floor. Her smile is sad.

'Am I dying, Mama? Is that what's wrong with me?'

Mama never answers.

My Uncle comes in the evening, his hat still on, cigar smoke and brandy on his breath. He moves the chair away from the bed and closer to the door. I trace my father's sharp chin on Uncle Song's face but the wine-flushed skin is wrong.

'Uncle, do you think I'm getting better?'

His words skitter to a halt, the language of money and ships, tea and taxes, jumbled into a great heap of vowels and consonants.

'Yes, of course,' he grumbles. 'You'll be better soon enough. The doctor says so.'

'Did he say that? He never speaks to me.'

'That's proper,' my Uncle says. 'What business does a man have asking impertinent questions to a young lady of class?'

'How can he make me better if he doesn't know what's wrong?'

To that question, my Uncle can only stare.


The doctor arrives in the morning. He speaks to me now and his voice is kind.

'Your legs are healing well, Lady. They would heal even faster if you let the wounds dry in the open air. If you put your chair here before the window, you could sun yourself like a cat. Can you do that?'

To the amah, the doctor is stern.

'I will not come back. You must take over now. The Lady must be washed every day, especially here between her legs. You must use only water that has been freshly boiled and then cooled. Here, take this sponge and show me on my own arm how you would do it.'

The amah grinds the sponge into the doctor's outstretched arm as if it were caked in mud.

'No! You'll reopen all her wounds. Do it like this, gently, in circles first one way and then the other. If the wounds become infected, the Lady could die.'

They work together, the doctor and the amah, cleaning and bandaging my body. When they finish, I reach out to touch his arm.

I say, 'Doctor, please, no one will talk to me. No one will tell me what's wrong. Can you?'

The doctor blushes like a schoolboy. I think he's going to lie like all the rest. Instead he sends Nian out of the room and closes the door.

'It's not proper but I think you should know,' he says.

He points at the sketchbook next to my bed.

'You like to draw?' he asks.

I nod.

He picks up the book. 'May I?'

I smile and he opens the book to a clean page.

'I draw too,' he says. 'It helps me think.'

He takes a stub of a pencil from his pocket. He licks it and begins to draw.

'Let me show you what happened,' he says.


*Cho*

We go for a ride today. We don't venture far, just to the British Public Gardens. Normally, the Sikh guards will refuse Chinese visitors but the guard on duty knows my father's name. I push open the wrought iron gate.

'Don't linger,' the guard whispers. 'I could lose my job if anyone sees you here.'

The garden is deserted, the roses long beheaded by the wind and the rain. Anyi and I walk a few steps but the wind is too heavy for her. It buffets her long cloak, whipping it up into my face. I want to turn back. She refuses. Her nostrils flare at the electricity in the air.

'Take me to the sea wall,' she cries.

I carry her there. A fragile railing and a few crumbling steps are all that stop us from falling into the river's white caps.

'Let me down,' she commands.

She puts her hands on the rusty bar and leans far over the railing. The water foams and seethes in hunger below.

'Be careful, Anyi!'

But the wind catches my warning and flings it back into my face. She lets go of the railing and falls forward.

23

I grab her cloak, her arm. I've got my fingers around her waist. I pull, propelling the two of us away from the river, up and back into the garden, onto the hard yellow stones. She lands on top of me, a long sigh of air escaping her mouth.

The Sikh guard is already running, pebbles spitting from under his heavy boots.

'Are you all right, sir? Madam? Can I give you a hand up?'

She stares into the distance, her eyes large and empty. The Sikh helps me to my feet but I can't let him touch her. I carry her away in my arms and lift her into the rickshaw.

She lays her head in my lap. My hand strokes her cheek. She speaks though her head is turned away.

'Do you think I'm dirty?' she asks.

'No,' I say.

She sleeps now. Her braid has come loose and her hair spills out around her sleeping face like flames from the sun. I take a strand of her hair and hold it against my cheek. It smells sweet like her skin. I reach out to trace her jawbone but stop. I don't dare wake her. She hardly ever cries out in the night any more but I can't take the chance. And even if I didn't startle her, what would I say if she asked, what do you want from me, Cho?

*Anyi*

The doctor's sketch haunts me: the two legs that should join smoothly at the top and that place in between, gouged and gashed, that will never heal.

And his words: 'You'll never be able to bear a child, Lady. Your body won't tolerate it.'

My memory stretches, a thread that grows ever taut between my wounds and their makers, my journey and its end. Why didn't they just leave me to the dogs?

I don't know how long I lay in the leaves but I remember it was cold. I heard the sound of wheels turning and thought I had died. Instead, it was the farmer and his wife coming back in the cart I'd given them. They found my coat with Uncle's

24

address pinned inside. The farmer and his wife argued for a long time whether to make the journey into town. The wife didn't think I'd survive it. The farmer thought Uncle might offer a reward. I don't know whether they were paid or even thanked. Not by me, in any event.

Auntie comes into the room. She wants to cut my hair. They get me out of bed and lead me to the middle of the room where I stand in my stocking feet. Nian holds the metal bowl while Auntie snips at my hair. When she's done, she sits heavily on my bed.

'That's better,' Auntie says. 'Now you'll be presentable.'

'For whom?' I ask.

'Your Uncle and I have a wide circle of friends,' Auntie says. 'It's time you started meeting some of them.'

'Are they Cho's friends too?'

Auntie chuckles. 'No, these men are closer in age to your Uncle than to Cho.'

'They won't want to talk to me.'

'You're right. How you look is of much more interest to them.'

I stare at my Aunt.

Her voice hardens, 'It's time, Anyi. You need to marry before it's too late.'

'I don't want to marry,' I say, though even to me my voice sounds childish.

'Your parents have spoiled you,' Auntie says. 'They've allowed you to have wild ideas. Women of our family marry. It's the proper thing to do.'

'What man would want to marry me now that I've been raped?'

Auntie Song slaps me across the face, first the right cheek then the left.

'Never use that word again,' she hisses. 'No one must know. No one needs to know. It never happened, you see, because you're a good girl from a good family. Something like that doesn't happen to people like us.'

But it did. I can see their faces now as clearly as Auntie

Song's. They grin at me as she chatters about hair oil and bed slippers and a new robe, even as she wanders out of my room and down the stairs.

'These things don't happen to good girls,' the soldiers say.

'What have I done wrong?' I cry.

'You disobeyed your Uncle. He told you to wait. You deserted the graves of your parents. Who will sweep their headstones now? You deserve to be punished,' the soldiers say.

They climb on to me then and do their business.


*Blossom*

The maid was warm and relaxed, snuggled close to the fire in the kitchen, her mending abandoned at her side when the housekeeper came stomping in.

'The Young Master wants to go out,' she shouted. 'Find Driver Zhang!'

Blossom ran outdoors but Driver Zhang was already in the courtyard, muffling the bells to avoid disturbing those inside the house. They stood together to watch the sun hang heavy on the horizon.

'It'll be hours before any of the clubs open,' Blossom said. 'What's the Young Master up to this time?'

The driver shrugged. 'How far will I have to pedal tonight before the Young Master is satisfied?'

The door into the house stood open. They could see Mistress Song waiting by the front door as the Young Master came down the stairs, carrying the broken girl in his arms.

Blossom had been at her normal hiding spot beside the upstairs window when the broken girl first arrived. She saw the housekeeper question the farmer and his wife and heard Mistress Song's cries when she learned who the girl was. Driver Zhang was the one who brought the girl into the house. She had blood on her face and one eye was swollen shut. She was wrapped in an old horse blanket that the housekeeper later ordered Blossom to burn. Why had Mistress Song allowed death to enter her home?

'Where are you going today, Young Master?' Blossom asked.

'I want to take my cousin for a ride, show her the sights of Shanghai,' he said.

'Shouldn't she be resting? I could go with you instead if you'd like some company on your ride.'

He turned away from the maid as if he'd never heard of such a thing before, as if the two of them hadn't taken dozens of rides about town, as if Blossom was nothing more than his servant.

'Get ready,' he barked at Zhang.

Driver Zhang bowed. He lit the little red lanterns that dangled alongside the carriage. They were no help in navigating. Old Master Song thought they made the carriage look pretty.

Old Master Song could have lived in Frenchtown like all the other rich Chinese but he said, 'This is my family home. My son and his sons and their sons will live in this house and I will become an ancestor.'

Inside the house, Mistress Song was causing a commotion. She called the driver inside to discuss the routes with the least number of bumps on the road while Blossom scurried back and forth with cloaks and scarves and hats, her face as sour as a fishwife's.

Mistress Song wailed, 'Are you sure she's strong enough for this? Is it too cold? Driver Zhang, do you think it will rain?'

Blossom sniffed. Driver Zhang would never answer a question like that. It wasn't his place. The Songs paid him to pull the rickshaw, not predict the future.

In the end, the Young Master had to concede: the girl was still too weak. Blossom watched him carry her back upstairs. She waited a long time for him to come down but there were dishes to be warmed and a table to be set. Pouting, Blossom returned to the kitchen. Driver Zhang had taken her seat by the fire.

'Just as well,' he said to the housekeeper. 'It looked like rain to me.'

# Chapter Three

# Playing Games

*Cho*

'Shall we play a game?'

Before Anyi can answer, I say, 'Mah-jong is hard with just two but we can try. Or shall I fetch a deck of cards and you can tell my fortune? I already know that I'll be very rich. I want to know if my wife will be fat and how many sons we'll have. Can you tell me?'

She struggles to sit upright in her bed. For a moment, her sleeping gown gapes open. She says, 'Get me that deck of cards.'

Her hands are bed-soft and weak. Cards spill on to the floor. In time, her fingers grow nimble and soon the cards rapidly change from one hand to the other. She separates the cards into five neat stacks.

'Choose.'

The stack with the chrysanthemum flower on top glows. It must be a good omen. Anyi holds the cards in her hand, as if weighing the severity of their message.

'Let me see,' she says as she spreads the cards face up on the bed table. Then she clears her throat loudly and begins to speak in an exact imitation of my father's impatient tones. 'You are a man of little industry,' she says. 'This will not change. You will lose one fortune and find another. I see many, many women in your future but only one son. Perhaps you will be the father of many daughters or husband to many wives.'

Anyi stops suddenly, one card trembling in her hand. Her voice is her own again though smaller and more timid. 'I know this card. I've seen blood in my future, too. You will die a violent death,' she whispers.

I laugh. 'Where did you learn that?'

'My amah used to tell my fortune all the time.'

'No, your voice! How are you able to imitate my father?'

'Oh that,' Anyi says, as she sweeps up the cards. 'Ever since I was a little child, I could mimic sounds. I started with birds. Then it was stories. Once, I told Kang about a dragon that comes to the village to eat little boys. I told it in the scariest voice I could manage and it sounded exactly like my father. Would you like to hear it?'

I throw myself on top of Anyi's bed, my body curled around her legs and my head propped up by one arm. I swing the other arm in the air like a conductor. 'I'll give you the name of someone and you give me the voice,' I cry. 'My mother!'

*Blossom*

All afternoon, laughter floated down the stairs. It followed Blossom as she dusted in the parlour and while she beat the mats in the kitchen yard. She could find no place in the house to hide from the sound of the Young Master enjoying himself so she sat at the bottom of the stairs to listen and sigh for a while. On her return to the kitchen, she felt baffled and angry. 'It sounds like a crowd of people in that room,' she reported. 'I didn't let any guests into the house, did you?'

The housekeeper grumbled, 'I don't hear the Young Mistress. It's the Young Master who's laughing his head off.'

Cook cocked his ear. 'It's good to hear some joy in this house again.'

'He should go out, not stay inside a sick room all day. It's not healthy for him,' Blossom sniffed.

Cook laughed. 'You never complained when he stayed in his room all morning if you could join him there.'

'Hush,' Blossom cried, red spots now high on her cheeks. 'The Mistress mustn't know!'

Cook spat out his toothpick. When the housekeeper glared at him, he bent down to retrieve it from the gleaming floor and slipped it into his pocket.

'Of course the Mistress knows,' he growled. 'Why else would she keep you here?'

For how long, Blossom wondered. The maid was only sixteen though already cunning enough to understand her value to the Song household. As long as she continued to amuse the Young Master, she would have a home. But it had been days, maybe weeks, since the Young Master had tossed a glance in her direction. It was all the fault of the broken girl!

Too restless to sit, she wandered into the hallway. The door to the Old Master's study was closed and she could hear voices inside.

Old Master Song was saying, 'Anyi must be married before everyone in town finds out about her shame and her marriage price rises to the heavens.'

Good Old Master Song, Blossom thought. He's wise to get rid of the broken girl.

'Where's your list of candidates?' he asked. 'I have a few names of my own I can add. We'll show Anyi to them as soon as she's presentable and then we'll choose.'

'What about Kang?' Mistress Song asked. 'Shouldn't he decide? He's the oldest male in the family, even if he's only her brother.'

'You think we should call him back from America?'

'He's the head of his family now. Let him take the responsibility.'

Blossom now squinted through the keyhole. She could see Mistress Song moving agitatedly around the room while the Old Master watched her from behind his desk. He didn't normally take any notice of what the Mistress said. 'You're right,' he replied at last. 'I'll send Kang a telegram. As soon as he reaches Shanghai, Anyi can be married.'

'Will he be here for the Mid-Autumn Festival?' Mistress Song asked.

'The ocean crossing will take two weeks. If the winter storms are early this year, it might take even longer. Let's say Kang will be here in a month.'

A month! The Young Master will have forgotten all about Blossom by then. She had to get him away from the broken girl. Now, how to do that?

In the evening, just before the lamps were lit, Blossom went searching for Mistress Song. She found her in the winter garden, the only place in the house the mistress found warm enough.

'Excuse me, Mistress, may I disturb you for a moment?'

Mistress Song looked up. Blossom took that for permission. 'It's not my place, I know, to offer advice,' she started, haltingly.

Mistress Song snorted.

'And I don't want to be presumptuous.'

Mistress Song shifted her weight in the cane chair. Curtly, she said, 'Speak your mind and be done.'

Blossom spoke, slowly and carefully, repeating the words her aunt had taught her just hours ago with such great care. 'We all know that massage is good for the body. It allows the chi to flow freely. It can be beneficial to healing injuries, especially where blood is involved,' Blossom said.

Mistress Song's mouth hung open and her face darkened. 'What are you talking about? What do you know about it?' the Mistress demanded.

Blossom answered, 'Of course I don't know anything. Please forgive me for interfering. It's just that I have an aunt. Everyone calls her Auntie Wen. She's very famous around town for her massage. She can heal almost anyone of anything.'

Mistress Song's face relaxed as she laughed in the maid's face. 'I don't take recommendations from housemaids. Now, go away. I'm sure there's something you should be doing.'

Blossom hung her head and shuffled toward the door. Auntie

31

Wen had predicted how this conversation would go, down to the exact words Mistress Song would use. Blossom was enjoying herself now, an actress who had learned her lines by heart and knew what was coming next.

She stood before the door, one hand on the doorknob. When she spoke again, it was with her back toward Mistress Song. 'The Young Mistress heals so slowly. She must suffer a great deal. The women at the fish market were asking about her this morning.'

Blossom heard the chair creak. She knew her mistress was sitting up now. Auntie Wen had warned her, 'Don't be impatient. Mistress Song might need time to think. It could take hours, days even.' But her aunt's prediction was wrong.

'What was the name of this masseuse?' Mistress Song asked.

*Anyi*

Auntie Song sends a masseuse to me. Blind, like all of her profession, her skin is nut-brown and so are her teeth. She says, 'I am here to help. Call me Auntie Wen.'

I'm afraid. Her palms are hard. I arch my back to take the first blow.

She clucks her tongue and whispers, 'Let your hips sink into the mattress, relax your tongue, soften your eyes, trust me.'

Her hands move. Her fingers wrap around my ankles, my calves, my thighs. I feel her hand enter me. I cannot bear it. She pushes in, farther and farther, like the tide on the beach, until I break into a million bubbles of foam on the sand.

When I open my eyes, there is blood on her hands and a smile on her face.

'What happened?' I ask.

'You're learning to be a woman,' she says.

'Don't I need a son for that?'

Auntie Wen chuckles. 'Yes, this gate leads down that path. But there are other roads, too.'

'What others?'

The pinpoints where her eyes once were grow dark. She

places one hard hand on my belly and pushes deeply. 'Here is the path to marriage and many healthy children. I can teach you to use your lips and your hands and your gully to extract every seed your husband has. Do you want that?'

My mother and father were rarely apart. Wherever she was, he was always nearby, his face against her soft hair. Their happiness seems so far away now, a fairy tale no longer possible for me.

'No children,' I say.

Auntie Wen releases my belly and strokes my hair. 'Then pleasure, if you like,' the masseuse says. 'Few women of your class will ever experience it. Imagine how it could feel to have your whole body thrill to the touch of a man.'

'No men!'

My words shatter against the windowpanes. Auntie Wen cocks her head to one side, as if suddenly interested in what I have to say.

'You would prefer a woman?' she asks.

'How can I desire pleasure when I feel nothing?' I cry.

'But you do feel,' she says. 'You just did.'

'I felt pain.'

'Is that what you want?'

My heart howls. The soldiers laugh. They poke me in the face, the mouth, my bleeding hole. They shout, 'You should never have been on that road alone. You must be punished for disobeying your elders.'

'Yes,' I tell Auntie Wen. 'I want pain.'

The masseuse rises. Her movements are confident as she cleans her hand with oil and a cloth. Back at my side, she uses the same oil to knead the knots in my back. She leans down to whisper in my ear. The smell of her breath is rank.

'I'll come again, tomorrow, around this time of the day. We must be left alone. Can you arrange it?'

'No one comes into my room except my amah and my cousin.'

'Your cousin is Song Cho?'

'Yes.'

'The amah will do as you say and I will take care of your cousin. There is a housemaid here who is my niece. Her name is Blossom. She'll keep your cousin away.'

Auntie Wen rubs my neck, the back of my head, the space between my eyebrows. She murmurs under her breath: a chant or a song? The tune is so far away. She's gone before I can catch the melody.

I sleep. I dream. A moon shines full on my face. An old moon, one I have known before. The candle sputters. I hear its fat spray all around. I cry out and Nian rises from her bedroll on the floor.

'Hush,' she says.

Nian fetches a new candle, squashing the soft old one under the heel of the new. For a moment, the world goes black until once more a candle burns and the corners of the room expand.

'Hush, Young Mistress,' she says. 'You're safe now.'

### Blossom

Last night, sleet turned the streets to ice. All day, the servants were locked up inside the house, no one allowed to leave, not even Driver Zhang. The maid had finished her chores and the housekeeper could find no other task for her so the housekeeper gave Blossom permission to go upstairs to watch people try to cross the street.

A truck bearing pigs had stalled in front of the house gate. Coolies emerged in their bare feet and tried to push the truck along. The ice cut into their soles. Their cries filled the street and Blossom laughed.

Downstairs, the grandfather clock struck three. A rickshaw entered the courtyard, one of the few to brave the weather. It was Auntie Wen come to take care of the broken girl. She had told Blossom she would need for two hours. 'Keep him away from the girl's room,' Auntie Wen had said. 'Do whatever you must.'

Blossom found the Young Master pacing in his room. She moved to the window, careful to position herself so that the winter light fell on her face and made her skin shimmer.

'Did you call for me, Young Master?' she asked.

'No, I didn't. But now that you're here, tell me why I'm not allowed to see Anyi.'

'The masseuse is with her.'

The Young Master bit his lip. 'I want to see Anyi.'

'Mistress Song said they were not to be disturbed.'

Blossom stepped forward. She placed her soft-shod feet carefully on top of his shoes. He looked down in surprise. 'What are you doing?'

She pushed hard, toppling the Young Master on to the bed. The wooden joints of the frame groaned as he fell on his back. She followed, landing softly on his chest.

'Are you sure you want to disturb them?' she asked.

Cho rolled quickly, pinning Blossom on the bed, then grinned. 'You have a point,' he said.

He rolled once more, now on to his back, pulling Blossom with him so that she was again on top.

'In fact,' he said. 'I'm feeling a little faint. I could use some nursing too. Who could I ask to help?'

'Why, Young Master, I would be happy to help you in any way I can,' Blossom said, as her hand crept down his body.

'You're such a good maid,' he said. 'But close the door first.'

*Anyi*

'When will Kang arrive?' I ask Auntie Song.

We sit on opposite sides of the breakfast table, an army of dishes lying ravaged between us. I watch the young housemaid clear the table. She wears her hair braided in one long rope that hangs down the length of her back though no braid can tame the loose tendrils that soften her heart-shaped face. I see the girl looking at herself in the mirrored wall. She must know how pretty she is.

'Just a few more weeks,' Auntie Song says. 'You must get well so that when your brother arrives, you're looking pretty for him. And for your new husband too.'

The maid is careless. She clatters the thin china plates together and whenever she thinks no one is looking, she dips her finger in the egg yolk left congealing on the tablecloth. She makes her way around the table, eating whatever she can find, while I turn my face to the wall to hide my tears. My Aunt hates it when I cry. She's told me often.

'Why do you want me to marry, Auntie? Am I a burden to you and Uncle?'

Auntie Song's hands flutter apologetically around her face but there's a sour line to her lips. 'Of course not, child.'

'You're ashamed of me?' I ask in a low voice. 'Is that why you've sent for Kang?'

'Why don't you go out for a ride with Cho?'

Driver Zhang pedals slowly. Cho points out the sights as we head in the direction of the Bund. We pass a long street hung full with banners: Very Best Merchandise! Sincere Prices! Air-conditioned Ballrooms!

'That's Nanking Road,' Cho explains. 'It's where my mother buys her clothes. Shall we take a look?'

But the clamour and colour are too much for me. The driver steers away, back down the Bund where I watch the Whangpoo River lap quietly along the road. Cho points across the water. 'That's the fishing village of Pootung. When you're stronger, we can take a boat ride from there. Would you like that?' he asks.

I should run away now while I still have the chance. When Kang arrives, will he let me out of his sight? Or will my last taste of freedom be as a bride, seated in my wedding sedan headed for my new husband's home?

Cho taps the driver on his shoulder. 'My cousin is tired. Let's go home.'

# Chapter Four

# Nanking Road

*Cho*

The rain falls in sheets. It bounces so high that the water sprays into the rickshaw, staining the fine calf leather of my shoes.

'Can't you pedal any faster?' I ask Driver Zhang. His feet are bare. His legs are too. He doesn't have to worry about ruining his good shoes.

Anyi stirs beside me. I begged Mama this morning to let her go out again. 'She needs clothes,' I said. 'I can't take her out on the town looking like this.'

Mama finally agreed but only after Driver Zhang had swaddled Anyi so tightly that now all I can see is her face peeking out from the blankets.

'Let's stop there.' She points at the first store on Nanking Road.

Driver Zhang slows, his face a question mark as he turns to look at me.

'Drive on!' I say to him.

'That one's not good enough for you,' I say to her.

'Look at that mannequin!' Anyi shouts as we move into the heart of the shopping district. 'She's wearing a gown just like in the magazines.'

The mannequin wears a dress with a mandarin collar so heavily embroidered it flashes in the dim light. The dress swells over the breasts and slides down the hips, one side slit up to the thigh.

'You've discovered the trademark dress of Shanghai,' I tell her. 'It's called a ch'i p'ao. Shall we go inside and see if we can have one made for you?'

Driver Zhang stops in the road but I wave him on. He lifts the rickshaw on to the sidewalk and drags it closer to the shop.

'Can't you get this rickshaw under the awning? I don't want the Young Mistress to get wet.'

But she's already out of her blankets and on the wet pavement where she laughs as she splashes in the puddles. I hold the shop door open and bow her inside. Instead she turns back to the driver, still on his bicycle seat, hunched over in the pouring rain.

'Come with us,' she calls out. 'You'll drown out there.'

Anyi strokes the large circular couch that wraps around a palm tree growing up to the high ceiling. Her eyes shine at the sight of the walls filled with glass display cases and brass handles. Driver Zhang creeps far into the corner where he can avoid touching anything with his dirty hands.

Miss Wang, the saleswoman, emerges from behind a heavy velvet curtain. She wears a dress like the mannequin's. I know her well. Her lips are soft and full.

'Has your mother sent you to pick up something?' Miss Wang asks sweetly.

'You know my mother spent all her allowance the last time we were here. I have a new customer for you. This is my cousin, Song Anyi, newly arrived from Soochow. Look at her! Eighteen years old and she's still dressed like a girl from the country. I want to make her into a lady of Shanghai. Can you help?'

Now the seamstress comes into the showroom too, a bent old woman whose only value lies in the nimbleness of her fingers. She and Miss Wang look Anyi up and down as if she were a turnip and they two ravenous crows. Then the seamstress starts picking out rolls of silk for Miss Wang to place next to Anyi's pale face.

Miss Wang mutters, 'These soft pastel colours are no good.

38

Orange is too harsh, blue too common. Wait, what about this one, so very hard to wear?'

She runs to fetch the roll herself, cradling it in her arms like the heir to the throne. It's an iridescent green silk heavily worked in threads of different shades to create the impression of light through bamboo leaves.

'That's the one!' the women cry together.

The seamstress measures Anyi, already pinning the fabric into shape. 'Come back in one hour,' she mumbles through a mouth full of pins.

The rain has stopped and the street gleams like the barrel of a rifle.

'Where now, Young Master?' the driver asks.

'Sun Sun Department Store.'

'What kind of place is that?' Anyi wants to know. 'We don't have department stores in Soochow.'

'Nothing in Soochow can compare to Shanghai! From the top floor of the Sun Sun Department Store, you can see all of Shanghai sprawling like a lazy cat at your feet. At night, you can dance under the stars. We can have coffee now and then do some more shopping. One new dress won't be enough.'

When we've finished, an army of shop boys follow us with the parcels. We have everything that a lady of quality needs: blouses, skirts and sweaters, shoes, a hat, hosiery, lingerie. I've been shopping often enough with Mama to know a good piece of merchandise when I see it.

'Send the boxes home in another rickshaw,' I tell the head clerk.

'Now take us back to the dress shop,' I order Driver Zhang.

'So much money,' Anyi whispers. 'How can you afford it?'

'This isn't my money, though it will be soon enough. Everyone in Shanghai knows who my father is. They know I'm allowed to sign bills with his personal seal. Then the bills get sent home for my mother to pay.'

Anyi looks troubled. She turns her face away though I can still see her teeth gnaw her lower lip.

'Would you like to see his seal?' I hold out the slim ivory stick, the characters of his name still stained in red ink.

'I know what a seal looks like. I have my own.' Anyi pulls a stick out of her purse that looks exactly like my father's, though hers has been carved out of ebony. 'I used my seal to pay bills for Baba's silk shop.'

'Then you know how it works. Why the grumpy face?'

'I don't want to be a burden.'

'My parents want you to look pretty.'

'Your parents care a lot about appearances,' Anyi bites back. Then she places both hands on my arm, as if to pray. When she speaks again, her voice is meek. 'Should I wear my new dress tonight at dinner?'

I don't like her meek. I don't want her to be afraid. I want Anyi to wake up. I put my hands on her shoulders and say heartily, 'We need a better occasion than that. Cousin, do you know how to dance?'

'Of course!'

'Then let's go dancing.'

'Tonight?'

'No. Let me think first about the best place to take you.'

*Anyi*

Auntie Wen approves of my new clothing.

'You'll fit in well,' she says.

She comes to me every day. It's her task now to make sure that I walk. She leads me around the perimeter of my room like an elephant in a parade. While we walk, she teaches me other things too, like how to pleasure a man with pain. The parade suddenly halts and Auntie Wen roughly pushes me into the corner of the room.

'Get down on your knees,' she says. 'Let me show you how it will feel. Then you can remember with your skin.'

40

From my room to the hallway and the hallway to the stairs, step after faltering step, my world expands. Now I'm the guide and she, the blind one, must trust my words.

Uncle Song doesn't like us to roam about the house. He says, 'The sun is shining today. Walk in the garden.'

The trees have lost almost all their leaves. The ground is covered in yellow, a carpet of gold where I could lie down and die. But Auntie Wen won't let me.

'After all our work, you want to give up?'

'When will you give me my first customer?'

'Soon. As soon as you're ready.'

I wait. At night, when Nian is fast asleep, I stand at the window and talk to the moon. It'll be full and fat soon. I can feel my blood frothing already.

The moon shines on the bowl of fruit that Nian brings to my room every day, together with a plate and the small knife that gleams in the silver light. It's surprisingly sharp. A bead of blood swells at my fingertip. Yes, why not? I make cuts, no bigger than a fingernail, down the length of one pale thigh. The pain is exquisite.

Today I begin. I help her down the stairs and out into the street, but once she hears the traffic, the blind masseuse needs no guide.

'Where are we going?' I ask.

'Jing 'An Temple.'

'He wants to meet us where the Buddhists pray?'

'These places are public,' Auntie Wen explains. 'No one pays any attention to who comes or goes.'

Her strides are quick and purposeful, the only moment of hesitation when we negotiate the high wooden threshold into the temple. Auntie Wen drops two copper coins into the offering box and motions with her hand that I should follow.

I've forgotten that this world exists. It's the ordinary

assortment of mothers with children, old men who've come for the free tea, a few young couples in love and yet to me they seem so strange. We wander past the memorial hall with its row of stone tablets. At the shrine to Guanyin, parents and abandoned lovers knock their heads to the floor, praying loudly for divine intervention. We come finally to a solitary porch, containing nothing but a single stone bench and some pots half-filled with dead earth. Auntie Wen sits down with a sigh.

'He'll be here soon. I feel the sun on my forehead.'

I sit. A shiver runs through me. Will this man be as satisfying as the knife? Auntie Wen rubs my back.

'Every man is different. And yet, all men are the same. Remember what I have taught you.'

My first customer is a trader of coffee and spices. He leads me to the farthest end of the temple grounds while Auntie Wen trails behind.

'I'll be your look-out,' she tells the trader.

He nods, looking for a suitable spot. He chooses a stone building that must be some sort of storage place. He's younger than I expected, with smooth taut skin and hard muscles. He places his large hands on my shoulders then slowly tightens his grip until his ten fingers close around my neck.

'No bruising,' Auntie Wen says quietly.

The man lets go and the blackness in my eyes seeps away. Auntie Wen is standing just inside the doorway, her face tilted toward the afternoon sun.

'I can't do anything if you watch,' the man barks.

Auntie Wen laughs. 'I can't see anything, remember? But I can hear better than most. You know the rules. No bruising, no cuts to the face or arms. The rest is up to you.'

The man grunts. He pushes me to the ground, carefully poking my belly with the toe of his boot. Then he kicks hard, once, twice, until I cry out.

'Do that again,' he mutters to me. 'I like the screaming.'

When we walk home from the temple, it's Auntie Wen who supports me. We stop frequently so that I can rest. She seems anxious.

'Are you going to be strong enough?' she asks.

'Yes.'

'Do you want more?'

'Oh, yes,' I say. 'Now, where is my share of the price?'

Auntie Wen shakes her head, fluttering her hands like the old woman she now pretends to be.

'I held up my side of the deal. You heard the man squeal in pleasure.'

In the end, we divide the money as agreed, three silver coins for her as procuress and seven silver coins for me. I bite each one carefully to be sure the old woman hasn't tricked me but she plays fair this time.

'When will you come again?' I ask.

'Tomorrow, like always.'

'Will you have a customer then?'

Auntie Wen chuckles. She pats my cheek as if I were a precocious child. 'Rest, Anyi. There will always be men who want what you have to offer. More than you could ever handle.'

We arrive at the Song family home at the same time as the bill for my clothes. That night at the dinner table, Auntie Song complains bitterly to Uncle Song. Then she scolds Cho.

'I think she looks pretty now, don't you?'

'It doesn't matter what I think,' Auntie Song screeches back. 'She needs to be presentable for a suitor.'

'What suitor?' Cho asks, bewildered.

Auntie and Uncle Song exchange a look. Cho's face turns red. My mind goes distant. I promise myself then and there: I will not be a burden. I won't depend on any of them, least of all a husband.

I send Nian out the next day to purchase a lockbox. I tell her exactly what I want and she does well. The lockbox is light but sturdy, made of leather and metal studs. It's small enough to fit underneath my bed. I count my silver coins one more time before putting them inside the lockbox and turning the key. Auntie and Uncle Song don't come into my room any more but I won't take any chances.

I push the lockbox into the farthest corner of the room. I hang the key on a string around my neck. I count the number of men I need to service before my lockbox will be full.

For the first time since I arrived in Shanghai, I sleep through the night.

# Chapter Five

# In the Mood

*Cho*

The band plays a two-step, slow and sad, perfect for holding your partner tight in your arms. Her steps are light, one note after the other in tune with the bass of my feet. She turns away, revealing her body gleaming in green silk, hiding it once more when she returns to my embrace.

When the band stops, her eyes are closed and her lips half-parted. She smiles like a child waking from a peaceful night's sleep.

'That was lovely, Cho. Can we dance again? Oh, the band is taking a break? All right, let's have a seat here by the window. I'm so very warm.'

She fans herself while I gaze at the crowd. Men nod their heads in acknowledgment and women smile but tonight I have eyes only for Anyi. The band strikes up, this time a tango. I pull her to her feet.

'Let's see how good you are!' I taunt.

She leaps ahead, a dragon kite darting in the wind, propelled by the rhythm of the music. She waits for me in the centre of the dance floor, laughing, 'Don't flatter yourself, Cousin. I'll show you what I can do.'

Our bodies circle each other. Every three beats we meet, just long enough for me to feel the tips of her breasts press into my chest. Our legs stab out: hers wrapping around mine, mine supporting her whole body as she loses herself to the violence of the dance.

When the band finally retires for the night and the lights in the ballroom flare up, I ask, 'Are you ready for the next stop?'

We drive to the outskirts of Frenchtown, to a long alley at the end of which stands a simple two-storied building. There's only one sign, a word carved into the wooden gate: Ciro.

Inside, there's a small entry hall where the girl takes our hats and coats. On either side of the booth, two doors stand wide open. One leads to the casino. That's for another time.

'In here,' I say. 'There's a show tonight.'

The stage is empty and the air in the room sour. I pick a table close to the wall where I can rock my chair on to its back legs. A waitress wearing only a bra and tap pants comes to take the order. Anyi stares.

'Where are the women?' she asks.

'This is intermission,' the waitress says. 'The show will start again soon.'

'I mean the other customers,' she whispers to me. 'Why are there only men in the audience?'

I grin and say nothing. I watch the waitress strut away, the cheeks of her buttocks jiggling out the bottom of her pants.

The curtain comes up but the stage remains dark. There's shouting then a light flickers on. Canned music plays while two women enter the stage. It's our waitress and another woman dressed exactly the same. They dance for a while, with each other and alone. The audience ignores them.

'Why are we here?' Anyi asks.

The dancers leave. A jazz trio appears; their music is livelier. The audience wakes up. They clap their hands and stamp their feet. There's a spotlight now, crawling across the stage and into the audience. For a brief moment, it shines full on Anyi's face. There's a murmur in the crowd and once more she turns to me, her hand clutching my forearm.

'What's happening?'

Another woman enters the stage. This one is a dancer wearing more than underwear, a diaphanous dress that reveals as much as it hides. The audience roars.

The dancer bows gracefully then twirls across the stage, the multi-coloured layers of her dress rising and falling with each step. A filmy shawl floats to the floor. An overskirt unwinds to reveal long bare legs and a tight sarong.

The dancer steps off the stage and into the audience, her hips circling slowly as she peels off each new layer. Sometimes, she pauses to wrap a silken garment around the flushed neck of a customer. The other men whistle and wave wads of money at her to lure her to their table.

Instead of them, she chooses our table. In two long steps she's standing in front of Anyi. The dancer undulates quickly now. Each thrust of her hips sets off a wave of heat. The heat strikes my face until my body glows. Anyi must feel it too. Blotches of red mark her face.

Maybe that's why the dancer reaches out for Anyi's hands and places them on her breasts. Maybe that's why the dancer rubs Anyi's palms round and round until the dancer's nipples are as hard as bullets. Why the dancer laughs then and kisses Anyi long and hard on the mouth.

*Anyi*

I run out of the room. Everywhere I turn, there are doors and behind those doors, danger waits for me, I'm sure of it. I slide down to the floor, my head against the wall, my eyes closed, waiting for what will come.

'Are you all right, Anyi?' Cho asks. His cheeks are still flushed though his eyes telegraph worry. 'I thought you would enjoy the show.'

'Get me out of here!' I cry.

'Wait here,' he says. 'Let me get the hats and coats.' He's on the other side of the narrow hall in plain sight when a man in evening clothes pulls me to my feet and drags me out of the foyer and into the casino. He's got a fistful of money in his hand and he's yelling at me, his spittle flying in my face. I remember him now. He was the second, no, the third customer after the coffee trader. He was the one who sprayed his seed on my face. He wants to do it again, right now.

'How much money do you want? I'll give you cash upfront.'

Cho drives his fist into the man's cheek, the crunch of bone sickeningly loud.

The man squeals in pain and surprise. 'Hey, get your own girl!' he shouts.

Cho swings again, this time breaking the long line of the man's nose. Blood spurts and the man staggers back, stunned by the flow. A crowd forms around us ready to lay bets.

Cho's yelling. 'She belongs to me. This is my cousin.'

The man fumbles with his handkerchief, his voice now nasal and thin. 'Your cousin, huh? You've a fine family. Where does your mother work?'

Cho swings for a third time but the man ducks under Cho's elbow and disappears into the cabaret. Cho bundles me into my coat and propels me out of the nightclub to the line of rickshaws waiting by the side of the road. He pushes me in one door; I scramble out the other side. He grabs me again, pins me on to the seat and shouts to the driver to start pedalling. I'm sobbing now.

'That man was going to hurt you,' he shouts angrily. 'I'm just trying to protect you.'

'That man is a customer,' I yell back.

Cho loosens his grip. He stares at me from the darkness of the rickshaw.

'What kind of customer, Anyi?'

How do I explain? Where should I begin? He knows what's happened. Why do I have to say out loud what must be obvious to the world? I tell him about Auntie Wen, the beatings, the silver coins in my lockbox. He wants facts: how many men, where do we go, what do they do to me. Then the question he's been holding inside bursts out like a sob. 'But why?' he asks.

Soldiers, full moons, silver knives that cut so well. I don't need to cut if I have a man who'll knock me down. As long as one of them is around, the soldiers will stay away. No more ghosts in my room and not in my bed, either. Can't you understand, dear Cho? Then his body pulls away from mine and my heart hardens.

'You told me I needed to fight back. To stand up for myself,' I remind him.

'Not this way! Let me take care of you.'

'I want to take care of myself.'

'You can't. This madness of yours is proof. It's sick and wrong and you must stop right now. Please, Anyi.'

'Why should I?'

'Because I love you, Song Anyi.'

A tiny flame of hope lights the cavern of my heart. Here is someone who wants to love me, filthy as I am. Could I wear a marriage headdress after all, the beads hanging heavy in my eyes and the red silk gleaming in the sun?

No, it could never happen. We would be breaking the law. Our fathers are brothers and the penalty for incest is public strangulation. My throat thickens at the prospect of death but I cannot bear to put him at risk. He smells so good, my dear Cousin Cho, the way a man should. No sweat, no blood, no taste of dry leaves.

'You want me?' I ask.

He presses his body into mine. I feel his length.

'Then you shall have me,' I promise.


*Cho*

She balances on her tailbone, arms and legs reaching for the ceiling. Four slender limbs float in the heavy air. I look carefully from all sides, trying not to breathe too hard on her ivory skin.

49

I can find no blemish, no sign that she cuts herself the way she says.

'You're perfect,' I proclaim.

White tulips stand in a vase on her nightstand. She asked for them as soon as she learned that none were to be found in Shanghai. I scoured the city: every farmer at the market with his roots and vegetables, every ruddy-faced flower girl on the street. I succeeded. I will do whatever she asks.

I straddle the wooden chair, my naked back pressed against the slats. I invite her to approach, using nothing more than a smile.

She scrambles off the bed, kicking aside her sleeping robe. She's a real Shanghai lady now. Her hair is cut and curled into the latest fashion. Her body is lithe and her figure willow thin. She plants her bare feet in front of mine. Her breasts tilt so close to my mouth I have to bite my lip. Her nipples are dusky rose, just like the inside of her mouth. I can't stand it any more.

'Come and sit here,' I beg.

She points at my knees, trembling with effort.

'There?'

'Here!' I cry. 'On top of me. Please!'

She sinks on to me. Her legs wrap around my waist. She hooks her feet through the slats and giggles. I feel her laughter deep inside my belly. She leans forward to rest her head on my shoulder. I almost weep.

'I feel so safe with you, Cho.'

I place my hands under her buttocks. My palms are slick.

'Look at me,' I command.

She straightens her back like an obedient child.

'I promise to be gentle. Do you believe me?'

'Yes.'

'The minute it starts to hurt, you tell me and I'll stop. All right?'

'But I want you to hurt me.'

'Don't say that! I don't want to cause you pain. And I won't

50

let anyone else hurt you. On the graves of all my ancestors, I swear it!'

She doesn't seem to hear me. Her eyes are shut tight. She must be ready for me. I pull her close, so close that when the gasp leaves her mouth it fills my lungs. I try to move slowly, I really do.

# Chapter Six

# Homecoming

*Kang*

Four weeks of travel, by train from Ohio to New York, then the steamer to Shanghai, every day wondering whether Anyi was alive or dead. Each morning Kang woke, determined to be hopeful. He would open once more his Uncle's telegram and read: *Anyi recovered. Marriage proposals received. Come home.*

Kang had called his Uncle as soon as the telegram arrived.

'Recovered from what? Why is Anyi in Shanghai?'

They talked for a long time, his Uncle sharing every gruesome detail of the marks left on Anyi's body. In his dreams, Kang saw his little sister splayed on a bed of leaves, tortured by beasts masquerading as men. How could any human being survive such an attack?

Yet for all the fulsome detail of her attack, Uncle Song was strangely cagey about the marriage proposals that followed. 'We'll discuss it after you arrive. Once you get to know the men, you'll understand,' Uncle said.

It was a lie, Kang was sure of it. He was convinced that the duty Uncle demanded from him was not to arrange his sister's marriage but her funeral. They would keep her body on ice until an auspicious day for the funeral had been chosen. They would wait for him to lay the yellow cloth on her dead face. Or was her body so ravaged that no amount of skill could keep her whole? When his thoughts reached this inevitable end, the optimism of the morning flew out of his hands like the shreds of his Uncle's telegram, yellow flecks floating in the ocean air.

How could this happen? As a child, Anyi had been fearless. Two years his junior, Anyi could match Kang in any feat: running, jumping, riding a horse. They had lived together like that, comrades in arms, through the golden days of their childhood. Then the tutor came and their roads parted.

Kang was banished to their father's study to memorise Confucian texts. Outside the study door, Anyi raged.

'Baba, why won't you let me study like Kang?'

Kang would have liked nothing better and even Mama agreed.

She said to Baba, 'Girls these days should be taught to read and write. And to make their sums too.'

'I can already do those things,' Anyi retorted ungratefully. 'I want to learn what Kang knows.'

Baba refused. 'No good ever came from educating a pretty girl.'

Anyi ran into the orchard then and refused to come back. In the years that followed, she grew tall and strong and wild, while Kang left home, first for Shanghai, then America. He had been gone for four years now, wonderful years released from family and duty and all the expectations weighted down on the shoulders of an only son.

Kang didn't belong any more in China; America was his home now. He had quarrelled bitterly with his father about his refusal to go back. So deep was Kang's resentment that neither the death of his mother last summer nor of his father's weeks later was reason enough for Kang to return. But Anyi!

Kang sat on the ship deck, willing the horizon to near. Day after day, it refused to move. The grey seas slapped the sides of the ship. He grew weary and fractious and all hope sank.

Then, overnight, the sameness of the western horizon changed. What was once a thick black line now dissolved into a landmass.

With every passing hour the ship seemed to gain speed so that the next day, Kang could already see buildings, a grillwork of city streets, hundreds of tiny figures milling about the docks.

The steamer eased into port, the guy ropes were fastened and the huge engine silenced at last. Sailors rushed forward to lower the gangplanks: first class, second-class, steerage. Kang rubbed his eyes hard and thought he saw a ghost. He leaned over the railing.

'Anyi!'

She was alive. She held no crutch and could stand on her own. She was thin though, so thin that the sea breeze could have knocked her over if Cho hadn't been at her side. Her coat flapped around her knees and Kang could see a flash of colour inside. His Uncle had not lied after all. Anyi was alive and well.

In one delirious rush his fears fled and he almost fell, suddenly off-balance, empty and unsure. His hands gripped the steel railing as he tried to align himself with this new situation. He had come for a funeral. Now, instead, he would have to think of her marriage.

He pushed his way forward, through the coolies and the passengers crowding the top deck. From the opposite side, Anyi made her way up the gangplank and when they finally met, he held her back by the shoulders so that he could first look his fill. Her eyes held his without shame or fear. This was the daredevil little sister Kang remembered. His heart grew so full that all he could do was fold her into his arms.

'You smell like home,' he said into the collar of her coat.

'You need a haircut,' she admonished. 'And a shave too.'

'I have to pinch you to see if you're real.'

He took her nose between his fingers and pretended to twist them tight. She shrieked then laughed, dancing all the way down the gangplank and on to the pier. Cho was waiting there with their old American friend, Max Lazerich.

'You're here for good?' Max asked.

Kang shook his head ever so slightly, motioning with his eyes towards Anyi as she and Cho chattered like carefree children.

'I'm here to handle my sister's affairs. It won't take long by the looks of it. I can't believe she's recovered so well. Let me introduce you.'

But Anyi scowled, crossing her arms tightly across her chest.

'What is that barbarian doing here?'

'Anyi! What kind of a word is that?'

'It's what Father called them, all of them, those foreigners who live on our soil as if it were their own.'

'Don't talk like that,' Kang said angrily. 'Father's brainwashed you.'

'Hush, he can hear you!' she cried.

She was staring past Kang, as if listening to someone speaking to her and flinching at the volley of harsh words.

'Come, Baba is waiting,' she said abruptly to Kang. 'Cho can take care of the luggage. We'll take a pedicab home.'

Kang whirled around. His father was dead but Kang felt a fear as real as if the old man were alive and standing before him, brandishing his fists. He scoured the faces of the crowd milling about the docks and when he turned back, he saw Max staring too.

'You know, you've told me so much about your father, I hoped he really was here so I could meet him at last,' Max said.

'Then you'll have to go to his grave in Soochow,' Anyi spat. Imperiously, she tugged Kang away toward the street.

There was no time to say goodbye to Max, no time to wonder about Anyi, no time to explain that the two suitcases he carried were all that he had brought from America. Like a tugboat navigating the Whangpoo River, Anyi was taking Kang into the heart of Shanghai.

*Anyi*

We sit in the back of the rickshaw, Kang and Baba and me. Kang waits for me to speak but I've left all my words behind on the docks. I open my handbag, fishing for courage.

'Here,' I say. 'This is for you.'

Kang opens the thin box. He spreads the delicate spines of the fan across his knees.

'Mother's?'

'Her favourite.'

'It's broken.' He examines the two slats of carved sandalwood crushed into one. 'Did she leave it for me?'

What shall I tell him, Baba? That neither you nor Mama left any gift for Kang? That you died with his name on your lips and a curse in your heart?

Baba doesn't answer. He wants the fan, his hands white-knuckled, ready to do battle.

'The fan was damaged on the journey from Soochow.'

Kang turns to me, his face anxious and care-worn. I try to smooth the wrinkles from his forehead with my thumb. He pulls down my hand, presses his lips into the back of it.

'I thought you were dead,' he whispers.

'I'm not. And now that you're here, I know I'll get better.'

'Where? I mean, how?' Kang stutters to a halt, his face red.

I lean back into the seat, looking for the words to explain.

'Never mind. You don't have to say anything. Not now. I'm sorry I asked.'

His face turns away from me. The Whangpoo River snakes under the road as we cross Garden Bridge. Soon we'll be in the home of our Aunt and Uncle. Soon, there will be no more time to talk. Words pour from my mouth, foolish and irrelevant, yet surely somewhere among the polite phrases there must be a few nuggets of truth?

'I can walk easily now. Cho has been showing me the sights. During the day, I'm fine. At night, it's hard to sleep, especially when there's a full moon.'

I lean my head on his shoulder. His body shudders. Does he, too, think I'm dirty? I raise my head to look at him. His eyes are large and wet. He doesn't speak. He holds my hand and squeezes it.

*Kang*

Anyi went to her room as soon as we arrived.

'It often happens. Don't worry,' Cho said. 'She'll be better in the morning.' He too disappeared upstairs, leaving Kang to dine alone with his Aunt and Uncle.

Uncle spoke of the candidates he had interviewed and the bride price the men wanted from Kang. Auntie Song was not shy in pushing forward her favourite.

'Comprador Chen is as rich as an imperial eunuch. Anyi will be very well off.'

'I don't care about the money, Aunt. Will he be kind to her?'

Uncle Song snorted. 'You talk like a girl dreaming of moonlight and stars. If you're so worried, come meet him yourself at the Shanghai Race Club tomorrow. We're both members.'

'Don't you need to donate money to become a member? How old is this man?' Kang asked.

'Honourable Chen is your Uncle's age. That's what makes him so perfect,' Auntie Song gloated. 'He already has five children: three sons to carry on the family name and two daughters to pamper him at home. He won't need any more children from Anyi.'

Kang was silent for a long time. Finally, he asked, 'What about wedding guests?'

His Aunt and Uncle shook their heads. Uncle Song said, 'You don't realise how hard it's been to keep Anyi's reputation intact. The servants talk. It's only a matter of time before their masters begin to listen. We cannot afford to let the truth get out, not before the wedding takes place.'

'You mean Comprador Chen doesn't know what happened to her?' Kang blurted out.

'Of course not,' Auntie Song responded. 'What man in his right mind would want to marry such a girl? We told him that Anyi is a shy and modest child and so he agrees to everything. There will be no bridal sedan or wedding procession, just a quiet family dinner here at home. That concession we're willing to make out of respect for your father.'

They had thought of everything. The date, the time, the wedding clothes and trousseau, all of it planned with military precision.

'Does Anyi know?' Kang asked.

'She's met the man, of course. Comprador Chen would not make a proposal without seeing the bride for himself. Once you formally accept his proposal, you can tell her.'

Kang blanched. His Uncle was gruff though not unsympathetic.

'Anyi is a sensible girl,' he said. 'She'll agree soon enough if you find the right way to tell her. And, if not, well, just make sure there's no fuss.'

Kang searched for the right words while he mounted the stairs that night but he could find none. Anyi's door was shut tight and no light shone through the cracks though Kang had been told about the single candle that must be kept lit day and night.

Just as well, it was his first night in China. He wasn't ready to broach the topic of marriage. There would be other days, better times. If he had a good night's sleep, he might even find the way to convince his sister that marriage was the only solution.

He headed toward the bedroom the maid had prepared for him, next to his Uncle's room at the other end of the hall. The maid, Blossom, was there waiting. 'We've rearranged the Master's dressing room for you. It's small. I hope it's comfortable enough.'

Blossom began to unpack his suitcases but Kang sent her away. He wasn't used to servants any more and besides there was so little to do. Two suits, four shirts, three ties. Some sweaters and a coat. An old hat Cho had once given him and a pair of warm leather gloves. The rest of his belongings, he had placed in storage back in Ohio, under the watchful eye of his former employer.

He had only one small photograph of Helen and him. It wasn't a very good likeness. It had been taken at a fair with the shock of the flash printed across both their faces. He propped it on the nightstand between the washbasin and his eyeglasses case.

'I'll be back,' Kang whispered. 'Sooner than you think.'

He slept fitfully. Now that he was in China, his dreams returned to America. He saw the shimmer of wheat at sunset, the sharp line that divided the asphalt highway into coming and going, the spray of freckles down Helen's back. With a start, he woke. It was still dark and his watch told him that he'd slept only a few hours.

He got out of bed and walked down the hall. There were noises inside Anyi's room. Kang tapped lightly on the door.

Cho opened it. He shook his head at Kang. 'She's having a bad night. I'm trying to calm her. Why don't you come back in the morning?'

From inside the blackness of Anyi's room came a low moaning. Kang turned on his heel and hurried back to his room. Why hadn't he stayed in America, simply wired his Uncle instructions and money? Shaking, he sank into bed, clutching the soft mattress to calm himself.

He closed his eyes and thought of Helen. He had come back to China so that he could sort out his sister's affairs himself, like a brother should. Anyi needed to be protected and the only protection for a girl was marriage. Kang would meet this Comprador Chen. He would talk to him seriously. And if the man were a decent fellow who would treat her well, Kang would let them marry.

*Anyi*

I can't sleep. I open the curtains to look down on the night streets and find an old moon hanging low on the horizon. Every night now, I force myself to look. I watch it grow fat week by week. Surely this is the way to lose the fear the full moon holds for me. Yet, even as thin as this moon is, my body turns cold and I begin to shake. I fall to my knees and crawl, eyes closed, to the bed.

Nian finds me, as always.

She lifts me on to the bed. She piles quilts on top of my cold body. I drag them up to cover my face. It's warm and sour inside my cocoon but at least my breathing slows. When the sun drives away the moon's glow, I'll sleep again.

When I sleep, I dream and my dreams are always filled with men: Uncle wears a heavy woollen coat, Cho dances the two-step for strangers, men line up to slap my face while Kang directs traffic.

I'm a girl again. My old cloth shoes peek out from under a long brocade gown. I walk down a dusty street, worried that the yellow dirt will stain my new white socks. As I turn the corner, I hear the clanging of gongs and drums. A wedding!

The crowd thickens. Auntie is at the head of the procession. She wears all her fur coats, one on top of the other. Her lady friends throw watermelon seeds at her feet and Auntie tries to catch them with her pudgy hands. The crowd is in such good spirits. They pay no attention to me, the bride.

I walk and walk until the crowd is so thick I can go no further. There's a sudden hush and the procession halts. Silently, a row of men and women form on either side of a seashell path that leads into a wooded glade. The white pancake makeup creases and cracks on my cheeks. My left leg is warm with urine I can no longer control. It puddles inside my shoe.

They push me forwards on to the seashell path. I fall and the crowd grumbles, forcing me onwards on bloody knees. Someone pushes my face into the moulding leaves. I knock my head three times on the ground in prayer to whatever god is demanding so much sacrifice from me.

I lift my head and smell the sea and wood rot and stench of moist earth. The crowd has disappeared. There's no one in this wooded glade except for me, though I think it won't be for long.

I wake. Baba and Mama have come. They stand over my bed with sorrowful faces.

'Kang is here,' I remind them. 'He'll take care of me and you can rest then, I promise. Soon we'll all be at peace.'

# Chapter Seven

# Brotherly Love

*Cho*

The weather outside is cold and clear. The sun hits the table at just the right angle to make it glow. The breakfast room has never looked so cheerful, almost domestic. I have to laugh.

'Still the old bookworm, I see.'

Kang looks over the rims of his glasses, confused as always at my jokes. His newspaper has wilted over the steam of his coffee, threatening to invade his plate of congealed eggs.

Anyi understands and laughs too, though not at me.

'When we were kids, we always ate breakfast together, all four of us, and read the newspapers. Do you remember, Kang?'

'I do.'

She reaches out to place her hand on his and a fire burns in my belly. Is this jealousy? I've never felt it before, always happy to share my women with others as long as I could have what I wanted from them.

She pours his coffee and he smiles his thanks. Their chairs are so close she can read the paper over his shoulder. Softly, they talk about the news of the day.

'The Japanese have signed a treaty with Germany to fight against the Communists,' Kang reads out loud.

Anyi replies, 'The day is so beautiful. Let's not talk about such things.'

'The two of you sound like an old married couple,' I say. 'Why don't you go and live together?'

Her face lights up. 'That's exactly what I want. I've found the place already, a little yellow house in Frenchtown just right for two. Let's go out today and look!'

Kang mumbles about appointments, my father, things that he must do. Anyi's face shimmers for a moment longer then fades.

'Give me a newspaper,' she says.

Kang reaches into the pile my father's left behind and hands one to her.

'Not this,' she says, tossing the pink pages of the North China Daily News on top of Kang's plate. 'I won't read about barbarians.'

Kang pushes away from the table. His breast swells like a rooster's yet all that comes out is a mild cheep. 'I don't understand what's come over you. You didn't used to be so narrow-minded. We'll talk about it later. I've got to go.'

Anyi's face is mutinous. She stares at the paper but I know better.

'Come here,' I say.

She sits on my lap. It's only for a moment, but the fear of discovery is electric.

'You can take me to see this house of yours. I'll do anything you want, Song Anyi.'

*Kang*

The servants came laden with plates. Kang sat in the place of honour between Auntie and Uncle Song. She kept his plate well filled. Blossom hovered too, eager to serve. Soon enough, Kang lay down his chopsticks and placed one hand on his belly.

'No more, please. It's all so good, Auntie, but I couldn't eat another bite.'

Uncle continued to chew. He pointed with his chopsticks at his favourite dish of red braised pork. Blossom held it while

Uncle fished out the biggest piece of fatty meat. When he was done, he covered his rice bowl with his hand.

'No more food,' he said. 'Kang has an announcement to make. Blossom, you can go now. Close the dining room door behind you.'

Kang fumbled in his pocket and brought out a plain blue box, small inside the palm of his hand. He pushed it across the table toward Anyi and prayed that she would like what was inside.

She opened the box and crowed, showing them all a pair of pearl earrings. 'They're just like the ones Mother used to wear,' she said, happily fastening them to her ears.

'You like them? I'm glad. I bought them today. A gift for you.'

'Why? It's not my birthday and I have nothing to give in return!'

She rose from her chair to kiss him on both cheeks. He thought he saw tears in her eyes and the speech he had so carefully composed dried to dust in his mouth.

'I want you to marry Comprador Chen,' Kang said quickly.

'Who?'

She asked the question, all the while backing away from the table until the mirrored walls of the dining room allowed her to go no farther. Her eyes flitted from one face to the other like a rabbit trapped by the dogs.

'He came to dinner three times in one week,' Auntie Song reminded her. 'He brought you a box of candied plums.'

'He's a good friend of mine. I've known him for years,' Uncle Song added.

'You want Anyi to marry that old man?' Cho shouted. 'Why?'

'For face,' Uncle and Auntie said in unison.

'I won't do it,' Anyi replied. 'If I'm such a disgrace to the family, I'll leave, get a job. I can be a clerk, just like Kang was when he first came to Shanghai, or a secretary at one of the banks. You know I'm good at numbers. I can read and write too. Surely someone in this city can use my skills?'

63

Auntie and Uncle laughed. His low rolling rumbles blended oddly with her high tittering wheezes. They looked surprised to hear themselves laughing together and that made them laugh even more. Then abruptly, they both stopped.

'What will people say?' Auntie asked in a chill voice.

'That I'm a stingy man,' Uncle answered. 'Is that what you want, Niece?'

Anyi's eyes locked onto Kang's face. She whispered to him, 'We could grow old together. Wouldn't you like that?'

Kang cast his eyes down at the table as Anyi fled the room.

### Blossom

The maid ran, slipping and sliding across the polished wooden floors until she reached the back door of the house. She threw it open and sprinted across the beaten dirt courtyard, past the corrugated tin shacks where she and the other servants slept, into the warm, yeasty environment of the kitchen.

They were all gathered there on overturned wooden tubs to eat the evening meal: Cook, the housekeeper, the driver and Nian.

'They're done already?' Cook looked up.

'Are there any leftovers?' the housekeeper asked.

'Never mind about that!' Blossom yelled. 'The broken girl is leaving. Hurrah!'

'It's about time,' the housekeeper acknowledged. 'It's scandalous to have a soiled girl like that in our household.'

Blossom laughed and danced about the kitchen. Cook smiled to see such joy but the housekeeper's face turned sour.

'This doesn't mean the Young Master will want you back in his bed,' the housekeeper said.

Blossom's eyes shone. 'We'll see.'

She crept back into the house and up the stairs. Old Master Song had left the house soon after dinner. The brother was pacing in the dressing room. As usual Mistress Song had fallen asleep with the gramophone still playing. Blossom would take the needle off the record though not yet.

She knelt by the keyhole to the Young Master's bedroom and tried to look in. It was dark. Could he be asleep already? Then from the next room where the broken girl slept came the creaking of wooden bed legs and the sounds of their coupling, in plain hearing of all their family. The housekeeper was right: the girl was shameful.

'Go away!' Blossom whispered. 'Go now.'

*Anyi*

The house sleeps. I creep down the stairs. Cook used to get up from his bedroll, a heavy cleaver in each hand, when he heard me lurking downstairs. Now he knows that I like to wander when sleep is more frightening to me than a dark house.

The door to the winter garden stands open. The warm humid air seeps into the hallway. I slip inside and close the door behind me.

Water drips from every surface: elephant leaves, fern fronds, orchids by the dozen. Auntie loves these flowers but to me they smell like death. I prefer the fruit trees, even in their leafless and forlorn state.

Once upon a time, we too had a winter garden. It was my favourite place with its view of the flowers and the orchards beyond. When Mother was still well, we would sit there together to sew and talk. Later, when she grew too ill to leave her bed, I would go there to dance with my reflection in the glass, dreaming of the day when I would follow Kang to Shanghai.

I curtsy to a row of bamboo seedlings. I smile at the sunflower who leans his handsome head down to greet me. I sit at the wrought iron table and eat cakes with Baba and Mama. Their ghosts need no chairs though they do like food. Mama licks her fingers then disappears into the ferns. Baba soon follows.

When Mama died, I locked the door to our winter garden and let everything that was once green die too.

New ghosts crowd into the winter garden. Mama and Baba huddle behind the ferns. They don't like to watch. The soldiers line up beside the kumquat tree. I get down on the floor, cold and stony, and let them come. It hardly hurts any more.

When the soldiers are done, Baba says, 'This is Helen's fault.'

Helen: the straw-haired whore whose American wiles had captured Kang's soul. She was the reason Kang had refused to come home.

'Is he going back, Baba? How do you know?'

My father doesn't have to give me an answer. I can see the signs too: the two suitcases with clothes suitable only for winter. Kang isn't here to stay. Helen is already luring him back, back to America where I'll never see him again.

'He's in China now,' Baba says. 'Here's your chance, Anyi. It's up to you to keep him here.'

'How can I stop him?'

'You know your brother better than anyone. Find his weak spot; do whatever is necessary. Keep him here. Save him.'

The air in Kang's room is chill. He murmurs, tossing from side to side. Finally his eyes open and he asks, 'Is that you, Anyi?'

He fumbles in the dark for his glasses. His hand brushes against a plate of oranges on the nightstand and the fruit knife clatters to the floor. Kang finds his glasses and a match too. He strikes it and light leaps into the room.

'Please don't make me marry,' I say.

'You cannot live alone.'

'I don't want to live alone. I want to live with you.'

We argue, our voices low and our tempers high.

'I am the head of the family now. You must obey me,' Kang decrees.

'What right do you have to order me around? Where were you when Mama was dying, when all she wanted was to have you at her side?'

'Don't say that, Anyi!'

Kang reels as if I've physically hurt him, now fatally wounded. How could I have done such a thing? There's only one way to make amends, the only form of penitence I know. With numb fingers I open my sleeping gown and pull it over my head.

'What are you doing?' he cries.

I'm naked now and moving forward until all that separates me from my brother is a winter quilt. Kang reaches for his shirt, crumpled on his chair. He holds it out to me, averting his eyes.

'Put this on,' he commands.

'No. Let me get into your bed. Let me show you how much I love you.'

The soldiers, Auntie Wen's customers and my own dear Cho: they all want what I have to offer. Why not my brother too? Yet he pushes me away. He cringes at my touch. My brother doesn't want my unclean hands on him.

'Why did you come back?' I whisper.

'I came back for you.'

'But not to stay.'

'I don't belong here any more. My home is in America.'

'With the straw-haired whore?'

'Don't call her that!' Kang shouts.

He struggles for control, a childhood weakness that Baba tried to beat out of him. This time Kang succeeds in taming his rage but only by covering his words in ice. 'You will be married, Anyi. And then I will go back to America.'

'No!' I scream. I fall to the ground on all fours. The fruit knife slides into my hand as if summoned. I hold the blade against my body and press. It's sharper than I thought and the blood flows quickly.

Kang rushes at me, struggling to catch hold of the knife. I writhe away until I can stand before the window.

'Stay with me for one year, here in Shanghai,' I cry.

'Why?'

'How could you forget?' I ask bitterly. 'All my life, this is what I wanted, to be a modern girl, to live in Shanghai. You got your chance, Kang. I never did.'

Kang's face shows no remorse. His eyes narrow with suspicion.

'And what happens after the year is over?'

'I'll do whatever you want, marry whoever you choose.'

'Will you come and live with me in America?'

I see Baba's ghost in the corner. He glares at me, his fists on his hips, violently shaking his head.

'I agree,' I say.

'Very well. You promise to come with me in a year. And I'll be the one to tell Aunt and Uncle.'

*Kang*

He was convinced now: Anyi was mad. He could not give her away to become another man's burden. He would take care of her himself. They would leave as soon as she was stable enough to survive the long ocean crossing, in a week or a month or a year. For now, she would have to be watched night and day though Kang shivered at the thought of Anyi trying to enter his bed once more.

As children they had often crept into bed together, huddled under a blanket to play cards by the light of the moon. It must have been that. He had got it all wrong. Anyi's mind was still muddled. She needed time to become herself again. He would never mention the incident. Why disturb her with it? He was ashamed to have thought such a thing of his own sister.

Now that there was enough light to see, Kang got out of bed and sat down to write. The letter was short but polite. Kang stood by the window watching as the old rickshaw driver carried the note away. By the time his Aunt and Uncle came down to breakfast that morning, the deed would be done. Kang leaned his forehead against the cold glass. He thought he had escaped China. Now the trap had opened and he was caught.

He sat down to write again. *My dearest Helen, the situation is worse than we feared. Anyi lives but is no longer herself. She will require constant care and I am the only one left to give it. Forgive me. I will return in a year's time. If I can, sooner. Then I'll bring you a sister to love who will love you in return. Wait for me.*

Kang had Helen's letter inside his pocket when he came downstairs. His Uncle was in the breakfast room noisily slurping his bowl of congee, the gruel splattering the pages of the newspaper as he read. Cho whistled as he dug his ivory spoon into the soft yolk in front of him. Kang sipped coffee, black and bitter, while he waited for his Aunt to arrive. One announcement would serve for all. Driver Zhang returned first, his hat in one hand and a note in the other. Kang read the words, as biting as he had expected them to be.

When his Aunt finally came to the table, Kang said, 'I have refused Comprador Chen's proposal by letter this morning. Here is his acknowledgement.'

Kang passed the sheet of paper across the table. The look of outrage on Uncle's face grew as his eyes moved down the brief note.

'Fool! Ingrate!' he screamed, throwing the note at his wife. Cho leaned over his mother's shoulder, craning to see what Comprador Chen had written, to witness the bitterness of a suitor scorned.

'You think that good husbands are like walnuts that fall from the trees? Your Aunt and I have exerted every ounce of our influence and the good name of this family to secure this engagement. Go now to Comprador Chen's house and beg him on your hands and knees to reconsider.'

'No,' Kang said.

His Uncle's mouth opened but the only sound Kang could hear was the grandfather clock, ticking away. Cho hid behind a newspaper, as red-faced as his father, the sheets of paper shaking with his laughter.

'Stubborn!' Uncle Song raged.

'Reckless!' Auntie Song cried.

Uncle Song stood. 'You have no value for family. Your father once said as much but I never wanted to believe him. So be it. If family is nothing to you then you are nothing to me. Get out of my house. I wash my hands of you both.'

Uncle left the dining room. Kang closed his eyes. He needed a moment's rest. Why had he not foreseen how badly Uncle would take the news?

Aunt eyed him coldly. 'You'll never find a husband for that girl. Soon, everyone in town will know about her. Then what will you do?'

'I'll support her.'

'How?'

'I'll start my own business. I wanted to ask Uncle for a loan.'

'No money. Not now. If you like, I can talk to him. I might convince him to let you and your sister stay here a little longer.'

'Please don't trouble yourself. We'll move out right away,' Kang said stiffly.

'As you wish,' Aunt said. Then she too left the room.

Cho lowered his newspaper and wiped his grinning face with a handkerchief. 'I've never seen anything like it. You were brave to face up to them. But what are you going to do now?'

# Part Two: The Dancing Girl

# Chapter Eight

# Metropole Gardens

*Cho*

Every time the door opens, a new gust of snow blows in. A waitress waits, ready to wipe away the melting flakes so that no customer can slip and fall in this finest of pastry shops. I wait too, trying not to look eager. Anyi sits in a booth, her eyes trained on the door, shredding napkins with a ferocious intensity.

A man enters. His hat is covered in snow and the brim is turned low to shield his face. He's got a little black notebook in his hand and he's scribbling madly. The waitress relieves him of his coat and hat and still the man goes on writing. When he finally stops, he puts his pencil into his trouser pocket while the notebook goes into the breast pocket of his jacket. He pats it one more time as if pressing it ever closer to his heart.

'Manager Lin!' I say warmly.

The man peers into my face. His eyes take in my clothes: a suit with fashionably wide shoulders and high-waisted trousers cinched tightly around my narrow body. Manager Lin eyes my wide tie with its burnt orange spots. Immediately, I loosen the knot and hold it out.

'Manager Lin, I'm so glad you could make it. I see that we have similar tastes. This is my favourite tie. Please take it as my gift.'

Lin demurs just long enough to be polite. 'What was your name again?' he asks.

'Song Cho,' I remind him. 'Please come and meet my cousin, Song Anyi. She's the one I called you about.'

Anyi sweeps her paper shreds onto the floor where they assemble like another gust of snow. Her eyes are cast demurely downward, allowing Lin to appraise her obviously expensive dress. But he seems more interested in coffee and cake.

'You wouldn't believe how hard it is to find girls,' Lin says. 'The ones with the big names, with their pictures in the newspapers, they have exorbitant demands. They want a motorcar, a personal maid, a private dressing room, an unlimited clothes account. Do they think I want them as concubines to the emperor?'

Anyi shifts in her seat. Her fingers play with the little silver pastry fork. Lin studies her hands.

'Can you sing? Play any instrument?' he asks brusquely.

Anyi shakes her head.

'She's a dream on the dance floor,' I interject.

'What about the barbarian tongues?' Lin asks. 'Can you speak any of those?'

Anyi replies with pride. 'I can read and write English.'

'I don't care if you've translated all the works of Confucius. Can you speak English?'

'Yes.'

The blaze in her eyes heats the air. Lin peruses Anyi's face for the first time.

'You have a temper,' he says. 'I prefer my women softer.'

I slide an envelope across the table. I leave it tucked beneath the saucer of Lin's empty coffee cup and turn away.

'Look, Anyi. It's snowing again.'

The envelope vanishes into Lin's breast pocket. His voice turns oily.

'It really is splendid to see you again, Song Cho, and an honour to meet your cousin.'

'When will the ballroom open?'

'In two more weeks. Barely enough time to get everything ready.'

'What do you need?' Anyi asks.

Lin holds out the stubby fingers of his hand, pressing them down one by one.

'Maids. Laundresses. Bus boys. A new bandstand. Cooks for every shift.'

'And the hostesses?' I prod gently.

Lin ignores the hint. 'Girls show up on my doorstep, day and night. They've no place to stay, no family or friends in town. The owners don't understand how much responsibility it is to be a dance floor manager.'

He rises abruptly.

'I've another appointment. Thanks for the coffee, Song. Nice meeting you, Miss.'

Lin signals to the waitress to bring his coat and hat. All is lost, I think, though there's a new fire in Anyi's eyes.

'Manager Lin,' she calls out. 'Do you know Auntie Wen?'

Lin returns to the table, his eyes bright.

'Are you one of her girls? That's a rare talent in this town, if you're strong enough to last.'

Lin reaches out one hand and clutches Anyi's upper arm. Angrily, she pulls away. Lin laughs.

He says, 'I want seventy-five per cent of your share of Auntie Wen's fee and the right to choose each customer.'

'Ten per cent,' Anyi counters. 'And the customers are mine to accept or decline.'

'Sixty-five per cent.' Lin pushes his face into Anyi's. 'And these customers of yours will never set foot inside the Metropole.'

In the end, they agree to split the fees evenly. We shake on it and I'm ready to leave but Anyi stays put.

'I want it in writing,' she insists.

They use Lin's notebook. She watches over his shoulder, mumbling under her breath about his terrible penmanship.

'You write it then,' he grumbles.

Her characters are strong and firm, flowing down the page

with a practised ease. She makes two copies and when she's done, she tears one sheet out and hands back the notebook.

'Why have you written this twice?' Manager Lin asks in a testy voice.

'So that we both know what we agreed. Is it correct, both copies?' she asks.

Manager Lin reads slowly then nods.

Anyi is the first to put her seal to each page, a tiny square of red ink that bears her full name. As a witness, I add my seal too. Finally, Lin affixes his mark to the bottom of each copy.

'We have a contract now,' Lin says. 'Legally binding and enforceable in any court, Chinese or barbarian.'

'When do I start?' Anyi asks, as she folds the sheet of paper into her handbag.

'Put on your coat,' Lin says. 'We have shopping to do.'


*Blossom*
The broken girl sat at the breakfast table. She was there when Blossom had risen at dawn to stoke the fire in the kitchen and she was still there now, waiting for the Young Master to come downstairs. He had gone out last night and the driver had not been summoned to bring the Young Master home until first light.

'My son is still sleeping,' Mistress Song said coldly to the girl. 'I forbid you to disturb him.'

'Then I'll go alone,' the girl said. She left the table and fetched her hat and coat. Mistress Song was waiting for her at the front door.

'Where are you going?'

'Into the city.'

'To do what?'

'I'm meeting someone.'

'Who?'

'What difference does it make?' the girl cried out.

Blossom peeked around the corner, one hand over her mouth to stifle the laughter.

'You may not leave this house unaccompanied. It's not proper for a young lady of your station.'

'I'm not a proper young lady,' the girl retorted. 'You said so yourself.'

Mistress Song leaned forward to clasp the girl's chin in her hand. 'As long as you're under my roof, you will obey me. You'll take the amah with you. That's what she's for.'

'Have you forgotten? Nian has gone home for the New Year. We're waiting for her to return so that we can move out of here.'

'Then Blossom will go with you.'

Blossom climbed into the backseat of the rickshaw where the girl had already installed herself. Truculently, the maid stared at the back of Driver Zhang as he pedalled hard over the hump of the bridge into the heart of the French Concession. She refused to enjoy the crisp winter air or even smile at the memory of the housekeeper's face when she was told about the day off.

Then the driver stopped and Blossom could mope no more. It was a palace fit for the emperor with wide marble steps and a great hall. A grand mosaic dominated the space with its blue, green and red tiles whose colours multiplied and refracted in the mirrors all around. So this was the Metropole Gardens that everyone was talking about, the dance hall to end all dance halls, soon to be opened any day now.

Blossom had never seen anything like it. Her fingers stroked the intricately carved panels, her feet sank into the soft plush carpet while her eyes lifted to ogle the crystal chandeliers overhead. The Song family home was nothing by comparison. Who knew such luxury existed?

Then Blossom realised that the girl was gone. She wasn't outside where the driver had parked the rickshaw to wait for their return. She wasn't in the hall of mirrors or the grand ballroom behind it. She was nowhere to be seen, no, wait, there she was, running up the stairs as if her life depended on it. Blossom quickly followed.

She found the Young Mistress with about twenty other girls all standing at the back of a huge room. A man approached Blossom, a long bamboo cane in one hand. With one savage stroke he cut the air. The girls pressed their backs into the wall. Blossom's eyes opened wide with fear.

'Who the hell are you?' the man barked at Blossom. 'Are you here for a job too?'

Before she could think of something to say, she heard the Young Mistress reply coolly, 'Manager Lin, this is my Aunt's maid. She's here to chaperone me.'

The man laughed. 'Not many of my girls come equipped with maids or such tender sensibilities.' Then he bent down to pinch Blossom's buttock and said, 'If you ever get tired of mopping the floors, you come and see me. Meanwhile, get out of the way.'

Blossom retreated to the far end of the room, unsure whether to sit or stand. There were no chairs, other than the tall barstool that the man kept for himself. After a while, she sank to her haunches to watch and learn.

Manager Lin was speaking to the girls. 'You are all here to become a dance hostess. You will make the Metropole proud or you will be fired. Your first lesson is walking.'

One by one, the girls crossed the wooden floor. At any sign of slouching or stiffness, the bamboo rod would lash out. One girl stumbled and fell to her knees. Her long braids brushed the floor. She began to cry, pulling at the Western style shoes on her feet.

'I can't wear these,' she moaned. 'My feet have just been unbound.'

She threw one wooden-soled shoe off. It clattered across the floor. Her bare toes were horribly misshapen. The long one was bleeding.

'Get out! I have no time for peasants!' Manager Lin screamed. He opened his notebook and crossed her name out. 'Next!'

After lunch, he paired them for dance lessons.

'In the beginning, you may not have many customers,' he explained. 'Or, the customers who have arrived will not be ready to dance. You will entertain them by dancing with each other. We will start with the waltz.'

There was no music, only the pounding of Lin's cane on the floor to mark the time. 'One, two, three. In, out, out.'

Some of the girls were so shy they couldn't bear to be touched. They giggled and murmured among themselves. The cane lashed out. The girls danced. All of them could follow but few could lead.

'You have to be able to do both. Not all men know how to dance,' he shouted. 'Now the two-step!'

They dipped and swirled, promenaded and lunged. He taught them how to fan their faces without disturbing their hair and to sit to show the greatest length of leg. He badgered and bellowed. And, as needed, he would knock a girl to the ground.

One of them could not get up after Lin had slapped her so hard he had broken the skin of her face. He called two workers to carry her out of the building.

'What do we do with her, Manager Lin?' they asked.

'Wherever you want,' he said.

On the ride home, neither girl spoke. The Young Mistress looked exhausted and her right hand shook. Blossom too had been drained by the experience. She had heard of the dancing world though never knew anyone who belonged there. Blossom had always thought of it as a glamorous kind of life full of pretty dresses and glasses of champagne. Now she recalled the parting words of advice her own mother had given when she left home.

'Be grateful for this position with the Song family. Most girls in Shanghai must content themselves with far less. You can become a seamstress or a shop girl or work on a factory floor. Or, you can slip into the cesspool of Shanghai and turn to prostitution. Not everyone has the skill or patience to do better than that. Beware!'

*Anyi*
The girls here are so young. One of them twines her fingers into mine, her hand so small I could crush it. There are more of them in the ballroom, standing well outside the pools of light that demarcate the dancing from the sitting, the illusion from reality. Manager Lin barks and the child shuffles away into her position close to the exit. Her dress is simple but expensive, a sheath that a man can easily pull over her head with one hand or simply bunch at the waist if he were in a hurry.

This girl must be one of the whores hired by Manager Lin for the men who come here to dance and then demand more. We, the dancing girls, are the gazelles who draw the predators out of the high grass. The whores are the dead meat to be flung to the lions.

There are only ten of us left, most from Soochow though I know none of them. Their parents were servants like their fathers before them. These girls could have grown old as amahs or chambermaids or kitchen helps, safe and maybe even loved in the world they knew. They wanted more, apparently. We all do.

A bell sounds. The practice is over. It was all just a show for the Cantonese owners of the Metropole Garden who sit in one of the balconies that jut out high above the dance floor. The wife fans herself violently, her head averted from the action below, while her husband carries a pair of opera glasses, raising them from time to time to examine the wares.

I feel his gaze on me now: my shoes, the sheer silk stockings, the curve of my hips cocked slightly to one side, just as Manager Lin taught us.

'Some men's eyes will never reach your face,' he said just that morning. 'All they can think of is the yin inside.'

But this Cantonese man is different. He likes breasts, the rounder the better. His gaze swivels from one dancing girl to the next until he finds what he wants.

Rosa came from the Paramount and is our star. It's her name and face on the flyers that litter Nanking Road this week. She's as Chinese as the rest of us but Rosa wears only Western clothes: a low-cut bodice cinched tightly up the back and a skirt cunningly flared so that when Rosa spins across the dance floor, the skirt lifts to reveal the lace garters underneath.

She has a following of her own. Mobsters, they say. Members of the Green Gang or some other triad who will dance only with her, all of them southerners just like the owner now leaning over the balcony above. He's paid a lot for her contract, more than the rest of us combined. How long will it take Rosa to repay her debt? Manager Lin will lend money, though his interest rates are higher than any moneylender in the street. Clothing, hairdressers, even the use of the tiny closet he calls a dressing room come at a price to us and a fee for him.

'I won't pay it,' I say. 'We have a contract, remember? It says here that you will not charge me for these things.'

He squints at my copy of the contract. He opens his mouth in protest but I lay one manicured fingernail beside his seal on the page.

'It doesn't say anything about a dressing room,' he points out.

'Very well. What does it cost?'

Manager Lin's face gleams with avarice and sweat. 'Don't worry your pretty head about it. I'll deduct the amount from your monthly salary. You'll never notice it.'

'I prefer to pay up front. Name your price.'

He sputters. He feigns ignorance of such matters. He says he'll need to ask the bookkeeper but Manager Lin knows the price of a jar of rouge, down to the last copper fen. Finally, he names an astronomical sum. I open my handbag and hand over my coins. His eyes bulge at the sight of so much silver, then he blanches, his eyes darting into all corners of the room, his greed turned cold with fear. He thrusts the coins hastily deep into his pockets and makes ready to leave.

'Wait,' I say.

He stops, his eyes wary once more.

'Write it down,' I say. 'Dressing room paid in full.'

He does as I ask but there will be a price to pay some day. If money doesn't give him a hold over me, he must find another way. What will he choose?

# Chapter Nine

# On the Town

*Kang*

Anyi was like a child in those days. Everything was new: the apartment Cho found for her, the freedom of waking when she liked, the novelty of a servant answerable only to her, for Nian had come along with the hat boxes and the new dresses and some old furniture Auntie Song had bequeathed to Anyi in a fit of generosity.

The apartment was in one of the new high-rise buildings that had begun to sprout like oversized mushrooms around Jing 'An Temple. It was nothing to compare, of course, with the skyscrapers Kang had seen in New York but here in Shanghai, five story apartment buildings cast unnatural shadows across the low brick complexes of the shikumen house where Kang now lived.

Kang knew that Anyi had long been the de facto mistress of their parents' home, ever since their mother fell ill. He expected, then, the order and calm of their childhood household. Instead, he found her boxes still unpacked and stacked high in the hallway. Clothes were piled on top of tables and chairs. When it was time to eat, she went out.

At first, he had objected strenuously to Anyi living alone. But as Cho said, beggars could not be choosers. He had arranged for Kang to live with Max, a good host, generous and discreet, who had cleared out a room and given Kang free rein to use the house and the servants as he wished. Good old Max, what luck to have found such a friend! Yet there were limits and so Cho had found an apartment for Anyi a few short blocks away.

'Who will pay the rent?' Kang asked.

'Don't worry. I'll take care of that too,' Cho assured Kang.

Whenever Kang visited his sister, he found Cho there with his suspenders over the back of a chair and his bare feet on top of a table. With Cho kindly keeping his sister company, Kang no longer felt that the burden of watching over her was his alone. And Anyi was getting better. Kang would never be able to thank Cho enough.

Kang knocked on the door. The amah opened it but Anyi wasn't far behind.

'Come in!' she pulled him with both hands into the sitting room and down to the couch.

Kang told stories then about his time in America, how the country was so grand and the people so kind. Anyi no longer complained about barbarian talk. She listened instead, her eyes round with amazement, her hands cupped around her face, her elbows planted on her big brother's knees.

Or, they would slide on to the floor, giggling like children, and sit cross-legged before the low coffee table. He made drawings for her just like he had in school: bridges, dams, river locks. She drew too, though it was landscapes she liked to capture: clusters of trees dark and threatening. They'd sit like that for hours, he with his pencil and she with her brush and ink, covering sheet after sheet of shiny white paper.

When Kang left, Cho was there to see him to the door.

'She's so much better when you're around,' Kang said.

'That's what I keep telling her,' Cho laughed. 'See, Anyi, even your brother agrees.'

Kang soon found work. His old company in Ohio appointed him as their agent in the Pacific. His task was to sell lathes and hones, saws and planers, all the tools necessary to make machines to whomever would buy them. He had no more time to visit his sister.

So Anyi would run over barefoot to borrow a book or just to say good morning to Kang. He would look up from his desk, the one he had borrowed from Max, glad to see her shining face, happy to break the monotony of shipping times and price lists and product specifications. And even after he had buried himself once more in his paperwork, Anyi lingered, poking her head into his boxes, pulling out a lug or a screw bigger than her hand. When she tired of that, she explored the rest of the house. If Max had been home, maybe she would have refrained. Since he wasn't, she opened his closets and sniffed inside his drawers.

The houseboy didn't like that. He stood in the doorway, ready to intervene at the first sign of danger. But Anyi was careful. Whatever she touched, she put back in exactly the same place: the glasses Max wore to read at night, his toothbrush angled at the corner of the sink, the slippers half-hidden under his bed.

'What time does the American come home?' she asked.

The houseboy wouldn't answer and Kang didn't know. She wandered into the garden and stood so close to the koi pond that Kang was afraid she would fall in. Instead, she squished the warm mud between her toes.

'Look, Kang, there are tadpoles here.'

The houseboy wouldn't let her back into the house with her muddy feet so she turned around and left.

'Come back for dinner tonight,' Kang called after her.

Anyi waved her hand over her head but she didn't come that night or any other night. Kang didn't know where she went or what she did and the amah wouldn't say.


*Anyi*

We spread out quickly across the parquet floor, drifting into pairs, just as Lin taught us. It's easier for two women to snare a man if they work together. First, you ask for champagne and then some small bites, purchased at ruinous prices from the

84

dim sum carts that circle the room. Then the man must dance with each girl at his table, in order to save face for all. Each girl requires a ticket, each ticket good for one dance only. Lin has explained the rules to all his girls.

The clock chimes eight times. The heavy metal doors swing open and a sea of men rushes in. The tide stops abruptly at the perimeter of the dance floor where the men stand as if enchanted by our fresh faces, the pastel coloured dresses and so many bare limbs.

One man works up the nerve to approach a group of girls. Soon, the tables are filled and the dance floor too. I haven't been picked yet. I ask the bellhop, 'Who's that fellow over there?'

The boy says without hesitation, 'That's Stirling Fessenden, the head of the Municipal Council.'

'And the man he's talking to?'

'Du Yuesheng, the gangster.'

None of us expected to attract the cream of Shanghai society, yet somehow the Metropole Gardens is an overnight sensation. Newspapers follow intently the goings and comings of Rosa, the star dancer. I read about her every day at breakfast. Journalists arrive each night and talk to Manager Lin. Once they're gone, he too writes in the black notebook he holds ready at all times.

'What are you writing?' I ask him.

'Names, dates, anything unusual or useful. I collect information like a miser hoards coins. Why aren't you dancing, Song Anyi?'

He waits with me afterwards, outside the Metropole Gardens, even on the nights I tell him Auntie Wen will not come. He doesn't trust me yet just as I don't trust either of them. They talk about me as if I were not there, as if I were a bolt of cloth to be cut into as many pieces as would yield the greatest profit.

Last night, Auntie Wen told Lin the name of my customer and the fee she had negotiated for the night.

'How can you charge so much?' Lin asked in wonder. 'You've doubled her price in the course of one week.'

'She's special, this one. She doesn't break,' Auntie Wen answered with pride.

There are nights when Auntie Wen shows up at the bottom of the stairs of the Metropole Gardens simply for the pleasure of talking to Manager Lin. No one cares that I'm standing by in a thin silken sheath or that the perspiration on my body cools quickly in the night air. Auntie Wen will suck on her pipe and Lin will loosen his tie. They'll gossip like fishwives, rivals in the trade of female flesh.

Lin tells me he admires Auntie Wen's ability to survive in their world, but he would never admit such a thing to her face.

'And don't you tell her either,' he warns me. 'Don't make me look weak.'


*Kang*

They had agreed to meet: Max, Cho and himself, just like in the old days. It was Cho who had arranged everything: the table, the food and the drinks.

'The place has been mobbed since opening night. I had to pull a few strings to get us in,' Cho said.

'What about Anyi?' Kang asked. 'Will she come too?'

'You bet,' Cho replied with a strange smile on his face.

Kang was the first to arrive. He sat in one of the red leather booths set close to the dance floor where he could see everyone coming or going. The orchestra struck up a tune that he and Helen used to dance to back home, her hips matching his exactly.

Max arrived next and slid into the booth next to Kang.

'Sorry I'm late. Work has been murder lately. There's a new Inspector General and he's decided to visit all the custom houses in the country. He should arrive in Shanghai any day now. We're all in a spin trying to get ready.'

The band moved on to a livelier tune, with plenty of beat. A singer appeared in a long white sheath that shimmered as she swayed from side to side. Pairs of dancers shimmied across the floor, some in time with the music and others not at all. It was a jumble of fine gowns and dark wool suits.

'Hey, isn't that your sister over there?' Max asked. He pointed at a slim figure in a jade green dress, gliding across the polished wooden floor.

Kang looked. These days it was hard to know for certain if it was his sister or not. Her clothes and hair changed by the hour. The woman Max was pointing at wore her hair brushed high on top of her head, exposing the long expanse of her naked back.

'Can't be,' Kang said, averting his gaze from so much female flesh.

Max hesitated. 'I only saw her the one time at the docks but it sure does look like her face.'

Kang stared this time, waiting for the woman to turn towards him. Her body was certainly thin enough. He had always considered Anyi's figure to be boyish whereas this woman's was anything but.

Cho slid into the booth on the other side of Kang. He and Max shook hands over the table. Kang was too distracted to be polite.

'What are you looking at?' Cho asked.

'Max thinks that's Anyi out there on the dance floor but that can't be right. I don't recognise the man and Anyi wouldn't dance with a stranger.'

'Sure she would,' Cho said. 'That's what dance hostesses do, if you have a ticket that is. Shall I buy you some so you can dance with her too?'

Kang was standing now on the leather seat of the booth. It *was* her. He couldn't believe it. He waved his hands, trying to catch Anyi's attention. And when that failed, he tried to climb over the back.

'Where are you going?' Cho asked. 'You're not going to try to dance with Anyi without a ticket? They don't like turtles here. That's what they call free riders, don't you know?' Cho laughed at Kang's discomfort.

Anyi changed partners, now a fat man in a tight brown suit. He pressed his shiny face against hers and when she did not resist, he dropped one hand and began to grope her rear end.

Kang tried to push his way out of the booth. Cho threw an arm around his shoulder, holding him tight. 'That's called catching a dead crab,' he said, pointing at the fat man. 'The patron is allowed to do whatever he pleases as long as he's paid the price. Within reason, of course.'

'How dare they treat my sister like that?' Kang stormed.

Max put a hand on Kang's arm. 'I think Cho is trying to tell you that Anyi works here,' he said quietly.

Kang fell back into the booth.

'It's true, old man,' Cho was jovial.

'It's not safe!' Kang cried.

'Of course it is. Whoever got hurt on a dance floor?' Cho retorted.

'But afterwards, you know.' Kang blushed up to the receding roots of his hair.

Cho shook his head. 'I'm surprised at you, Kang, to think such a thing of your own sister.'

'I'm not worried about Anyi's morals. I'm concerned about these men! They're not all decent like us. What if one of them tries to force himself on her?'

'That's why I'm here, every night, to watch over her and make sure she gets home safely. You can rely on me, Cousin.'

When Kang's face remained stony, Cho pointed at a man standing at the back of the ballroom, flanked on either side by bouncers. 'See that man down there? That's the manager, Honourable Lin. I've explained to him what Anyi is allowed to do and he's promised that as long as Anyi is inside the Metropole, she'll dance and nothing else.'

'He's agreed to that?' Kang and Max asked in chorus.

'Of course he has,' Cho said stoutly. 'Lin and I understand

each other. I've got it all in writing. Anyi will come to no harm here.'

The shiny-faced man had danced Anyi into a corner, where he was now rubbing his body up and down hers. Anyi's face was blank, calm and averted, as if she were standing by the road waiting for a bus.

'You're a better man than me if you believe this Lin,' Max muttered. 'I'd thrash any man who handled my little sister like that.'

Kang stared at Anyi, rage and despair chasing each other across his face.

Cho leaned toward him. 'She's made up her mind. You know how she is. You can't stop her now.'

'It's not right,' Kang muttered. 'What will your parents say?'

'What does that matter? You're the head of the family now.'

'Then Anyi should do what I say.'

All three watched as Anyi swirled past their table.

'You should be proud of her,' Cho said. 'She's a dancing girl now.'

### Nian

The brother came to visit. He didn't bother to take off his coat or hat or to greet anyone. Nian stood behind the door and waited for the fireworks to begin.

'How could you?' he asked the Lady.

Nian called her the Lady now that there were no other mistresses to heed. She devoted herself to the Lady, trying to anticipate her every wish, as a good amah should. She watched now as the Lady turned on her heel and marched into the sitting room, her brother trailing close behind. Nian closed the front door and stood in the hallway, just out of eyesight, to watch and listen.

The Lady sat in an armchair, calm and cool. She said, 'You told me I would be free for one year to do as I like. This is what I want to do.'

'It's scandalous,' he shouted. 'What will people say?'

'Why does it matter, Kang?'

The brother paced the room, waving his arms about and shouting. 'People will talk. They'll say things about you. That you're a bad person.'

'Do you think I'm bad?' the Lady asked, leaning forward.

Abruptly, he stopped pacing and for a long moment said nothing. When he did speak, his voice was strained. 'Of course not.'

The brother remained with his back facing the Lady and in time the Lady leaned back in her chair and grew still. Then the brother started pacing again, this time pounding one fist into the other.

'You must hand in your notice,' he demanded.

The Lady smiled.

'Right away,' he shouted.

He whirled to face the Lady and with every word leant farther down over her chair. 'Tonight. I'll go with you. I'll talk to this Manager Lin. Tell him it was all a mistake. He can't force you to work at that place.'

'I signed a contract, Kang. We sealed it with our chops.'

'You're still a child!'

'I'm not, Kang. You've been away for too long. I'm a woman.'

He looked at her then. It wasn't more than a glance, as if the sight of her would burn his eyes.

'You won't do as I say?' he asked heavily.

'No.'

The brother didn't answer that. He just stood up to leave. The Lady followed him to the door.

He said, 'I don't know why I'm here, Anyi. You won't let me take care of you. I might as well go back to America alone.'

Before he left, the brother leaned down and kissed his sister on her forehead. She stood there for a long time afterwards, her head against the door.

'Nian!' she finally called.

The amah came and helped the Lady back into her chair, trying to read the signs. Her body wasn't as limp as when she cut herself, nor as taut as the nights when she had seen Auntie Wen. Yet her face was bleak and Nian could sense the weariness in her bones.

'Talk to me, Nian. Tell me the gossip you heard at the market today.'

The amah sat down on her haunches and thought. 'There are a lot of northerners in town,' she said. 'Looking for any work they can find to pay for passage out of the country.'

'Why?'

'They say war is coming again to China. Do you believe that too?'

The Lady shrugged. Nian waited in silence.

'Will you be home for dinner tonight?'

'Maybe,' the Lady said. 'I'm tired now, Nian. I think I'll take a nap.'

'I need money for the shopping,' Nian called after her.

'My purse is in the sitting room. Take what you need.'

It wasn't the first time the Lady had given Nian free rein over the money and it was hard to resist slipping a coin or two into her pocket.

There was a boy from Henan who had a market stall close to the shop where Nian bought the Lady's brush and ink. He had a sweet smile and soft lips. Whenever Nian stopped by, he would close his stall and they would walk to the river and lie down among the rushes. It had been almost a month since the last time, a month since she had learned of the child she was now carrying.

The bells from the Jing 'An Temple began to peal. If Nian hurried, there would be time enough to buy a fish and some vegetables and still stop by his stall. Quietly, she crept down the hallway to peek at the Lady. Her breathing was soft and regular.

Nian moved silently toward the dressing table, her eyes

searching the jumble of pots and potions for the one she wanted. The rouge jar was open, its cake still soft. Nian pushed one grimy finger in and smeared the red across her forehead and cheeks. She smiled at the sight of herself in the mirror and then, at the sound of one more peal of the temple bells, she hurried out the door.

# Chapter Ten

# Carlton Café

*Anyi*

Kang is still angry. He doesn't care about the money I save him. It's the looks he hates: in the street and in the teahouse around the corner. Everyone seems to know my name. He's dead-set against me dancing at the Metropole Gardens but I can't give it up, not yet. The men I meet there pay well. My lockbox is filling quickly now though it's nowhere near full. When it's full, I'll stop dancing and Kang will love me again.

It's been weeks since I last saw him. The houseboy tries to pretend I'm a stranger.

'Is my brother at home?' I ask.

Kang appears, a sheaf of papers in one hand. 'Why are you here?' he asks stiffly.

'To invite you to dinner.'

'At a restaurant?'

'My home. I'll have Nian cook all your favourite dishes.'

'You're trying to bribe me.'

'I'm trying to be nice!'

Kang's eyes drop and his hands retreat into his pockets. 'Will you invite others?'

'If you like.'

'Let's keep it small,' Kang says. 'Just Max and Cho.'

'All right, I'll tell Nian there will be four for dinner.'

'Five,' Kang corrects me. 'Max will want to bring Jin, his lady friend.'

'Another American?'

'Chinese.'

'Her family allows her to be seen with a barbarian?'

'She has no family. She was sold as a child to Master Feng. He's the owner of Del Monte House,' Kang explains.

'Isn't that a whore house?' I ask, laughing.

'You're a fine one to talk. Jin is the First Cook,' Kang bites back. 'Not a whore.'

That night, when the knock comes, I open the door myself. Kang hasn't forgiven me yet. I can see it in the hunch of his shoulders but he smiles for the sake of the barbarian and his slave girl. She's ugly, a fitting mate for Max. She walks with a cane, unable to place weight on her tiny bound feet. She must come from the countryside where the mothers still bind the feet of their infant daughters in the hope of selling them for the highest price. The slave girl limps into the apartment, one hand on her cane and the other on Max's arm.

The meal is a success. Kang praises each dish. He says, 'Max, let's send the cook over to get these recipes.'

Nian glows. Maybe that's why she pours the after dinner drinks with such generosity. Before long, the men are loud and their faces red. I sit on the couch and watch. Then Jin leans across and touches my hand.

'May I say something to you? In private?' Jin whispers.

We walk out of the apartment and into the night. The scent of magnolia fills the air. Crickets and frogs burst into full song. Jin and I stand under a street lantern that radiates heat. The incinerated remains of insects shower our heads.

'What do you want?' I ask.

She bows deeply, one hand on her knee, the other clutching her cane.

'I want to thank you for this gown. Max told me it was a

gift from you. I have never owned anything so beautiful before. Please know that I will treasure it always.'

I stare into her face, so placid, so very ugly. Now I recognise the torn right shoulder, so badly mended that Nian should have thrown it out weeks ago. Instead she left the rag hanging on the back of a chair where Kang found it.

'Can I give this to Jin?' he had asked.

Now, here in the dark, Jin's eyes are so bright I have to turn away but she won't let me escape. She moves a little closer, close enough now to touch my forearm with her hardened palm.

'Your brother told me that he and I were born in the same year. That makes us both two years older than you,' she says.

Her hand is warm. She's crept so close that her toes touch mine. What does she want from me? I'll never know because now the men are ready to leave for Carlton Café. They call to me, to both of us.

'It's time to go!' Cho cries.

The man in front of the casino is so tall that he has to stoop under the awning that hangs over the front door. Yet he stands as sturdy as the oldest tree, his legs planted well apart. I've never been this close to a Negro before.

Cho steps forward. The Negro's face is bland, unreadable, as he scans Cho's face. I move forward too and the Negro's eyes light up.

'Welcome to Carlton Café, Miss Song. My name is Beauregard.'

He steps aside. His breadth hides an entire entryway. He reaches down to fling the door open.

Cho spurts past the black man, disappearing into the teeming crowd. Kang and Max and Jin follow. I come last, stepping carefully over the threshold.

I say, 'Thank you, Beauregard. Let me introduce my brother, Song Kang, his friend, Max Lazerich, and Jin.' I laugh. 'As for my cousin, Song Cho, you can see he knows his way around this place.'

Some say it was a Buddhist monastery in what was once the countryside outside of Shanghai. Now they call this part of town the Badlands. Altars have given way to craps tables. In the alcoves where a statue of Guanyin might have once stood, a roulette wheel hangs. Cigarette girls crisscross the rooms.

Cho sits at the roulette table. Already he has an impressive pile of chips. As soon as he catches sight of me, he cries out to the crowd. 'This is my cousin, Song Anyi, the famous dance hostess from the Metropole Gardens.'

*Cho*

I love the glow of attention, the pop of the flashbulbs wherever we go. Anyi doesn't like to talk to the journalists so they come to me and I spin tales. They don't care how preposterous my stories are because they make good copy and good copy sells. Every morning, Anyi and I read the newspapers together and we laugh. Then the amah knows it's time to bring in breakfast or lunch or a pot of steaming tea. She's a good servant, that Nian, keeping her eyes discreetly down so that she can't see the rumpled sheets or Anyi's gleaming skin.

I don't bother to go home any more. Driver Zhang brings me everything I need: clothes, a cricket bat, a new pair of dancing shoes. Nian delivers my lists to the driver and he obliges the very same day.

'Your mother was asking about you,' Driver Zhang says as he carefully places an armload of gramophone records on the table. 'She wants to know where you're hiding.'

'What did you say?'

'That you told me not to say,' Driver Zhang answers.

It doesn't take Mama long to figure things out. She arrives the next morning, pounding on the front door, with Baba at her side. They're bickering as always and their shouting is loud enough to pierce all the doors.

'This is your fault,' Baba says to Mama. 'If you hadn't indulged our son from the very first day, he would have known better.'

'If you hadn't taken that dirty girl into our home, Cho would never have been tempted to behave like this.'

Nian is too frightened to let my parents in. She squeezes herself between the wall and the great wardrobe and refuses to come out. I can hardly stand for laughing so it's Anyi who opens the front door, brandishing my cricket bat. She whacks both my parents and sends them back home.

'You didn't want me in your house,' she calls after them. 'Why should I let you into mine?'

Mama sends me notes, pleading with me to come home. She writes about Comprador Chen, a laughing stock now for having tried to capture such a pretty young butterfly in his old man's net.

Kang smiles to hear that story as we stand before the roulette table.

The ball is in play. All eyes watch as the numbers blur into a white halo then dissolve once more into simple digits. When the ball finally drops into its slot, I leap out of my chair in triumph.

'Drinks all around!'

I throw my arm around Anyi's shoulders and squeeze her tight. I smile at the crowd of cheering men and women, every one of them envious of Anyi and me.

*Anyi*

We're gamblers now. The Lido, the Cosmos, the New Paradise: we know them all. I don't care to play as much as Cho. I'd just as soon talk to the men who crowd around but I have to be careful not to make Cho jealous. I place a gentle hand on the shoulder of the man who gets a little too close. I open my fan to waft away the breath of the man who's drunk too much. I press my thigh against Cho's but he doesn't notice. He's seated at the roulette table, red-faced and eager.

Kang disapproves. I can see it in the set of his mouth, that thin line of disapproval so like Baba's. He decided at the last minute to join us and bring along his American pal too.

'My treat,' he said before we even stepped inside. Now I can see him adding up the tab in his head, appalled at the expense.

The Negro is watching me again but he's too practised to let me catch his eye. He turns his attention instead to the tall American and the dowdy Chinese girl at his side. What does he make of this odd pair? Jin is too plain to be a prostitute, at least not the kind that frequents a place like Carlton Café. She clings to Max's arm while her eyes are fixed on me.

So many eyes watching, what do they want? There are two, three, four customers of mine in here. They flick their eyes at me but give no other sign of recognition. I don't mind. I want their money not their attention. No, that's not true. I long for the oblivion that comes from the violence they wreak on me: the open-palmed slaps, the clopping of blood under the skin, the bruising the next day. Blood money, that's what I should call it.

Cho is winning tonight. That's good. His mood is foul when he loses and then I have to humour him. Tell him how manly he is, how much I love him, how glad I am we have this apartment for ourselves and most nights, it's true. He's weak, my Cho, easily discouraged. Lucky for him his family has money. He would never be able to survive on his own. He's not like me. No one is.

Now it's the owner who's eying me from her booth at the far end of the casino, a chain-smoking, horse-faced white woman utterly out of place in Shanghai. Cho says she has a reputation for being a sharp businesswoman. I suppose I should admire her for that.

She stares at me and I stare back. Those pale eyes of hers don't even blink. I want her to flush, to look away, to concede that I am more brazen than she. But the crowd at the roulette table grows raucous and Cho demands my attention.

*Kang*
They were hemmed in on all sides, the other gamblers eager to press Cho's flesh now that he was winning. No one else

98

was willing to put down a chit. It was just Cho against the bank.

'Give me the dice,' He cried.

He threw all six of them down the long green baize. The crowd leaned forward to watch them spin and tumble. Kang could hardly breathe and when he looked over, he saw Anyi's body slipping toward the ground.

'Make way!' he shouted, as he pulled Anyi away from the table, out of the overheated room and into the deserted garden. He brought her to a bench made of cold stone, lit by a startlingly new moon. They sat there, side by side, in silence, for a long time.

Anyi leaned her head on Kang's shoulder and murmured, 'You saved me.'

Jin appeared silently at Anyi's side, bearing a cup of warm water. Anyi smiled and drank eagerly, returning the cup to Jin once she had drunk her fill.

'Leave us, Jin,' Kang said. 'I have something to discuss with my sister.'

'No, stay,' Anyi insisted. 'Jin and I are sisters now. We just agreed. There can be no secrets among family.'

Jin looked surprised. And when Anyi reached out to hold her hand, she blushed deeply. Kang had never seen his sister close to another woman. This was a good sign, wasn't it? First Cho and now Jin, so many friends to take care of Anyi.

'I'm leaving for America,' Kang began bravely.

Anyi gazed calmly. 'Yes, I know. We agreed we'd leave after a year.'

Jin listened intently, the moonlight painting her fingers as white as bone.

'I mean now,' Kang continued. 'I can be my own man in America. There's no one to tell me how to behave. No one's expectations to meet.'

'Our parents are dead now,' she said tartly. 'You're just as free in Shanghai as you'd ever be in America.'

'Helen is all alone.'

'What about me?'

'You've got Cho and Max. And Jin, right here beside you. You don't need me.'

Anyi sat up straighter. The night clouds had shifted so that the moon now lit only one half of her face, the half that stared at Kang in pain.

'You promised to stay with me,' she said.

'I'm only going ahead to make the preparations so that when you follow in the New Year there'll be a home waiting for you.'

There was a long silence, broken only by the sound of motorcars passing. It was long enough for Kang to summon up some hope.

'Anyi?'

She screamed then. Jin dropped the cup, shattering it on the flagstones.

'What did you do to her?' Kang shouted at Jin.

'Nothing!'

His sister was standing now, talking into the night to someone or something out by the trees. It was gibberish.

'Mama, Baba, don't hurt him, I'll fix it, I promise, no don't hurt him!'

Anyi raised her arms to shield Kang's face, crying out in pain, her face tilted up to the moon.

A man came running out of the casino, big and black and determined. He leaned over her and said quietly, 'Remember me, Miss? It's Beauregard.'

Anyi stopped screaming. The Negro scooped her into his arms and faced Kang.

'You should take your sister home,' he said. 'Follow me.'

He led them out of the garden and into the kitchen yard where the rickshaw drivers gathered to wait for their fares. The Negro whistled through his teeth and a pedicab rolled forward. As gently as any mother, he arranged Anyi's limp body on the back seat of the cab, gesturing with his head that

Kang should sit up front, next to the driver. When Jin too tried to get in, Kang shook his head.

'You go back inside and find Max and Cho. Tell them what happened. There's no need for you to come too. Anyi is my responsibility. I'll take care of her.'

# Chapter Eleven

# In the Mirror

*Anyi*

Jin gets out of the rickshaw as Baba and Mama scramble in. I move across as far as I can, right behind Kang who's seated beside the driver and exposed to the elements. He turns up the collar of his coat.

He says, 'Lie down.'

'Where will Baba and Mama sit?' I ask.

Kang turns in his seat, his knees knocking against the driver's elbow.

Carefully, he says, 'Anyi, Mama and Baba are dead.'

'I know that! I was there and you weren't.'

Kang faces the front once more. I can see his jaw clenching from my corner of the rickshaw.

'If they're dead,' he says loudly. 'How can they be here?'

Mama leans forward and places one cold hand on Kang's shoulder. He jerks away and glares at me angrily.

'Stop playing tricks, Anyi!'

A growl begins low in Baba's throat. He raises both hands, ready to strike his own son dead. I scream and the driver swerves and the rickshaw tips on to its side, spilling us all into the street. The driver doesn't bother to help us up. He rights his vehicle and pedals away. Kang and I stand in the street, alone. His coat sleeve is torn and there's blood on his lip. Now I'm not the only one suffering.

'Let's walk,' I say. 'My apartment isn't far and I can patch you up there.'

Kang takes hold of my hand, too tightly at first but I have no desire to run. I wish we could walk like this forever, Kang and me, to wherever it is that Mama and Baba sleep, where we could all rest in peace. Kang draws my arm through his.

'You see their ghosts,' he says. 'They come to visit you.'

There's no question in his voice so no need to respond.

'What do they say to you, Anyi? Is there any message for me?'

'You know what they want. You knew it when they were still alive. Stay with me, Kang, here in Shanghai.'

'And Helen?'

'You'll find another woman, someone who will give her life for you, who'll care for you for the rest of your days.'

Kang stops suddenly. His hand is rough as he takes my chin and turns it to face him. 'Tell me now, Anyi. That promise you made, to return with me to America. Are you going to keep it or not?'

I rise on tiptoes and tilt my face upwards. I kiss Kang on the tip of his nose. 'If you keep your promise, I'll keep mine. One year together in Shanghai, Kang, remember that.'

*Kang*

His life turned grey. He wrote to Helen, putting off all their plans to some distant point in the future.

He wrote: *As soon as we arrive. Try to look on the bright side. You'll have more time to collect your trousseau.*

Kang put all his energy into making money. Factories surrounded Shanghai and every one of them needed the kind of tools Kang sold. But Kang was in a hurry. He decided to limit his business to only those customers willing and able to pay in cash. It pleased him immensely to see his bank account grow. Every month, he sent the balance to a joint account in his name and Helen's, ready to be used as soon as they were married. Then they would buy only American products to furnish their new American life.

Kang grew miserly that spring, hoarding his yuan notes and silver coins the way a child collects pebbles. He refused to buy new clothes for himself, laundering his own shirts night after night. There were no movies, no dance halls, no trips to the countryside. He had only two indulgences: the books he continued to buy, though their prices rocketed higher every day, and lunch with Anyi in a restaurant once a week.

Cho came too of course. He was all the family they had left. They took turns to pay the bill. This week it was Kang's. He chose a small, clean restaurant, unusual because it had tablecloths and napkins. It was close to the docks too, a place where he could visit customers after lunch, his suit still neat and his tie clean. He ordered quickly and simply, steamed rice with a little fish and some sautéed vegetables. The waiter had hardly left the table before Anyi and Kang started bickering. It seemed to be all they did these days. Nothing he said could please her and certainly nothing she did would please him.

'Why do you have to sell to the Japanese?' she asked.

Cho sipped his tea. When Kang did not reply, Cho said, 'My father likes to trade with the Japanese. He says they're the only ones who pay on time.'

'Our Baba hated them,' Anyi muttered. 'He wouldn't sell his silk to them when the Japanese invaded in 1931. Everyone in Soochow praised his valour.'

'Did it help us win the war?' Kang bit at her.

'He stood up for his principles!'

'He was narrow-minded and a racist,' Kang shot back.

'How can you dishonour your father like that?' Anyi's voice grew shrill and loud, the red in her cheeks high and hot. Cho tapped his fingernail against his teacup.

'Cousins, please, a little restraint while we're in public. People are staring.'

It was true, Kang could see. Men and women were glaring

104

at him and that only infuriated him more. The war was long over. When would the Chinese let go of their grudges and prejudices, this foolish idea that they were better than all others?

'We should think for ourselves like the Americans do, rather than parrot the ideas of others,' he lectured.

Before Kang had a chance to wax eloquent on the virtues of an independent mind, Cho asked, 'What do the Japanners do with your tools?'

'They make gun barrels!' Anyi shouted.

'They turn table legs,' Kang yelled back. 'That's what it says on the trans-shipment papers. I know!'

Anyi rose then and without a word or a glance at Kang, she left the restaurant. Her handbag still stood on the floor beside her chair. Cho picked it up and, with an apologetic shrug to Kang, rushed into the street in search of her.

Kang tried to cancel the order but he couldn't catch the eye of any waiter. He resigned himself to eating it all, slowly and alone. He opened his briefcase and took out his black book, a diary and an agenda and a place to store business cards, all bound together in a heavy cord of twine. He unwound his package and opened the calendar. Once again, Kang counted the days left in the year.

*Cho*

She's not on the street or in the tram into town or at her apartment or in any of the stores on Nanking Road. I find her finally at the Metropole Gardens, asleep in her dressing room. She's stretched out on the divan, the largest object in this coffin of a room, aside from the mirror of course. I try to join her on the divan but she gets up and removes the long gown she wears only for Kang, shapeless and dull, kicking it into the corner with the other ones like it. Her wardrobe in this place is crowded with sequins and lace, though she seems uninterested in clothing today. She pulls out the first dress that comes to hand, a lavender sheath with a bouquet of pink camellias printed on one shoulder.

Now that she's dressed again, her focus returns. She seats herself at the dressing table, handling the rouge, the eyeliner and the lip pencil. Her concentration is intense and before my eyes, Anyi transforms herself into a sophisticated woman – glamorous and beautiful and utterly frightening.

She stands now to study her reflection in the mirror. It used to make us laugh when Anyi first got the room. She would make faces or I would flex my muscles. For weeks, we made love on the divan, fighting over who would get to face the mirror. It was risky, of course. Manager Lin likes to walk in unannounced. As a precaution we would jam a chair under the flimsy doorknob but most of the time, we didn't bother. It was more fun that way.

Now the mirror is just a nuisance. Neither of us can see her face any more, only its constituent parts: the carefully pencilled eyebrows, the powdered skin, the red bow of her lips.

'I'm a dancing girl,' she says.

I look up but it seems Anyi wants no answer. She talks to herself a lot these days, muttering under her breath, shouting sometimes too.

'They used to call me the broken girl,' she says. This time she's staring at me with a smile on her face. I open my mouth to deny it but she won't give me the chance.

'I heard the servants gossiping. Even your mother called me that when she thought I was asleep. You don't think I'm broken now. Do you, Cho?'

She turns her face from side to side. She no longer wears her hair in tight curls. It's cut in one heavy blunt line that swings along her jawline.

Before I can reply, she answers herself. 'Oh, you're so wrong. I *am* broken, torn into a million ragged edges, but no one cares about that. You and Kang and Manager Lin, all you worry about is how I am on the outside. You all want me to look pretty and smile.'

She smiles at the mirror. The points of her eyeteeth penetrate her lower lip. Now there's blood in her mouth. She wipes it away like a child with the back of her hand and soon it's on her face, too. 'Pretty, pretty, pretty,' she sings to herself.

'Stop that, Anyi.'

Her singing grows louder, higher, falser. I've heard her voice change like this before.

'You'd better get ready,' I warn. 'Lin will dock your pay if you're late again.'

'Money, money, money,' she sings now. Her voice quavers. The tune rises past any natural range into the pitch of hysteria. I slap her, not hard, but loudly. She doesn't even blink.

'I need earrings for this dress,' she says petulantly. She walks back to her dressing table and opens the drawer. A long tangle of costume jewellery falls to the floor and, on top of it all, rolls a small blue box. Anyi crouches down and opens it.

'Kang's pearls,' she says smiling and puts on the studs.

I reach down for a pair of jadeite earrings and hand them to her. 'These look better with your dress.'

'Don't tell me what to do,' Anyi bites back.

I hold my tongue. It's better not to rile her when she's in this mood. She combs her hair once more and pulls on her shoes. She leans down to pick up a handbag from the floor, filling it with bandages, liniment and a clean cloth.

'You're going out afterwards?' I ask. 'Why don't you come home with me?'

She looks at me now, her eyes grazing the full length of my body. She steps closer and lays one hand on my flat belly before working her fingers into my shirt. I feel the heat rising. Ten more minutes before opening, hardly enough time to make love properly, though if that's what she wants, I'm game.

'Hurt me,' she says. 'Now. Will you? I'll never leave you again.'

She clings to me, her body hot and limp against mine. I hate this song she sings, over and over.

'How can you ask me that? What's wrong with you, Anyi?'

107

She doesn't answer. She never does. She only ever says: 'You can use a whip. Beat me with your fists. Anything you like, any way at all!'

I look at her face. Those fine cheekbones, that fragile jaw. I could shatter them both with the flick of my hand and send her crashing into the mirror. Turn her back into the half corpse she was when she first came into my life. I won't do it! I've worked so hard to make her into what she is today: beautiful, fierce, mine.

Oh, I know about those other men, the ones who beat her. I don't care. She gives me what I want no matter how late she comes home at night. And I know that she doesn't care about any of them. All she wants is their money. She doesn't even know their names. How could I let myself become one of them?

I have to stop this nonsense once and for all. I screw up my nerve. I turn my face into a mask. I say to her in slow and cold words, 'Don't ask me again, Anyi. You insult me.'

The bell rings. Final call. All the dancing girls must be present when the doors to the ballroom open. If she doesn't show herself to Manager Lin soon, he may fire her.

'Come home with me,' I whisper under my breath.

She's opened the dressing room door. She's already halfway down the narrow hallway when she turns back, her face bright with hope. 'What did you say, my love?'

'Don't bring those men home. I don't want to see any of it.'

# Chapter Twelve

# Day and Night

*Anyi*

I emerge from the ballroom damp from the sweat of bodies pressed against mine all night long. My skin cools in the night air and my knees shake. I wonder if this is a sign that I'm ill. I am, of course, but not in that way.

Tonight, my customer has violated the rules. He's waiting in the foyer of the Metropole Gardens, trying to look at himself in the mirrors that hang on all sides. I don't recognise him until he turns around with a broad smile on his brown face. The Japanese attaché. I mimic his girlish voice almost every night, attracting a group of British boys who hang around my table to listen to my imitations.

'I don't service Eastern devils,' I say to him.

The man stiffens. 'Auntie Wen warned me you'd say that. I'm willing to pay double.'

'No.'

For one electric moment, we stare at each other. Then the man laughs, long and hard.

'I like you,' he says. 'You have spirit. Very well, I'll leave you in peace though I suspect we'll meet again.'

The Japanese attaché swaggers out the front doors. Baba is pleased. He nods as I leave the Metropole Gardens but he wasn't so pleased this afternoon when I showed him my coins.

'Look, Baba!' I had thrown open my lockbox. 'See how

much I've earned? And none of it is in paper money whose value can plummet on the whim of a government official. Smuggler's bars and bullion, things that cannot change in value, heavy things that weigh a person down, like the copper coins I put on your eyelids so that you could buy snacks in the afterlife. Have you eaten today, Baba? And how is Mama?'

Baba rarely speaks these days though he accompanies me everywhere. He stands now in the corner of the hotel room where Auntie Wen has lodged my next customer. I like this place, the Cathay Hotel. The walls are thick and the curtains heavy. No sound can escape. The customers who have no time for a hotel room take me in rickshaws or the alleys of the old walled city where my cries mingle with the agony of a thousand others.

This customer tonight, I've seen him before. He comes from Shandong and trades in wine. He opens his suitcase and takes out a whip.

'Not the face or arms,' I remind him. 'The rest is all yours.'

Auntie Wen is asleep on the sofa when I return. She and Nian help me into a chair. I open my purse and pull out the coins I've earned with so much blood. They spill on to the coffee table and the glint of their silver shines in Auntie Wen's eyes. Customers pay me now. Not Auntie Wen. I count out loud, slapping each coin onto the table so Auntie Wen can count with me. Only when she's satisfied that she's received her fair share will she open her breast cloth and secrete her money there.

'Come,' she says, rising from the sofa. 'Let me massage away your pain.'

She leads me into my bedroom where I finally give in to the pull of sleep. Her hands are sure. They know my body so well now. There's no need tonight for Nian's cup of bitter tea. I dream of whips and horses and dead leaves.

*Nian*
The sun had climbed high into the sky and was already on its way back down and still the Lady slept. She'd have to be

110

woken soon. It took longer each time for her to surface. Nian tried calling her name and even jostling her shoulder but the Lady slept on. In the end she had no choice. She went into the kitchen and pulled down from a high cupboard a small blue ceramic jar Auntie Wen had brought together with a red one.

'The blue one is for daytime, when the Lady needs to wake and go out,' she had explained. 'The other is to help her rest and sleep. Don't mix them up!'

Nian shook out a handful of the dark leaves from the blue jar and placed them in a teapot. She set the kettle to boil while she carefully washed her hands. When the brew was ready, she took it to the Lady on a tray with two almond cookies.

'She may not like the bitter taste at first but she must drink it all,' Auntie Wen had instructed. 'Give her something sweet to nibble on and that will help her keep the tea down.'

'Wouldn't it be better to feed the Lady?' Nian asked. 'Her blood needs to be replenished and her yang nourished. She needs eel and deer meat and goat milk.'

'Do as I say,' the blind woman snapped. 'All she needs is this tea.'

Nian suspected this wasn't tea at all because its effect was so immediate. The Lady's eyes grew bright and glittering. Her movements became ill judged and her moods skittish. She would knock over glasses and walk into walls, no longer able to control her fingers to fasten her own clothing.

Nian dressed her. Then she went out into the street to hail the pedicab. Back and forth she trudged to help the Lady prepare for another night of dancing and pain.

When the rickshaw left, Nian didn't stop to rest. She collected the tea, the cup and the teapot and threw away the dregs, not tempted to drink the brew herself. Her kind may be doomed to defeat but she had no desire to court death as well.

Nian was asleep on the sofa when the apartment door opened. She thought it was the Young Master who came and

111

went as he pleased. Instead, it was the Lady who'd come home early for a change.

'No message from Auntie Wen?' she asked.

The amah shook her head. She watched as the Lady went into her bedroom and closed the door. It was hard to tell, from night to night, how easily the Lady would fall asleep. Nian waited until long after the Drum Tower had sounded the alarm. The gates to the old walled city would be closed now. Surely the Lady was asleep.

Nian crept into the room. She shook out her bedroll and laid it on top of the heap of clothing that cluttered the floor. She had just closed her eyes when she heard the Lady move.

From her spot on the floor, the amah watched. The Lady reached under her mattress and pulled out the knife. It was in a different hiding place every night. It had become a game they played. Nian had handled that knife many times. It was small, easy to hold in one hand, something you could use to peel an apple.

The Lady opened the knife and began to cut crosshatches down the length of her thigh in the soft white flesh that she thought no one could see. Soon enough, the blood began to flow, staining her pale skin and the white sheets below. It was impossible to stop her. Nian had tried. The Lady would simply wait for Nian to fall asleep and then the blood would flow once more.

Nian lay on her bedroll, watching and waiting.

*Anyi*

I have a table of foolish young men to entertain tonight, all employees of the barbarian trader, Jardine Matheson. They're boys, some probably still virgins. They think their time in the East will make them men. They drink heavily. They call me Annie.

'Give us one of your imitations, Annie. We want a show tonight,' they beg.

I crawl onto the table. I crouch on my hands and knees long enough to be sure that all eyes are locked on my breasts. I stand and make a small pirouette, a fast one to whip open the slit in my dress. Now I have the attention of all the tables around me. Now I can perform.

I start with the British ambassador, a pompous old man with an unfortunate habit of ending each sentence with a loud harrumph!

Then his French counterpart, a slightly built man with lovely feminine hands that will wander as far as you allow him to go.

The German, the American even the Russian ambassador, not one of them is spared.

My grand finale is the political attaché from the Japanese Legation, all martial rectitude in a high squeaky voice. They call him The Crow. They say he screams like a girl when he ejaculates. I wouldn't know.

Cho watches from a table close to the dance floor. He comes every night as he promised. He enjoys my shows too, though he teases me about the British boys at my table.

'I thought you hated all barbarians,' he says.

And I always answer, 'I want their money. And besides, Manager Lin says I must.'

Tonight he asks, 'Does Auntie Wen make you take barbarian customers too?'

'Never! No one can make me do that.'

My show is over and the applause is gratifying. Manager Lin smiles in his shadowy corner of the room. Cho is gone.

One of the Brits whispers into my ear, 'Come out with us tonight, Annie. We're off gambling in the Badlands. Wouldn't you like to come?'

I smile and let him fondle me a little longer on the dance floor. I make no promises. While he's fetching the coats, I head for the street. It's time to find a rickshaw. I have a new client waiting.

It's almost dawn by the time I arrive at the Carlton Café. Most of the gamblers are gone, out of luck or money or both. Cho is asleep in an armchair tucked behind the roulette wheel. It takes a long time to wake him.

'Where have you been?' he asks in a querulous tone. 'No, don't tell me. I can guess.'

I try to pull him to his feet but he loses his balance. The Negro Beauregard comes to the rescue. When Cho is standing, the Negro smiles and holds out one big hand.

'You've got a bill to pay, don't you remember, Mr. Song?' the Negro says. His voice is kind but his eyes are sharp. They see the panic in Cho's face. 'Don't try running. Won't do you any good.'

'How much is it this time?' I ask.

I go with the Negro to the end of the casino designed to look like a bank from the Old American West. Eve Arnold sits behind the teller's window, her face as sallow as the faux golden bars. She counts my money and gives me the change. 'Pleased to do business with you, Miss Song. Why don't you try your luck sometime too?'

Cho has revived and demands the same thing. 'Come on, Anyi. Let's play a few hands of blackjack. Just to finish off the night.'

'I'm tired, Cho, I need to go to bed.'

He pouts. It's a look I've seen many times, a tactic that never failed to work on his mother, though not on me. Maybe it's the sun peeking through the windows of this casino. Maybe it's the pain that throbs down my back, the marks of the lash seeping into my blouse. I can't humour Cho any more. I can't humour any man right now.

Cho's mood turns black. He shouts. He waves his fists in the air. But I know that Cho is all bark and no bite.

'Give me money, then, if you won't spend any time with me,' he says.

I take out my wallet, remove one bill, and give the rest to

114

Cho. He takes it without a word, neither thanks nor a curse. I sink into a seat, unable to stand any longer.

'How about if I take you home?' Beauregard appears at my side.

He drives Eve's Model T with care. He waits patiently for a herd of bedraggled cattle to cross the street on their way to the slaughterhouse. He stops at my apartment building even though I haven't told him where I live.

He shrugs. 'I must have heard it. It's not a secret, is it?'

I'm too tired to challenge him. He helps me out of the car and when we've both made it onto the sidewalk, I turn back to thank him for the first kindness I've been shown today.

Then he asks me, 'Are you sure you know what you're doing?'

His eyes are yellow and large. They seem sad. What does he know about my life?

'You've heard rumours?'

'No, ma'am. Just what my own eyes can see.'

He places one soft hand under my elbow and we ascend the stairs to my apartment. I don't know why but he makes me feel strong.

Nian is waiting for me at the door. She clucks her tongue as she pads back down the hall to run the bath. 'Auntie Wen was here to give you a massage but couldn't wait any longer. She'll be back tomorrow night.'

'I don't need her help,' I say. 'I'm young and strong. Just give me a hot bath and some sleep.'

A cup of tea steams invitingly beside my bed. Nian stands over me, waiting until I swallow the last dregs. Only then am I allowed to crawl under the sheets.

The light is dim. One candle burns. I peer through the haze that inhabits my room day and night. Mama and Baba nod happily at me from inside the wardrobe. They like the sight of me in an empty bed. Even the soldiers who line the back wall are appeased when Nian comes in to collect the last of the bloody bandages. I close my eyes and sleep a dreamless sleep.

*Cho*

I like this place. The minute I step foot inside the dark antechamber, a manservant rushes forward to relieve me of my hat and coat and another stands ready to lead me down the hall. The trunk of a birch tree is embedded in the wall that marks the entrance to my private room. Already, three maids kneel on the floor, their dimpled faces reflected in the waxed wood.

'Welcome back, Master Song,' they sing.

I sit on the raised bed. Two of the maids bow and exit the room, leaving the third to remove my shoes. She adjusts the many silken pillows so that when I lie down, my head is supported at the proper angle. By the time she's done, the others have returned, one bearing a tray with tea and small bites and the other with the opium I crave.

'Leave us,' I say to the two maids.

The one with the opium places the paraphernalia on the tray at my side: the spirit lamp, some matches, an ornate silver box and the long pipe. She opens the box, spearing a drab brown ball with her silver fork. She lights the spirit lamp and the smell of roasting opium fills the air. It takes no time at all. They're professionals here at the Rising Cloud.

Today the maid fondles me while I use the pipe. I inhale as deeply as I can, holding the sweet smoke in my lungs while she strokes. We're getting quite proficient, she and I, my release and the floating of the opium coming together. I'm a leaf drifting on the water, spinning into an eddy and shooting back out into the current, directionless, heedless, free.

There were journalists tonight at the Carlton Café, a tight knot of buzzing attention. When I walked in the door, the flashbulbs went off in a series of explosions that almost deafened me. Then they figured out that Anyi wasn't with me and the cameras were packed up and the journalists moved on. They only want her.

If only they knew that she lies in a stupor for most of the day. There's a sourness that lingers in the sheets. She doesn't wake until night, after her amah has tipped another cup of that bitter brew into her waiting mouth and only then does she come alive, more gorgeous than ever, flitting and flirting and laughing. I want to hold her, tell her how much I adore her, but she won't stand still long enough for the words to form in my mouth.

This is the time when Anyi wakes. I know what she does every night, when the clock in the Custom House strikes two o'clock and all decent people are asleep. I don't understand the pleasure pain brings.

'Give me another pipe,' I say.

The maid obeys and when the pipe is in my hands, she opens the buttons on my trousers. Her breath is hot and moist but her mouth is strangely cool. When she's finished, she cleans me with a warm towel before rinsing out her mouth with cold tea. My mind is marvellously clear.

I miss the old Anyi. I miss the days when we would dance in the narrow space between her sitting room and the dining alcove, wide enough for two or three steps of the tango, the two of us naked in each other's arms. I want that Anyi back. I know what to do. I'll buy her earrings. They sell them at the Great Bazaar. I'll go as soon as I've rested a while. I just need to close my eyes for one moment first.

When I wake, a long envelope lies on my tray. The maid kneels on the floor, picks up the envelope with both hands and offers it to me. I open it: the amount is astronomical.

The maid bows meekly and murmurs, 'Honourable Song, we hope to serve you many times over once this pittance of a bill has been satisfied. Shall we deliver it to your mother, Madame Song?'

I stumble outdoors. There's rain on its way; the air is damp and cold. The long envelope crinkles against my chest. I feel a draft through my coat. My fly is still open. Passers-by laugh in my face.

Mama will be stunned. I haven't spoken to either of my parents in months, not since their visit to Anyi's apartment and the row that followed. Just last week, Baba sent me a letter warning that if I didn't leave Anyi, he'd cut off my allowance. I could wheedle Mama into paying my opium bill but Baba will want his pound of flesh. He'll make me come home. He'll force me to beg for my money.

I won't be treated like a child. I'll go home in my own good time. For now, I have a more pressing problem. How can I pay this bill?

I could ask Anyi for the money but she hates opium. She says her mother used it in the last months of her life. To her, opium smells like death. She'll try to talk me into breaking my habit. What habit? It's an amusement, that's all, like playing cards or taking a stroll. Give me something better to do and I'll forget all about it.

The envelope cracks and bends inside my coat as if it too is protesting. I don't want to hear Mama's whining or Anyi's reproaches. I need to find a different solution.

# Part Three: The Turtle

# Chapter Thirteen

# A New Friend

*Blossom*

The maid stood at the entrance to the ballroom, shivering with fear and anticipation. Mistress Song had sent her here in search of the Young Master with instructions to bring him home at all costs. The idea thrilled her. She imagined herself preening in the heat of the spotlights that now traced the outlines of the dance floor. But her blue cotton pants and tunic were no match even for the little tea boys so smart in their white uniforms. Blossom stepped deep inside the folds of the heavy velvet curtains and waited.

The Young Master appeared through a narrow hallway out of which dancers and waiters and prostitutes came and went. Blossom was startled to hear a soft curse uttered on the other side of the curtains. Carefully, she peeked around the fold.

Manager Lin stood an arm's length away. He wet his pencil with his tongue and added a black mark to a page in his notebook.

'What are you doing?' a voice asked.

An older man with a heavy southern accent now joined Manager Lin on the other side of the curtains. Manager Lin bowed deeply. Blossom held her breath.

'I was making a note to myself, Mr. Yip. There should be a new rule at the Metropole Garden against guests in the dressing area.'

Yip shrugged. He was much more interested in the dance hostesses now streaming on to the parquet floor. He liked the young ones, judging from the moist noises he made as they passed by fresh-faced and innocent, all of them dressed in shades of pink and peach, so close to their skin colour that they looked naked.

'Do you make enough money from the young ones?' Yip asked.

'Their tickets are cheap,' Manager Lin admitted. 'But they're easier to handle than a star like Rosa.'

'The young ones fall in love. I read about it all the time, even in the Hong Kong newspapers. *Poor woman jilted by a man she met on a dance floor!* Don't they know the difference between lust and love? And then they commit suicide. What a waste of time and money!'

The band started, playing a set of Chinese folk tunes rearranged for ballroom dancing.

'Everyone in town is copying you,' Yip noted.

'Men from the countryside like this kind of music. It encourages them to buy drinks.'

Grudgingly Yip said, 'Well done, Lin. I'll talk to you later.'

Blossom heaved a sigh of relief. Now that Manager Lin was alone once more, he turned his attention to the guests. A table of three men, hunched over in quiet conversation, caught his attention and he summoned the bellboy. 'Let me see the reservation book.' He turned the heavy pages until he found the one he wanted. 'So, Japanese and Kuomintang officials meet under my roof using false names. That's interesting.' He made a note.

Blossom couldn't care less about officials or their true names. She had spied her rival circling the dance floor alone. The broken girl hadn't changed. She nodded coolly to the other hostesses. She was as haughty here as she had been at home.

The Young Master, however, was clearly a favourite, flitting like a butterfly from bloom to bloom. Unlike the other men, he did not offer a dance ticket to anyone.

'Turtle!' Manager Lin suddenly yelled, waving a raised fist in the direction of the Young Master.

The tea boys gathered, children ranging in age from five to fifteen, their white caps perched at a precarious angle on their small heads. Manager Lin pointed out the Young Master and off they went, scrambling between the legs of the other dancers and over the ringside tabletops, trying to catch their quarry. The antics caught the attention of other guests, who were now cheering.

'The turtle is faster than the little bunnies tonight,' someone quipped.

The Young Master was finally trapped with his back against the bandstand by an army of red-faced tea boys. Most had lost their caps during the chase. He laughed and raised his hands in surrender, releasing the elegant dance hostess in his arms.

'I give up!' he cried. 'I'll go peacefully!'

'You promised to stay this time,' the dancer cried. 'Please, Cho, can't you dance a little longer?'

'Got to go, Rosa,' he announced.

He made his way slowly through the crowd, stopping to chat with an acquaintance in the crowd. Blossom monitored his progress, waiting until he was close enough for her to grab him.

But he turned instead, back toward the dance floor where a man was presenting himself to the broken girl, a dance ticket thrust out in one fat hand. She accepted the ticket. He wasn't much of a dancer. He clutched her awkwardly about the waist, attempting to steer her deeper into the dance floor. She smoothly took over, guiding the man with a nudge of her leg or a pull of the arm.

She didn't glance at the Young Master, not even when she sailed right past him. The fury on his face stuck like a knife deep inside Blossom's heart.

*Cho*
'She's at the Metropole every night but she won't dance with me unless I have a ticket.'

The dealer is normally chatty but tonight he just grunts. I'm winning and that makes him nervous. I feel the icy blue stare of Eve Arnold boring into my back.

'Hit me,' I say.

Twenty-one! The dealer's really sweating now as he counts out my chips. He doesn't have enough. He's got to ask Eve Arnold for more. I've seen her fire dealers for less.

She arrives with a new rack of chips and a fresh deck of cards, a move she makes whenever the dealer is paying out too much money. Most of the players leave the table when that happens. Luck is a delicate thing and the American woman knows it. She can turn a good hand bad just by leaning against the horseshoe table. But Eve Arnold doesn't scare me. There isn't a woman alive who can.

I say to the dealer, 'Anyi can't be seen any more with turtles like me. She says Manager Lin will fire her. Well, so what?'

Eve Arnold is taking her time. She's checking every card in the deck. She counts the rack of chips one more time.

'She doesn't think about me,' I continue. 'What am I supposed to do with all this time on my hands? All I can do is amuse myself with a bit of gambling and a little pipe of the sweet smoke.'

The dealer isn't listening. He's bent his ear down to Eve Arnold's tight mouth, listening to her instructions.

'There's no harm in a little opium, every now and again,' I say to the man on the stool next to me.

He and I are the only players left at this blackjack table. He smiles and listens and when I lose all my chips, he pushes his own pile towards me. Then, when I lose all his chips too, he laughs.

'I'm hungry,' the man says. 'Do you know a good noodle place?'

I take him to a shop close to the walled city that's open all night. The spices are so hot they numb your tongue but not this guy. He talks and talks, all about himself and the family he left behind in Kyoto, how he knows no one here in Shanghai.

123

'You know me,' I say, thrusting my hand at him. 'And I know all about Shanghai.'

We shake hands and laugh, downing our cold beers.

'I work all day,' he says. 'At night, my colleagues prefer to socialise with other Japanese. They won't venture into town like me.'

He's vague about his line of work, though to be honest I don't care. Once we've eaten and drunk our fill, I call for the tab. We struggle over the check, as we should, and I manage to pull it out of his hand. But when I reach for my wallet, it's gone and with it all my money.

'Someone must have picked your pocket. You're not such a man about town after all!' He laughs at me for a long time and I laugh too. His glee is infectious. 'You can treat me next time. There will be a next time, won't there?'

'Why not?' I answer.

He gives me the money for the rickshaw ride home. He promises to meet me in two days. 'Give me your address. I'll think of a place to meet and let you know.'

I do as he asks. Who could refuse such a generous fellow? I get into the rickshaw. The wheels have already started to turn when I remember what I've wanted to ask all evening. I turn back and call down the street.

'Remind me, my friend. What was your name?'

'I am called Tanizaki Haruki,' he shouts as the rickshaw rolls away.


*Tanizaki*

It was late by the time the rickshaw drove off, taking a drunken Song Cho to his next destination. Tanizaki had earned the luxury of rolling into bed too but he denied himself. He wanted to write while his impressions were still fresh. He removed his sweat-stained shirt first, grateful for the clean night air that swept across his skin.

Even as a child, Tanizaki was known for his meticulousness.

He would prepare for everything, no matter how trivial the event. There were far more interesting men in the Carlton Café but Tanizaki made sure he missed nothing. He had noticed that the Chinaman was well dressed and always flush with cash. There was a woman who accompanied him, his mistress some said, though lately Song had begun to appear alone at the casino. Tanizaki thought the man looked lonely. He wouldn't be a hard nut to crack though once the shell was open, would this Chinaman yield anything worthwhile?

Tanizaki opened the plain manila folder. Clipped to the left side was a brief biography of the Chinaman: his full name, no known aliases, a physical description. On the right side were blank sheets, the standard forms used for debriefing. In one column, Tanizaki noted the time, date and place of the first interview. He had nothing of substance to report, so he left the middle column blank. Soon enough, he hoped to fill that column too. The Chinaman liked to talk.

Tanizaki had just closed the file when he heard footsteps in the hallway. He was inside the warren of bedroom-cum-offices that filled the second floor of the Japanese Legation. He should have been safe there but he knew he couldn't depend on it. He waited calmly with one hand resting on the dagger he carried with him at all times. There was a discreet knock on the paper screen, followed by the shoji door sliding open. Kokoro knelt in the door opening, her head bowed low.

'The Chinaman has been located at the opium den called Rising Cloud. The proprietor says he comes often. Do you wish him to be brought here to the Legation?'

Tanizaki shook his head. It would be so much better if Song Cho were to come to the Legation of his own accord.

The shoji door closed silently. Tanizaki opened the file again. He should have noted it – the yellowed eyes and the black fingertips. The Chinaman liked his opium. Tanizaki added the extra details. It would be a good reminder, to himself and any other interrogators, that the subject could turn unreliable.

*Cho*

Yuyuan Garden is damp with the ragged ends of a wet Shanghai winter. A servant brings a dry faggot, lights it, then plants it deep into the ground next to my chair. The light does little to dispel the bleak darkness but I can hear the clatter and splash of a water wheel close by.

The Japanner arrives, wearing a tuxedo.

'You look magnificent, my friend,' I cry. 'Do you have an audience with the queen of England?'

'Not of England, but of China,' Tanizaki counters.

'Ah, a courtesan, how unfortunate for you to have to pay for love!'

'Don't we all?'

'Not me,' I say with a grin. 'I'm a turtle, you see.'

'That's right! I remember your tale from the casino. I like this word for you. I will call you the Turtle!'

I pretend to be offended and Tanizaki looks contrite. He points and asks, 'Can you see the turtles in there?'

I shake my head.

'Here,' Tanizaki says. He leans down and picks one up. It's almost small enough to fit into his palm with a light-coloured shell and dark mottled legs. He holds the turtle carefully with both hands around the back of its shell where the turtle cannot reach his fingers with its snapping jaws.

'You're just like this little creature,' Tanizaki laughs. 'You think you're safe inside that shell you wear. Maybe you have a good job or an important wife or a father who has lots of money.'

'Exactly! I really am a turtle.'

Tanizaki turns the turtle on its back, pinning it to the ground with the leg of a chair. He pulls the burning faggot out of the ground and holds it against the creature's white belly. Its arms and legs wave wildly and an unpleasant smell rises from the burning shell.

Tanizaki grins. 'The underside of the turtle is its weakest part. Hold it to a flame long enough and it will crack.'

Tanizaki thrusts the faggot into my face. The heat singes my hair.

'You're crazy!' I shout.

Tanizaki laughs once more. He throws the burning faggot into the water where it hisses angrily before sinking the garden into utter darkness. 'Come, come, a little heat like that scares you? If that's the case, maybe we should cancel our plans for tonight.'

'What did you have in mind?'

'Greyhound races at Luna Park or cockfights by the waterfront. It's your choice,' Tanizaki answers.

I hesitate. Anyi and I had planned to meet at Carlton Café. She said around three o'clock in the morning, but she's usually late. Maybe this time I should let her wait for me.

'Why not do both?' I say. 'Let's go!'


*Anyi*

The floor boils under my feet. I stumble, trying to reach the row of blackjack tables before the heat consumes me.

'Have you seen Song Cho?' I ask the dealer. 'Is my cousin here?'

It's long past closing time. The gamblers are all gone. It's just Beauregard and the cleaners still on the main floor. Eve Arnold should be in bed by now but there she is, in her nightgown and wrap, her mouth set in an angry line.

'Go away,' she yells at me. 'We're closed!'

I don't like her voice. The twang hurts my ears. I try to move away but trip over a piece of carpet, pulling three stools down with me as I hit the floor hard. Beauregard is there in a flash, soothing, cajoling. Eve Arnold follows.

'Throw her out.'

'Let her rest,' he pleads. 'Can't you see the state she's in?'

'This is not a home for stray dogs. Get her out of my sight!'

He leans down to pick me up in his strong arms but the American woman won't let him. She yanks on his arm with one white claw, startling him so much that he almost drops me.

'What the hell do you think you're doing?' he shouts.

'I could ask you the same,' she replies heatedly. 'Where are you going?'

'You said she had to leave so I'm taking her home.'

'Did I give you permission?'

A quake rumbles through Beauregard's body, whether of fear or anger I cannot tell.

'Put me down,' I say quietly.

He finds me a cab, not an open rickshaw but a proper automobile with doors and windows against the chill night air. He gives the driver my address, though there is no need.

'I know that woman,' the driver says. 'She lives on Hart Road. She's been in my cab plenty of times. Even used it on occasion to service one of her customers.'

Beauregard gives the driver a hard look but the man doesn't flinch.

'It wasn't me,' the driver laughs. 'She's too rich for my wallet. And besides, I don't enjoy beating my women.'

'Take her home,' Beauregard orders. 'No matter what she says, just get her home.'

# Chapter Fourteen

# Old Wars

*Cho*

We've taken to the streets, Tanizaki and I. It reminds of the days when Anyi first arrived, so eager to learn everything about Shanghai. But Tanizaki has no interest in dress shops or teahouses. He wants to know where the fun is. So we go into the walled city and rub shoulders with the people he so laughingly calls 'the locals'.

The locals don't laugh back. They don't like the sight of a Japanese man in their streets. When we walk into the cockfighting ring, the crowd goes sullen.

'Go home!' some mutter, though I hear them loud enough.

'Why did you bring the Eastern devil here?' the owner of this ragtag operation asks me. He's got one dead cock in his hand, freshly mangled from the last fight, its yellow feet still twitching. He won't take Tanizaki's money. He won't even take mine.

'The war is over!' I yell at the owner, ready to plough into the man. Tanizaki pulls me away. He sidesteps the few half-hearted punches aimed in his direction. A drunken gambler lurches at him. Tanizaki sends him to the floor with the twist of one hand, landing him in a cloud of blood and feathers.

When we get out, we shake our suits clean then, laugh hard and long. We can take care of ourselves, he and I, even among the riff-raff of Shanghai.

'I never realised the Chinese had such long memories,' he says. 'Or is it you,' he asks teasingly. 'Who has such a short one?'

'I've no axe to grind with the Japanese,' I say. 'The war happened so long ago. What is it now, five years?'

'Where were you at the time?' he wants to know.

'At home, here in Shanghai.'

'I'm sorry to hear that.'

'We were holed up for weeks inside the family compound. Mama had to send the driver out to forage for provisions while all Baba could think about was the merchandise going bad in his warehouses.'

'So you weren't in any danger?'

'Our house is close to the International Settlement. Baba knew you Japanese would never dare drop bombs on us.'

Tonight we go to Chapei. Tanizaki seems to prefer it to any other part of Shanghai. And who can blame him? The Japanese returned to this place after the war and rebuilt it from the ground up. The streets here are wide and clean. And the baths! What could be so wrong with a people who love cleanliness?

'In Japan,' he tells me. 'It's bad manners to pour your own sake.' So he pours for me and I pour for him though he doesn't drink much and I end up finishing the flask each night.

'Describe Anyi to me,' he says out of the blue. 'I want to see her through your eyes.'

I tell him about the dancing, the nights on the town, the journalists who trail us from casino to nightclub to home. The gleam of her eyes, the softness of her skin, the taut muscles below the surface. But when he asks me about our home life, I grow silent.

'You want more,' Tanizaki guesses. 'Buy her contract, then. Set her up in a golden house of her own.'

'The Metropole doesn't own Anyi. She's a free agent and she likes it that way.' Then the words come out slowly, as if I've just coined them, 'I want her to myself.'

'Marry her, then.'

'I can't. It's against the law.'

'That's not the reason. You could run away together. You have money enough. There's something else stopping you. Is it her or you?'

So I tell Tanizaki about Kang and her promise to return to America with him in a year's time.

I tell him about the men at the Metropole who ply her with drinks.

I tell him about Auntie Wen and the men she brings to Anyi at the doorstep of the Metropole Gardens. How they beat and whip and crush my beloved girl.

Tanizaki's eyes glitter. Are those tears? His compassion for Anyi overwhelms me.

'Some nights, the amah has to carry Anyi inside. It takes hours to tend to her wounds.'

'And you?' Tanizaki asks, his voice raw with emotion. 'Do you hit her too?'

'She's asked me many times. She says she deserves it.'

'And then?' Tanizaki presses.

'She gets angry. Look at this scar on my forearm. Can you see the curve of her jaw?' I point at the sickle-shaped line. 'When I refuse to hurt her, she tells me I'm not a real man.'

Tanizaki looks at me with pity in his eyes.

'I can't protect her any more. Sooner or later, she'll get her way. She'll find a man who'll hurt her the way she wants, someone who'll kill her.'

'I'd like to meet her. Let's go to the Metropole right now.'

The idea is preposterous. She won't let us on the dance floor when she finds out where Tanizaki is from. She might even have us thrown out of the Metropole. And she'll hurl cruel, crushing words about my choice of friends.

'Maybe some other time,' I say to placate him. 'Anyi has some peculiar ideas about your people.'

*Tanizaki*

The city amazed and disgusted him. Perversion was available on any street corner of Shanghai: girls and boys of every age, size and shape. But Tanizaki had a peculiar taste, one that few could appreciate, let alone share, something he would not be able to find on his own. So he sent Kokoro, his best agent, to reconnoitre. She was as well trained as any man and had followed Tanizaki from Kyoto to Tokyo to Peking and now to Shanghai for his current assignment. Her cover here was that of a housemaid. It took Kokoro three days to return with an answer.

'The person you're looking for is a blind masseuse,' she said. 'Though you must be wary of her. She's had dealings with our people in the past.'

The masseuse agreed to meet him at a teahouse near the Little East Gate, a run-down, crime-ridden part of the old city. Tanizaki preferred it that way. It was unlikely that anyone here would recognise him, but he took no chances. He made the old woman move from the seat at the open window into the dark recesses at the back of the teahouse.

Tanizaki was brief, his requirements clear. The old woman never blinked or sucked her teeth in surprise.

'Give me a few days to find the right girl. Where can I leave word for you?'

'Kokoro will find you. Give her your message,' he said.

The old procuress was true to her word, offering a name as well as a time and place to meet, far from the Japanese Legation. He agreed to all the terms, but Tanizaki refused to pay her exorbitant fee until he had tested the wares. The first girl was pliant enough though she didn't last long. Auntie Wen sent him a second and then a third. They slaked his thirst but not his hunger. Tanizaki needed more.

This time they met outside a synagogue, closer to the Japanese settlement than Tanizaki liked so he set Kokoro on watch. She knew the story about the synagogue, built by old Jacob Sassoon in memory of the wife he had loved. Tanizaki waited on a stone bench in the middle of a small bare plot of green, nothing that any self-respecting Japanese would call a garden, but something that a Westerner might accept as one.

Auntie Wen soon joined him. She sat down and tilted her face up to the sun, weak and watery as it was. She had remarkable patience for someone of her profession. She sat quietly, waiting for Tanizaki to be the first to speak. For Tanizaki, it was quite a novelty to be absolutely direct.

'There's a woman I want you to procure for me,' he said. 'Her name is Song Anyi.'

'Impossible! She hates foreigners, the Japanese most of all. Something to do with her father.'

'She dances with them. I've seen her.'

It had started as a whim. He didn't respect Cho's taste in women but there were only so many nights he could spend pent up in the Legation. He had a bond with Kokoro but she drew a line at sharing a bed with him.

'Why don't you look for this Song Anyi,' she suggested. 'From what I hear, you may like her better than you think.'

That night he went to the Metropole. He took a seat in the back, not wanting to be seen. He watched Anyi as she moved across the dance floor, graceful to be sure, but no more than the other hostesses. He was ready to leave when Anyi went to sit with a group of young men, Brits he thought, judging from the amount of noise they made. In moments, she had them in thrall. He moved closer to listen.

Anyi was a mimic, a wicked one, and it was her brilliant performance that was making the men laugh. Tanizaki was charmed by her infectious sense of humour. He recognised every man she mocked. He dealt with them day in, day out, in a world far from the dance floor. How could a mere hostess know such things?

She rose from the table now and began to strut in a

133

bow-legged gait that was strangely familiar. Then she began to speak in a high-pitched voice and to shake hands stiffly with the men round the table. She was imitating *him*. And doing it so well, women were pointing their fans at him while the men roared with laughter.

He fell for Song Anyi then and there. He had to have her, this woman who was unafraid to mock the world around her.

But Auntie Wen said, 'You're too rough. I can't afford any more of your *accidents*. The police won't turn a blind eye forever, no matter who you are.'

'I want her,' Tanizaki said.

'Give me time. Maybe I can convince her to accept you. I can't promise.'

'I want her now.'

'It can't be done.'

Heat flooded his face. He bit on his tongue just to taste the blood. Tanizaki didn't even realise his fist was clenched until the woman recoiled like a snake, her head bobbing on her corded neck. He had forgotten how sensitive the blind could be. Auntie Wen's instinct for danger was razor-sharp.

He got up and threw a wad of bills into the sparse grass. 'Here's the money for the last one and her burial costs,' he said.

He left without another word but when he reached the gate, he turned to look back. The old crone was already gone and all the money too.

*Blossom*

On her days off, Blossom normally went into town to gaze longingly at the clothes on display at Nanking Road. Today she had promised to visit Auntie Wen in her tiny apartment inside the walled city. She wound her way through the narrow alleys, sidestepping the rubbish left to block the gutters.

Inside, the apartment was dark and humid. Her aunt had

an insatiable need for warmth and, though the coal tripod glowed white-hot in the darkness, Auntie Wen was wrapped in a thick quilt, eating watermelon seeds and spitting the wet shells on to the coals.

'Sit down,' she said. 'Tell me what's new with you.'

'The Young Master doesn't come home any more. He's forgotten me.'

'What makes you think he ever gave you a thought in the first place? Women like us are toys for men like him. If it's a man you need, come and work for me.'

'I don't need help to find a man,' Blossom replied with scorn. 'Cook will be bedding me now that the housekeeper is leaving.'

'Where is she going?'

'Home. Her brother was killed and his wife ran away. Now there's no one to take care of the parents.'

Auntie Wen released a long belly laugh. 'Let me guess. The wife was having an affair and the lover killed the husband?'

'No.' Blossom's voice became grave. 'The letter said a Japanese soldier out on patrol killed him. It said war is coming.'

Auntie Wen's breath suddenly blew hot on Blossom's forehead. 'Where does this family live?'

'I don't know. Somewhere far away in the north.'

'Mukden?'

'Yes! That's it. How did you know?'

'Mukden is a Japanese stronghold now. If they invade Shanghai, it will be from the north.'

'Why would the Japanese invade?'

'How ignorant you are! The Japanese are animals. Believe me, I know.'

'Let them come! Shanghai has an army garrison and our soldiers are strong.'

'Stupid girl! Don't you know anything? The garrison was emptied, a concession demanded by the devils as the price to end the last war. Don't you remember Chapei burning?'

Blossom was flustered now. 'I was a child then.'

'You were eleven, old enough to know better.'

'I remember the smoke and the ashes that blew in my eyes.'

'And me?' Auntie Wen asked in a low voice. 'Do you remember I stayed in your house?'

Blossom took a moment to reply. 'I do. Mama said you had a fever and needed to rest. That was why I had to give up my bed and sleep with Mama and Baba. You made them close all the shutters and darken the lamps. You cried every morning when the sun came up.'

'It was all I could see by then. Those flashes of light were like needles through my eyes.'

'I thought you were born blind!' Blossom exclaimed.

Auntie Wen struck hard with both hands, pummelling the girl to the ground, slapping her so hard, her lip burst.

'Stop, Auntie Wen! Why are you hurting me?'

'I wasn't born this way! Japanese soldiers did this to me. They raped me and then they made sure I could never report them.'

The blind woman loosened her grip on Blossom. The girl scrambled away as far as she could from the old woman who sat wheezing on the floor. So Auntie Wen was just as dirty as the broken girl. Dirtier even, to be entered by the Eastern devils. No wonder Blossom had never been told the truth.

'They could have killed me,' Auntie Wen said to herself. 'I suppose I should be grateful they didn't.'

They sat like that for a long time. Then the voices in the street grew louder. A new night in Shanghai was beginning.

'Don't laugh at your housekeeper,' Auntie Wen said suddenly. 'She may be headed toward her death. Now help me get up.'

They wandered the streets, down to the alley where the food carts stood. Auntie Wen moved slowly and stumbled often even though she knew every crack and crevice of this part of town. She leaned heavily on Blossom's arm and the girl's strong back began to ache.

'Do you want to eat?' Auntie Wen asked.

'I've no appetite now.'

'Then leave me. I have work to do.'

When Blossom reached home, Cook and the housekeeper were still arguing.

'What would I do in the North? I'm a cook, not a farmer or a soldier. How many bowls of rice do you think I could earn there?'

'You're only worried about yourself. You don't care what happens to me?'

In the days that followed, the housekeeper was often out of the house, arranging train tickets and bus rides for the long journey home. She loaded herself down with gifts for her parents and anyone else she might still know. She muttered in her sleep about unreliable men while Blossom tossed and turned beside her, eager for the woman to be gone.

Mistress Song didn't replace the housekeeper. Blossom relayed her conversation word for word to the other servants that night in the kitchen.

'Mistress Song said she could manage the household herself. But her face was all red and puffy, as if she'd been drinking. And her voice was awfully loud. Squawk, squawk, squawk.'

Blossom strode about the kitchen flapping her arms. Cook laughed and pulled her on to his lap.

'Tell us more, naughty girl. What else did the Mistress have to say?'

'Well,' she said, imitating the Mistress's high-pitched voice, 'now that the Young Master is away so often, there's hardly any work to be done. Not for just the two of us.'

Cook grew sober then. 'True enough. It's too quiet here, now that you mention it.'

There were times when Mistress Song seemed lost. She would call for the driver, seat herself in the rickshaw then forget where she was heading. She grew fat and the driver complained bitterly.

'I can hardly steer and when there's a bridge to cross, I think my heart's going to explode.'

Blossom no longer slept alone. Some nights, Cook would come to her in the tin shed she had once shared with the housekeeper. But Blossom preferred to sleep in his room by the kitchen fire where it was warm and close enough to the courtyard for her to hear any sounds if the Young Master came back.

# Chapter Fifteen

## Dry Leaves

*Cho*

I take Tanizaki to the Metropole. He's as excited as a child on New Year's Day waiting for the candy and the red envelopes to be handed out.

'Have you been here before?' I ask.

'No,' he says. 'But I've heard a lot about it. Isn't this where your cousin works? Tell me her name again.'

So I tell him and he murmurs her name softly to himself. I don't want to promise him anything. My plan is to introduce them to each other when the time is right.

We take a table close to the bandstand where the light is brightest and we can see every girl on the floor. Tanizaki is busy taking in the scene. We can see everyone in the place and they can see us. Men come from all corners of the ballroom to say hello to my friend. Their eyes glide briefly over my face, as if they wonder why I am with him.

Baba doesn't wonder. He knows how important Tanizaki is. He tells me so himself.

For a week, I drove to the docks with Baba, promising to work. It was the only way for me to get money out of his tight fist. As soon as I got there, I sat in his chair, put my heels on his desk and tried to sleep. One day, a sudden swipe at my feet sent me almost to the floor. My fists were already clenched, ready for the fight, when I saw my friend's face beaming at me.

'What are you doing here?' Tanizaki grinned. 'You said you despise people who work for a living.'

'I do,' I said stoutly. 'What makes you think I'm working?'

Our loud voices must have alerted Baba because he rushed in, his shirt hanging open and water still glistening on his forearms. Seeing Tanizaki, Baba bowed lower than a whore. Then he slapped me across the back of my head.

'Look sharp, my son! This man is the political attaché of the Japanese Legation.'

I bowed and my father said in his mealiest voice, 'Your shipment has arrived, Honourable Tanizaki. I took care to clear customs myself, just as you requested.'

Tanizaki grunted, winking at me over my father's bent back.

'Load it into the car, then,' Tanizaki barked at Baba. Turning to me, he asked, 'Do you know a good place for dancing?'

'Go, my son!' Baba cried. 'Take the Honourable Tanazaki wherever he wants.'

'It may take a while,' I warned Baba. 'I may not be back until tomorrow.'

'Don't worry about that,' my father said in his most jovial voice. 'As long as the Honourable Tanizaki needs you, you stay by his side. Why are you gaping? Don't keep the man waiting!'


So here we are, me and the political attaché of the Japanese Legation. There are no flashbulbs or panting journalists to mark him as a celebrity, though there are plenty of eyes watching him, watching me, even that ingrate of a dance floor manager, what's his name, Lin, scribbling away in his little black notebook. Then I see her.

'There she is,' I shout. 'The one in the red ch'i p'ao.'

'Call her over,' Tanizaki says.

'Maybe later. It looks like she's busy right now.'

We laugh. We joke. We drink bad champagne with the dance

hostesses who've gathered at our table. All the while, I watch her, dying with every step she takes in another man's arms. I want to rush on to that dance floor and throw her over my shoulder, take her away and keep her hidden forever. I'll buy her a golden house and we'll live there together, just my songbird and me.

'You should have seen her when she first got to Shanghai. She was just a country girl, innocent and young. I made her into what she is now,' I say with pride.

Tanizaki looks at me with surprise.

'You don't think I'm the nurturing kind? Well, I don't blame you for thinking that. Look at her move. Can you feel the heat around her? She creates it and I bask in its afterglow.'

'Introduce us,' Tanizaki says.

But here's the waiter come to take our order. He knows who I am and treats me properly. 'Give me another beer,' I say.

By the time the man returns, I change my mind. 'Get me a cognac. No, wait, where are you going with my beer? I want both.'

I tell Tanizaki, 'We have the whole night ahead and I have plenty of money in my pocket. Drinks for everyone! Yes, you too, my friend, Tanizaki. It's my turn to treat you. You've already taken me to so many splendid places. You put me to shame, a newcomer like you, knowing your way around like an Old China Hand.'

Tanizaki drinks little sips, like a grandmother taking her medicine. He won't play Bottoms Up with me, and now that I think of it, I've never seen the man drunk. Has he no weaknesses? He asks again to meet Anyi.

'I'm afraid you're too late for that. Can't you see the dance floor is empty now? The hostesses are backstage and Old Lin won't let anyone in at this hour, especially me. He's afraid of us turtles, the ones who can con a free dance and more from a pretty girl.'

'Don't you mind being called that?'

'We turtles come in all sorts, you know. We're not all old and slow. Some of us are young and green, like this shot of crème de menthe. Beautiful, isn't it? I'll just swallow this and see, I'm a snapping turtle now. Fast and ferocious, you'd better move out of my way! Whatever I want, I get.'

Tanizaki giggles. This schoolgirl laugh of his is ridiculous but it takes years off his face.

'You should laugh more often. You're too serious.'

Then suddenly he turns on me. 'Where is Anyi? Why aren't you waiting to take her home like a good cousin? Don't you care about her any more?'

'Why do you say that? Of course I love Anyi.'

'You were angry just a little while ago, when the journalists came to take her picture.'

'All right, I envy her, just a little, in the same way I wish all my father's money was mine. Do you understand what I'm saying? Sometimes I'd like some attention too.'

We make our way out of the Metropole and into the night. He teases me, tells me I'm jealous. Maybe I am. I could throttle that man, the one who's pushing Anyi into his car, putting his sticky hands on her perfect body. I want to poke out Tanizaki's eyes because he's watching her too. Every man in Shanghai watches her. Can I kill them all? That would be a lot of work!

Sometimes I think of Anyi wrapped in a thin, gauzy film. I can see everything. I can feel her body through the fabric. But it's there and the film gets harder every day until it's not a cloth but a shell. I can't break it any more and I don't know why.

I've never had patience with things that don't come easily to me: toys, cars, women. I'm too impatient and let them go. But I can't do that with Anyi. She's caught hold of me. It's the fire that burns inside her, the excitement when it flares out of control. I must have that heat.

I say to Tanizaki, 'I've a date with Anyi later tonight. Now, what shall we do in the meantime?'

*Anyi*

It's four in the morning by the time I arrive at the Carlton Café. Cho is still sitting at the blackjack table with not even a dealer to keep him company. I lean against the back of his chair to take the weight off my bleeding legs but he won't sit still. He twists sideways in his stool. Back and forth. Back and forth.

'You said you would be here when you finished work,' he snarls.

'I'm here now, aren't I?' I snap back.

'Who were you with?'

'That's none of your business.'

'This was supposed to be our night out,' he cries.

For a moment I actually feel sorry for him. Then he grabs my arm and the pain I've been trying to hide explodes. I can't hold back my cry of anguish so I turn it into rage. 'Is that all you have left?' I point with my throbbing hand at the pitiful assortment of red and blue chips on the blackjack table.

'Why do you care?' he answers. 'It's not your money.'

'Whose is it, then? Did you go crawling home to your Mama?'

He lunges at me then, his hands tight around my neck. Finally! I throw my head back and laugh, a high thin wail that brings Beauregard to our side.

Cho drops his hands to his side. He buries his face in my hair and whispers, 'You make me crazy, Anyi. Please don't shut me out.'

He doesn't understand. He'll never give me what I need. The realisation fills my mouth with the taste of dry leaves and I almost gag on their sweetness. I push Cho away as gently as I can.

'I need to eat,' I say.

We order food from an all-night restaurant close by and have it brought to the Carlton Café: rice with dried shredded pork and some pickled vegetables. Cho complains about the meagreness of the meal. This time I won't rise to the bait.

'Better for your stomach if we eat something light now,' I say soothingly.

'How much money do you have with you?' he asks.

'Enough for dinner.'

'I'm going to need more.'

Now I see them: Beauregard and the other bouncers standing in a circle around our little table. Just outside the ring sits Eve Arnold. She fixes her cold blue eyes on Beauregard and nods. He moves, blocking the only exit from the room. More bouncers come to stand on his left and right. Eve Arnold walks quietly through the crowd. No one gets in her way.

'Evening,' Eve Arnold says as she places herself squarely in front of our table. 'It's time to call in your chits, Mr. Song. I'll take that money now, if you please.'

'How much money do you owe, Cho?'

He doesn't answer. I can see the sheen of sweat on his forehead. Beauregard gently places a stack of chits on our table. I count them: twenty-thousand yuan. A fortune.

My mind is spinning wildly, looking for a way out of this trap, but I'm too tired for schemes. I tug on my earlobe, an old habit from childhood, my way of wishing for good luck. My eyes search Cho's face for answers. He's staring at my hand. Suddenly, he's reaching out to close his thumb and forefinger around my earlobe, tugging at my earring.

'Aren't these pretty?' He looks at Eve Arnold.

'They're mine. How dare you?'

'You've got plenty of earrings. A whole drawer full.'

'Kang gave them to me.'

Cho is pulling so hard on my earring that it's starting to hurt. 'Let go!'

His hands drop into his lap. 'Anyi, look around. Do you understand what's going to happen if I don't settle this bill?' He casts another nervous glance at the bouncers but it's the look on Eve Arnold's face that scares him the most.

'Don't kill me,' Cho whispers.

Beauregard won't look at me. He stares at Eve Arnold, awaiting her command. We all watch and wait while she makes up her mind. Is Cho's debt worth a death?

I reach up to touch my tender lobe. Eve Arnold's dry fingers get there first.

'Yes, I'll take these in exchange for your debt.'

I won't let go. I kick and bite. I snarl at Eve Arnold until she moves aside. It's Beauregard who has to deliver the final blow. He places one large hand on my shoulder. Two fingers would have been enough to crush my neck. Maybe that's what Eve Arnold wants. I would welcome it. I stretch out my neck to make it easier for him. Beauregard has a different plan.

He bends down and speaks, gentle and low, into my ear, 'There's nothing more you can do about this. Just let them go, Miss. Better for everyone that way.'

*Nian*

The slamming of the door woke her. Or maybe the cry of rage that followed. Nian got up from her bedroll and went into the hall.

'What's going on?' she asked.

The Lady sat on the floor, her legs crooked. She was crying soundlessly. It was the Young Master who had bellowed. Nian could see him through the window, shaking his fist, pounding on the glass. The amah closed the blinds.

'Come to bed,' Nian said.

The amah lay back down on her bedroll, listening to the Lady toss and turn. She talked to herself or to the ghosts that crowded the room, something about earrings and debts.

'Kang will never forgive me,' she moaned.

Nian offered the Lady some tea or a massage or something to eat, anything to get her to settle. The child growing inside Nian was draining her of energy and she needed to sleep. If only the Lady would stop gabbling. Nian even got up to make

145

a pot of Auntie Wen's sleeping draught but the Lady wouldn't touch it. She continued to rant.

'I try to stop, I really do. What will I do if Kang ever finds out? He can't know about Cho or Auntie Wen or the men she brings me. He'll turn his face from me forever! He'll leave me behind and then who will be left to save me?'

Nian fell asleep listening to the Lady worry out loud about her brother and America and a woman named Helen. The last thing Nian remembered was her shouting, 'I need those earrings!'

In the morning, the blood had long dried and the Lady's body lay pale and limp on the bed. It had been weeks since she had cut herself. Nian had almost managed to forget the smell. She shook the Lady's arm, called out her name, slapped her face and belly. Had she finally succeeded in emptying her body of life?

The Lady groaned and pulled away. She buried her head under the pillows and fell into a restless sleep.

Nian picked up the knife and took it into the kitchen. She lit the fire and waited for the water to heat. The Lady would need to be washed soon: circular motions with a clean wash cloth dipped in water that had been boiled and allowed to cool. Nian remembered the doctor's instructions as if it were yesterday.

# Chapter Sixteen

# A Debt to Pay

*Anyi*

The gravel driveway is empty. So is the kitchen yard where the rickshaw drivers wait for their fares. I try every door and window but they're all locked. I suppose no one comes to the Carlton Café during the day. Is the entire household asleep?

There's a boy curled up in a ball under the porch. He must belong to the horse-faced woman.

'Fetch your mistress! The one who stole my earrings last night,' I scream at him.

The boy flees to the other side of the house. My yelling has worked. I can hear noises inside the house, the sound of heavy feet and a thin nasal voice. An upstairs curtain opens and there is Eve Arnold staring down at me. She's wearing a blue dressing gown and her hair is pinned into curls.

She says, 'Take her to the river and drown her.'

I hear no reply. Maybe her henchman is already on his way to do her bidding. But I'm not afraid. There's no one else in that house except Eve and her Negro bouncer and I can't believe Beauregard would hurt me.

The kitchen door swings open and there he is. He's even bigger in the light of day than he is at night, when his edges soften into the darkness.

Eve Arnold is standing behind him, whispering more

147

instructions. He tells her to go to bed, then walks out and shuts the door quietly behind him.

He walks down the wooden steps and into the kitchen yard. He stands a head and a half taller than me but I won't move a muscle, not even to smile back.

He says, 'I'm sorry, Miss Song. You've got to leave. Eve Arnold did you a favour last night. Don't be pushing your luck. She's not a good-tempered lady.'

It's no more than I expected. Still the line of my mouth grows thin. 'I have money with me,' I announce. 'I'll buy back my own earrings. For twice the amount Cho owed.'

Beauregard shakes his head. 'Just leave, you hear me? When you get home, you ask that cousin of yours to buy you a new pair.'

He takes a step closer, so close that now his shadow covers mine. I look up at him, in surprise not fear.

'How do you know he's my cousin?'

'You told me, don't you remember? I remember lots of things. I know you dance at the Metropole Gardens. Mighty popular too.'

'Is Beauregard your real name or a stage name?'

The Negro throws back his head and laughs. 'There's no stage big enough for the likes of me so I don't need a name for that.' Then Beauregard does something I would never have expected. He says, 'You look like you could use a friend.'

What does he mean? Does he want to beat me too like every other man I know? The disappointment craters me but I refuse to show it. Instead I chew words together to say something nasty, maybe something I'll later regret, some little thing to fill the loss I feel right now.

Before I can speak, he says, 'I'm not like those men at the Metropole Gardens. Or those fellows I see with Auntie Wen. I don't want any of that.'

'Why do you want to be my friend?'

'Tell you the truth?'

148

'Please.'

'Because you thanked me for letting you in that very first time you came and every time after that. Not many people do. In fact, you're the only one.'

I have to smile. And suddenly this little dirt yard feels like an oasis.

'I accept your offer, Beauregard. But a man like you and a woman like me, we can't be seen on the streets together. And I'll bet Eve Arnold won't want me inside your house either.'

We both look up now. We're just in time to catch a glimpse of a lace curtain slowly falling into place.

'True enough,' he says. 'It don't matter. We can have tea together, right here in this yard. How about that?'

He whistles long and hard. Before the echo has died in the yard, the kitchen boy appears with a pot of hot tea and two clean cups. We share it right there in the dirt, the Negro and the dancing girl. We must be a sight to see though there's nothing around but naked trees to spy on our wonder. We talk about life, his mostly, and all the strange places he's lived for a while. He tells his tale well and I'm happy to listen. He makes me feel like a girl once more.

The sun is already fading. It's time for me to leave, for both of us to get back to work, but he won't let me walk away without first taking my hand in both his large ones.

'It's an honour to be your friend, Song Anyi. And since I'm your friend now, I'll venture to give you a piece of advice. Don't be mad at Eve Arnold. She's just collecting a debt. If you want to blame someone, you take a good look at that cousin of yours.'

*Nian*

The amah was in the sitting room when she saw the Young Master pacing up and down the street. She'd never seen him awake so early in the morning, before even the fruit vendors had come into the streets with their heavy baskets. The Young Master saw her and ran up the stairs to the front door.

149

'Nian! Let me in!' he cried.

'What do I do?' the amah asked the Lady.

She too was awake at this unusual hour, though still in the clothes she had worn the night before. She sat in the easy chair with a magazine on her lap.

'Tell him to leave,' the Lady calmly said.

Nian obeyed. She yelled at the Young Master through the peephole.

'Go away!' she cried.

'Forever?'

Silently, Nian turned to the Lady.

'Forever,' she said. 'Unless he apologises for what he's done and makes amends!'

By the time Nian had returned to the peephole to convey this last message, the Young Master was gone.

The Lady went to bed then and so she never saw the basket of flowers the Young Master had left at the front door, a brilliant display of pink and white jasmine blossoms that Nian almost fell over on her way to market.

It must be an omen, Nian thought. My luck is changing. She ran back inside to smear a handful of rouge on her flushed cheeks then hurried back out again. With the blossoms in her shopping bag, Nian ran all the way to the market where her lover sold wooden carvings from his stall. She was certain that she'd find him this time to tell him about the child and the money she was saving for the three of them. Instead, she found a ruddy-cheeked woman in his stall, selling embroidered shoes.

'He's gone,' The shoemaker said. 'He sold me his place here. Said he was going south, that he wouldn't come back.'

Nian dropped her bag. The bazaar was suddenly warm and awfully close. She needed air, fresh air, and started to run.

'Hey, you!' the shoemaker cried. 'What about your things?'

The shoemaker ran after Nian, the bag banging against her fat calves, and caught up with her just outside the market.

Nian had stopped. What was the point of running away? What was the point of doing anything?

'Your jasmine is beautiful,' the shoemaker said.

'Do you want it?' Nian replied dully.

'How much money?'

Nian sold the flowers, placing the coins inside the cloth bag she kept on her body, day and night.

When she got home, she found a necklace hanging on the doorknob. She took it the next day to the same stall where the shoemaker now greeted her like a fellow peddler. Nian haggled long and hard.

The day after that, it was a box of chocolates that lay before the door as yet another offering to the goddess inside. Nian didn't sell the chocolates. She ate them, one after the other, before throwing up by the side of the road.

That evening, when her mistress asked whether the Young Master had come by, Nian said, 'I haven't seen him in ages.'

*Cho*

The front gate is barred when I arrive. Driver Zhang opens it for me.

'I've come home,' I say.

He peers behind me, looking for the luggage or all the things I took to Anyi's. I tell him not to worry because I'm only staying for a night or two or as long as it takes for Anyi to calm down.

'Are my parents home?' I ask.

Mama throws her arms around my neck, weeping and laughing and crying to Baba, 'See, I told you my baby would come back!'

Baba says nothing but I know that he's pleased. A parade of my favourite foods appears magically on the table, my parents grinning as they watch me eat. They've taken to eating in the small room Mama once reserved for her mah-jong parties.

'That round table was too large for just the two of us,'

151

Mama explains. 'Now that you're back, I'll open the dining room again.'

The dining table and chairs are shrouded in white sheets. Even the mirrored wall of the dining room is covered, making the space feel small and oppressive. The room hasn't been cleaned in weeks.

'Is the housekeeper sick?' I ask.

'Gone,' Mama responds.

'Where's the new one?'

Mama hums a tune under her breath. She wipes her fingers through the dust on the table, unable to stop herself from putting one grey finger into her mouth. She blanches then spits.

'I didn't think we needed one.'

Her eyes squint up at me. I'd forgotten how short she is. White strands of hair poke out of her bun at strange angles and her face is as ashen as the dust that still clings to her hands.

No one asks why I've come home. No one mentions Anyi, not Mama or Baba or any of the servants, though her room is exactly as she left it. There's even a stub of a candle waiting on the nightstand. The quilt is the same, a little dusty maybe but stretched tight and smooth across all four corners of the bed. I run my hand down its length, imagining her body warm inside. Then I stop. I feel eyes on me. It's Blossom standing in the doorway. Her eyes are strangely shy.

'What do you want?'

'I was looking for you,' she says.

I sit down hard on the bed, the wooden legs creaking like an old lullaby. I pat the bed beside me. 'Here I am.'

She's eager, soft in places where Anyi is hard. Only her hands are rough; I had forgotten that. She lays one calloused hand on my chest and asks, 'Young Master, are you here to stay?'

'Why not?' I answer.

I can visit Anyi from here. Driver Zhang can bring me. I'll go to every flower vendor in the city and buy all the tulips I can find. I'll bring hundreds to drop at Anyi's feet. I'll worship her like a household god. And once she's appeased, we'll get married.

*Blossom*
He slept with his mouth open. She could see the blackened tongue and smell the rot in his teeth. Their coupling had been so brief, a few thrusts and then it was over. Blossom curled herself into the Young Master's side, trying to satisfy herself with her own hands.

Sure that she could restore the Young Master's vigour, Blossom returned the next morning and every morning after that. Cook didn't like it. Blossom avoided the kitchen as much as she could, where Cook could be heard loudly thrashing among the pots and pans. She obeyed his every order, however unreasonable, and rose each day an hour earlier than usual to stoke the kitchen fire and draw the water for the breakfast meal.

Only then would Blossom creep upstairs and into the Young Master's room. She would slide under the warm quilt and stroke him awake. Some mornings, he would call Anyi's name, still half asleep. Blossom would straddle him then, pushing his flaccid member into her until he grew hard and his eyes flashed and he knew exactly who Blossom was.

At night, Blossom would lie on her side and watch him sleep. There was a time, not so long ago, when she wouldn't have let him rest. She would have taken him in her mouth or her hand to rouse him. And he would have responded, all night long and into the day.

Now his skin was yellow, jaundiced and loose. His belly was round and flaccid and when he stood, it hung over his yang like a thick blanket. He didn't seem to care any more about pleasing her or, for that matter, pleasing himself.

Blossom was worried. She badly needed advice and decided to turn to the one person she could trust in matters like this.

The next morning, she persuaded Cook to let her buy the fish for dinner that night. Instead of heading to the riverfront where the fish were pulled fresh from the sea, she went inland, to a park with a kidney-shaped lake flanked by a stone pagoda. There, Blossom found Auntie Wen playing mah-jong with other blind masseurs just like her.

Auntie Wen laughed when she heard Blossom's sad tale. 'So your Young Master has returned home at long last but you no longer fancy him as you once did?'

'He's gotten old and he smells bad though I would put up with all that if he could satisfy me the way he once did. What can I do to entice his yang?'

'Nothing,' Auntie Wen said. 'You're not the problem. Men who love the pipe can love nothing else.'

That night, Blossom listened to the Young Master snoring. The saliva in his throat gurgled with every breath. Sometimes he sounded like he was choking and for a moment Blossom thought she might welcome his passing. Then she knew: it was no use any more. She would have to find another patron. She wondered if Cook might take her back.

# Chapter Seventeen

# Lovers Quarrel

*Cho*

Anyi didn't dance tonight.

The lights on the bandstand wink out one by one as the weary musicians retire for the night. Other lights come on, harsh and bright. I count my dance tickets in their glare. I tear the tickets into tiny pieces and scatter them around my table. Some cling to the stained red tablecloth while others swirl in the air like angels, before dying on the dark sticky floor.

It's the last of my money, all I could wheedle out of Mama. She said, 'We must economise, my son. Your father said so this morning.'

The words barely registered. I was so eager to be off. But Mama needed to talk. She followed me around the house and into the yard where Driver Zhang was waiting, ready to go to the Metropole Gardens.

'Baba's business is doing badly. He's done something to affront his Japanese customers and now no one will do business with him. They run the city these days,' she told me.

I look at the white scraps on the floor. They look like snow, the snow that marked her first winter in Shanghai.

I carried Anyi in my arms that morning. She was still wearing her bed socks and bandages. We went out into the street where the snow banks were high. I laid her gently on top of the largest one. She was so light she hardly left a mark. Her black hair

155

glowed in the wintry sun and her lips were so red it hurt to look at them. She laughed, then, the full-throated laugh of a girl in love.

A bouncer comes to remove me from the ballroom. I don't know him but he speaks kindly to me anyway.

'Come with me, Honourable Song. You'll feel better in the fresh air.'

We walk away, steadily, from the ruins of my night.


*Blossom*

The clock seemed louder than normal, its ticking frightening the maid into silence. She followed Cook into the dining room, the two of them bearing the dishes for the evening meal. The Song family custom was that Cook announced each dish that he had so lovingly prepared: breakfast, lunch and dinner. Old Master Song always said it was the best part of his day. Now Cook spoke in vain as the Song family glared at each other across the table.

Blossom lingered by the liquor cabinet, gently pushing the crystal glasses from one side of the shelf to the other, her ears pricked to hear what the Songs would say.

Old Master Song growled, 'Tell your mother what you told me.'

The Young Master pushed the hair from his forehead, revealing his swiftly receding hairline. It shocked Blossom to see yet another sign of age marring the Young Master's once perfect body. It wouldn't be long now before his skin grew mottled and the thought of his old hands on her young skin made Blossom shudder.

'She won't talk to me, Mama. The amah won't even let me in the door.'

Mistress Song bristled at the insult but had to ask, 'Who?'

The Old Master knew. 'What son of mine would hang about a girl's doorway? Have you no pride? She may be family but in the end just a girl like any other.'

156

Mistress Song's face grew red. 'Are you talking about Anyi?' she screeched.

'If Anyi is so ungrateful that she won't see Cho then she'll have no more support from me,' the Old Master shouted.

'You don't give her anything now,' the Young Master shouted back.

Blossom chuckled then but that was a mistake. Three sets of black eyes locked on to hers. The entire Song family stared at the maid as if she were a snake.

'How dare you listen to our conversation?' Old Master Song thundered.

Even the Young Master shook his head at Blossom.

'Scandalous,' Mistress Song shouted as she threw her chopsticks at the maid. 'Get out!'

Blossom fled the room, letting the door swing shut behind her. She ran down the hallway and into the narrow alcove under the staircase. There she waited, panting, to see if anyone would chase after her. If it was Mistress Song, then Blossom would run upstairs, sure that her fat mistress would never follow. But if it were the Old Master, Blossom was determined to run out the front door and never come back to the Song family.

Some very small place in her heart still held hope that it might be the Young Master who would follow her into the dark hallway. If he were the one to come searching for her then there might still be reason to stay. But the door remained firmly closed and from inside the room, murmurs of conversation started up once more.

Blossom crept back down the hallway, to the dining room door. She placed her ear against it and listened as hard as she could.

'Does she please you still?' Mistress Song was asking.

'Answer your mother,' the Old Master barked. 'Don't just shrug your shoulders like that.'

The grandfather clock suddenly chimed. The maid jumped,

banging her head against the brass doorknob. A chair scraped inside the dining room and footsteps came towards the door. The maid ran, into the kitchen, through the kitchen yard and on to the tin shack where Blossom now slept alone.

She threw herself on the ground where her bedroll lay. She waited for the tongue-lashing or the beating she knew she deserved. When none came, the maid sat up with a sneer on her face. Master and Mistress Song weren't questioning Cho about her. They wanted to know about the broken girl.

'She's the dirty one,' the maid hissed to herself and the hissing echoed against the corrugated tin walls. 'Who knows how many men have emptied themselves into her?'

Blossom raised her fist and cried, 'I wish you had never come to Shanghai!'

*Anyi*

Cho and I are the news of the day. Everywhere I go, the murmurs and the snide looks follow. Some of the dance hostesses don't even bother lowering their voices. They speculate loudly about the cause of the spat. Rosa grows hopeful. The tea boys lay bets on how long our fight will last.

Here on the dance floor, Rosa is laughing. The spotlight shines on her powdered face, made soft by the collar of fur that frames her cunning face. With both hands, she pulls on Cho's arm, trying to draw him into her arms and on to the dance floor.

Cho won't say no, of course. I wonder whether he knows the word. Rosa is leading now. He drifts in whatever direction she points. Then a man nudges me awake, pulling me on to the floor. Cho watches and Rosa frowns. She stops dead in her tracks, almost causing Cho to crash into the couple dancing next to them.

'Hey, watch where you're going!' the man yells at Cho.

Cho yells at Rosa. She slaps him across the face. He stands there, the fool, while couples twirl all around him. If he's looking for me, he's got it all wrong.

I'm back to my table, loudly calling for champagne. The rules of the Metropole Gardens are clear. We're allowed to drink but only in modest amounts. Rules be damned. I'm the first hostess to drink and I'll be the last one too.

My British boys egg me on. They like it when I get drunk. So do the men Auntie Wen brings to me, sometimes as many as three in one night.

'No one else has ever managed that,' Auntie Wen gloats. 'You'll be rich soon, Song Anyi.'

I don't need Cho any more. Not his money nor his protection, not even the warmth of his body next to mine. I've plenty of replacements. Most of the men in this place have taken me to bed. Not even Auntie Wen knows about them all.

Another night begins at the Metropole Gardens and already I'm drunk. I stagger across the dance floor. I fall, time and again. Some customers think it's funny, a part of my act. They laugh as I sprawl on the parquet floor and I laugh back.

Other customers become embarrassed, convinced that they have caused this very public mishap. Manager Lin is careful to find those men before they can leave the ballroom. He plies them with drinks and compliments and new dancers, tender young girls who would never fight back.

He'll fire me soon, once he's done plucking every feather from me, his plush little chickadee.

*Cho*

My tuxedo is immaculate and my nails, well groomed. I've chosen a table just outside the spotlight that heats the hair pomade of the band members so that the oil drips on their shoulders. Here, in the shadow of the music, I can be both private and visible. Manager Lin brings me to the table himself, once I show him my fistful of dance tickets.

'Rosa was asking about you,' Lin says. 'Shall I send her over?'

His look is almost hopeful but neither of us doubts who it

159

is I want. I look across the room, seeking her out. Lin follows my gaze and nods.

'I'll send Anyi over as soon as she's free,' he promises.

She comes to my table, her face mutinous. Who knows what threat Lin used to drive her to my side. She sits down. We talk about the weather, the clear night sky and the prospect of a full moon tonight. Her gaze wanders.

'Dance with me?' I ask.

'Can you pay?'

I give her my tickets, all of them. She tucks them carefully inside her evening bag. She stands and holds out one white hand to me.

'Come,' she says.

She feels thinner than I remember, the ridges on her back more angular. The scent of jasmine lingers for a moment then disappears. She's as light as a dream. We don't speak as we dance. I don't want anything to ruin this moment. I could dance forever with her in my arms, the light sparkling on her face and shoulders, but the band stops and we have to go back to our table.

I dig into my pocket and pull out my offering. It was far more expensive than I had expected. It took every yuan I could dig out of Mama's hiding holes. She's taken to squirrelling cash away in the unlikeliest of places: ginger jars, cigar boxes, an old summer hat. I was afraid that I would have to take up Tanizaki's offer after all. He knew all about Baba's business woes and seemed so sorry. But I don't like the idea of borrowing money from him. My pride won't let me.

Better, then, to forego the fancy shops on Nanking Road. The Great Bazaar would have to do. I tried to haggle, but I don't know how. I bought Anyi a pair of earrings, as close to a replica of her own as I could find, that might just work if the lights are low enough.

I cup them in my hand like a pair of prayer sticks, ready to throw them at the feet of the gods. She takes the earrings out

160

of my hands, delicately pinching them between thumb and forefinger. A smile begins to form on her lips. Her eyes shine and she asks, 'How did you get them back?'

I can only shrug, unwilling to claim the merit, unable to disappoint her with the truth. But then she peers more closely at the baubles and her face slams shut.

'They're not mine,' she says.

She drops them into my champagne glass and stalks away.

The bubbles eat away at the paint. I finish my bottle of champagne and order another. The music hits my face in waves as the tears roll down my cheeks.

When the third bottle arrives, Manager Lin comes with it.

'Are you feeling all right, old man? Why don't you come with me to a cool, quiet place?'

I wave him away. I can't afford any distractions now. She sits at a table, surrounded by her usual crowd of braying Brits. Never once does she look my way. Never once do I let her out of my sight. The minute she leaves, I will too.

But there are so many people at her table, men and women from the Metropole Gardens. They jostle and joke. I lose sight of her for a moment and when the crowd thins, she's gone.

Did she leave the ballroom? Is she out in the street already? Is Auntie Wen luring Anyi away again?

I rush to the door hidden in the folds of the bandstand curtains. The door leads to the dressing rooms and, from there, an exit to the streets. Maybe she's inside still, changing her clothes. I could find her, talk to her, I just need to get her alone. If I could just hold her in my arms one more time, she'd understand.

But instead of Anyi, it's Manager Lin I find. He stands in the doorway and grins with all his teeth.

'Sorry, old boy, no guests allowed backstage,' he says.

I wait outside. The moon is so bright everything glitters. The streets are still clogged by cabs and rickshaws but soon enough it will be quiet. She'll be here any minute now. Hurry!

# Chapter Eighteen

# Moon

*Anyi*

The soldiers follow me wherever I go. They form a circle on the dance floor that tightens, step by step, until there's nowhere for me to go but down to the ground where they want me. Neither the young barbarians nor Manager Lin notice. They're too busy laughing. Cho would recognise the soldiers' faces but he's not looking. Instead, he says he has a surprise for me.

Cho, what kind of a joke are you playing on me now? Why do you offer me two skulls, the flesh half-eaten from the bone? He holds them in his palms while the skulls laugh at me. And when I fling the skulls away, Cho laughs too.

I run away. I hide in my dressing room and ask the great mirror, what's wrong with me? The face that looks back can't be mine. Then the soldiers appear again, one by one, until the mirror is filled with their grinning teeth.

Manager Lin finds me with my arms wrapped around the mirror. He lifts me from the floor. He wipes my face clean of tears and smudged lipstick. And when the heaving in my chest calms, he sends me back to the dance floor to entertain the young barbarians who hurry now to my side.

'Come with us, Annie!' they cry. 'Be our Lady Luck tonight!'

But the soldiers won't let me. They say it's time to go home, time to get down in the leaves and the dirt and atone for my sins. I leave the young barbarians and turn down Hart Road.

We march, click-clack, click-clack, with the moon lighting the way home.

The moonlight is a needle in my eye, sharp and cold and long. It'll enter my brain soon; it's been there before. Then the moonlight will burn and the soldiers will come and the pain will begin.

*Cho*

She's already at the apartment by the time I catch up. I can hear the scratch of metal against metal as she tries to insert the long latchkey in the dark. I hear her curse. By the time she finally manages to turn the lock, I'm at her side.

She shrieks, slaps and kicks, calling out loudly, 'Nian! Where are you?'

The gods smile on me tonight. The amah must have sneaked out again, gone to wherever it is that she goes so Anyi and I can be alone. But first we must appease the neighbours because we've woken them with all our shouting. Window shutters swing open and angry words spew out.

I want to apologise but before I can utter a word, Anyi's teeth sink into my hand. She seems as surprised as me when the flesh gapes open and the blood blooms on the cuff of my shirt. It should hurt, but it doesn't. She stares at the red hole. She digs a finger into my wound then puts it into her mouth, sucking.

'Blood,' she says.

I see the full moon reflected in her eyes. I can speak now, 'I love you, Anyi. You don't know how much. Please, let me come inside.'

I hook one arm behind her knees and catch her torso as she falls. I carry my beloved across the threshold. Her head tilts backward, her long white neck fully exposed.

'You've come to hurt me,' she says.

She's begged me for so long. Is that what I must do to make her love me again? I'll do it. Later I can love her the way I

163

want, tenderly and slowly. Look how she gives herself to me!
I'll love her, right here, right now. I'll take her and she'll be
mine forever.

I kick the door shut. Anyi squirms out of my arms. She runs,
her arms covering her face, muffling the words inside her chest.

But I know what she means to say. She wants me to hurt
her and so I will.


*Nian*

The amah had left the house as soon as the Lady departed.
She had already been to the train stations that left Shanghai
for points north, west and south. But there was no way to
trace the path her lover might have taken. She had no photo,
just his name, and that got her nowhere.

The docks were Nian's last resort. Steamships butted their
noses against the sturdy pier. Here was a ship headed for
Madagascar. There an identical ship casting off for Vladivostok,
places Nian hadn't ever heard of, but having learned the price
of a ticket to Hong Kong, she knew that her lover hadn't taken
this way out of the city.

She had heard rumours of a place in the bend of the
Whangpoo River, where passage on a seaworthy junk could be
booked for less money than a grand steamship or even bartered
in exchange for labour on board. She didn't know exactly
where this place was and no one she asked seemed to know
either.

It was midnight by the time fate led her to it. The smell of
the mudflats was awful. Half-dead fish lay all around, too
mangled by the nets to sell at any market, not even good enough
for the pigs rooting through the heaps of trash that lined this
sewer of the city. The water slapped pettishly at the sides of a
boat haphazardly drawn up on the shore.

These were no watermen, Nian decided, not like her own
people born and bred at sea. She had been raised in a place
like this, as an infant bound to her mother's back to prevent

her from rolling overboard and later, as a toddler, tied to the guy lines so that when she fell, she could eventually be hauled to safety. Nian had been taught that a boat was a haven and should be treasured as such.

But the two men arguing at water's edge had not been given the same lessons. They complained loudly about the sea and the work they were compelled to do, ferrying passengers for no more than a few silver coins.

'How can I feed my wife and children?' one of them wailed.

'That's your fault, fucking your wife night and day.'

'Are you calling my wife a whore?'

They fought then with their hands and feet. Nian watched them from afar with pity in her heart for the misery of their lives. Maybe she should have waited for them to calm down but she had to be home soon, before the Lady returned. And so she stepped into the fray and asked for help. Immediately, the men stopped fighting.

'Where do you want to go?' they asked. 'No luggage? That's good, the boat will move faster. Climb on board, little lady, and we'll be off!'

But Nian shook her head. All she wanted was information. She repeated her lover's name but they turned sullen and angry. They refused to say whether he had boarded one of their boats.

'Unless you can pay us for the information,' one of them scowled.

'I've no money to give you.'

'I'll give you something else then,' the other said and stepped forward to slap her face and belly.

'Stop,' she cried. 'I'm pregnant!'

'You too, hey? What is it with you women? Don't you know what a burden you are?'

They used sticks and rocks, anything that came to hand. And when they had exhausted those resources, they kicked her with their hard-toed feet, puncturing her skin.

Her first thought was for the child inside her womb. She

twisted madly to shield her belly from their blows. The men laughed. The more Nian fought, the harder they kicked until finally she lay limp and still. They abandoned her then. Maybe they thought she was dead. Maybe she was.

No one would miss her, not even the Lady. Auntie Wen and Manager Lin were feeding on her, just as the scuttling sand crabs would feast on *her* own body if she stayed here any longer.

And what of the child? It must be dead by now. If she waited a little longer, her body would expel the dead creature. Then she could give up its tiny carcass to the tide.

Nian stared at the full moon, now so swollen and heavy she could almost touch it with her finger. Full of promise like her own womb. If she got up now and made her way home, the child might still survive.

She rolled onto one side, working one leg to gain purchase in the soft mud. She crawled, whimpering with pain, until she could pull herself to standing by the rotting pier. She would go home first. If the child survived, she would give it to her parents to raise as their own. She would give them all her savings to cover the costs of the child's upkeep. Maybe she would visit the child as it grew older but as she staggered on, she struggled to envision a future that would make such a thing possible.

The moon was bright on her shaking hand as she tried to insert her long key into the lock. The door opened. Inside, the apartment was dark but she called out anyway. Once she was sure she was alone, she leaned her head against the door and let the hot tears seep out.

Where was the soft cushion for her aching head? Or the tender hands to rub ointment into her skin, so broken and bruised? Her flare of resentment was something she rarely let burn, now all the hotter for being hidden so long.

She made her way to the kitchen. She took a savage kick at the piles of clothing that littered the floor. Who could blame her? She took down the red jar and made herself a pot of the sleeping draught. If it was good enough for the Lady, it was good enough for her.

No sooner had she swallowed her first mouthful than her head grew heavy and her tongue thick. It was as if she had never left the mudflats. A slow tide ran over her body, sealing her eyes and blocking all breath. The weight on her trembling legs was monstrous.

She stumbled down the hall, the path to the bedroom suddenly long and strangely slick. It was almost more than she could do to open the bedroll. So this was where the Lady went to hide from her pain, Nian thought. She fell onto her side. No will to fight any more, she slept.

*Cho*

My neck is stiff and one leg tingles. Why am I lying on the cold stone floor? I try to push myself to sitting but my hand slips.

There's something wet on the floor. I can't see what it is because it's too dark in the hallway. Wasn't there a full moon tonight?

I wipe my hand on the tail of my dress shirt. I stand, slowly, shakily. My trousers are tangled around my ankles. I pull them up and begin to walk. My muscles feel sore, as if I've been running.

Where is Anyi?

I stumble against a spray of dried leaves, nestled in a vase on the floor. The vase shatters. Then I hear the moaning.

I turn the corner into the sitting room. Anyi lies on the floor, her face glowing in the moonlight. Is she dead? Is she hurt? I stumble closer to look.

Her dress is torn. It hangs in long strips quivering like leaves in the first breath of autumn. Her eyes are open; her mouth is too. Each moan bubbles up through her throat, bringing blood to her lips.

I kneel down. 'Anyi,' I whisper.

She doesn't answer. I touch her bare knee and she shrieks.

She crawls away like a crab on her hands and feet into the farthest corner of the room. Her cries echo through the apartment.

'Anyi, it's me. It's Cho.'

The sound that comes out of her mouth is rhythmic, a low-pitched keening. The amah comes running out of the bedroom. When did she get here? Nian stares at her mistress and then at me.

'What did you do to her?' the amah cries.

I stand on soft legs. I see the bloody trail Anyi has left on the floor. The moonlight illuminates the blood that runs in streaks down my shirt. But I have no wounds, no cuts or gashes other than the bite that's stiffening my hand. It's not my blood on the floor.

'I did what she wanted. She's begged me so many times. She said it's what she needed,' I answer, falling again to my knees. I crawl toward Anyi, so still, so broken.

'What do I do now?' I ask her.


*Anyi*

From far away comes the sound of a man weeping. Is that you, Baba? Mama is dead, her body in flames, tiny grey squares floating in the air. She's at peace now, Baba, don't call her back. Let her go. We all have to go.

The wind picks up. The ash swirls and the flames fan into a tower, a sword, a candle that tips dangerously over our heads. Watch out Baba! He rises into the air. His shoes fall and clatter to the ground. He dives into the flames hands first. He'll never weave silk again.

So much noise! Feet running, a shrill whistling, chatter chatter chatter. Comprehension floats just beyond my reach. Only the moon is clear.

I see them now. The worry written in Nian's hunched form. The white shock that's nailed Cho to a place on the floor. Oh Cho, how could you do this to me? How could you leave me alive?

168

# Part Four: Pieces of Silver

# Chapter Nineteen

# Morning, Noon and Night

*Nian*

The barbarian answered the phone, polite and calm, as if a call in the middle of the night was the most normal thing in the world.

'I need to speak to Song Kang,' the amah cried. 'Something terrible has happened.'

Nian heard the receiver thud to the floor, then the pounding of feet and shouting. When Kang spoke, his breath came hard and fast.

'I'll leave right now,' he said. 'I'll be there in five minutes. Call a doctor!'

She called the same doctor who had treated Anyi before. And when he too promised to come straightaway, Nian breathed easily for the first time that night. She returned to the sitting room where the Lady still lay, eyes staring into the moonlight that streamed through the open blinds. Nian closed the blinds and Anyi heaved a sigh.

'What shall I do?' Nian asked.

'Clean!' Cho screamed. He emerged from the bathroom wearing a shirt and pants that were not his. He carried his own bloodied clothes bunched in his hands and held as far as possible from his body.

'Burn these!' he shouted. 'Then go and fetch a mop. Never mind, you're too slow. I'll do it myself.'

Cho ran into the kitchen, returning with a pail of water and a rag. He emptied the pail onto the floor and got down on his hands and knees to scrub. Cho wiped the blood, wringing out his rag into the pail until the water turned rosy.

'Hurry,' he cried. 'Better clean up Anyi too!'

As light as the Lady was, the effort of lifting her body made Nian's head swim. But the Young Master would permit no delay. Nian carried the Lady to the bed and gently removed her clothes, cutting away the last bloody bits that had stuck to her skin. She took down the softest quilt she could find and covered her. Once Nian was sure that the Lady was as comfortable as she could make her, she sank to her haunches, her own limbs trembling. She couldn't decide whether it was fear or pain that made them shake so.

Would this be the day the Lady died?

*Cho*

There's a loud knock. How could Kang be here so soon? I turn out the light before opening the apartment door. His hair is sleep-tousled and he's trying to catch his breath. He runs down the hallway, his shoes making tacky noises on the wet floor until he reaches Anyi's room. There, he lets out a cry of anguish.

Max and Jin are right behind him but they stay with me in the sitting room, badgering me with questions though none of us listens to anything but the sound of Kang weeping.

As soon as the doctor arrives, Jin follows him down the dark hallway into the bedroom. Then Max. Should I go or stay? I go.

A thin line of drool drips from her open mouth. Traces of blood smudge her blanched cheeks. Damn that careless amah! The doctor takes Anyi's limp hand to feel the pulse. He shows Kang the blood under her fingernails. 'Someone, give me some light,' he orders.

The amah reaches for the candlestick beside the bed but her

171

hand misses the copper holder and she loses her balance, almost toppling onto Anyi.

'What's wrong with you?' I shout.

The doctor studies Nian for a moment, the perspiration beading on her ugly face and her body swaying as if at sea. 'Sit down,' he says brusquely. 'You must be in shock too.'

But the amah refuses. 'Someone has to help you.'

'I can do it,' Jin says, pushing Nian aside. She lights the candle and holds it steady above the bed.

The doctor removes the quilt. Anyi's white body is thinner than I remember, her nakedness shocking even to me. Bruises bloom everywhere, five points of contact on each arm, darker bruises on her narrow hips. The skin around her pubic bone is raw. The doctor takes a pen out of his pocket and nudges the frayed edges of skin. Blood streams quickly. I vomit in the corner of the room.

The doctor pays no attention to me. He's rolling Anyi onto her side. 'Lash marks!' he exclaims. 'But old and long healed.' The doctor folds his lips, as if afraid he might utter some unpleasant truth.

'Can you hear me?' he asks.

Anyi blinks her eyes.

'Do you know who I am?'

The crack of a smile forms around her lips.

'Do you remember what happened?'

My breath stops. Anyi closes her eyes.

The doctor turns to Kang. 'I don't have to tell you what happened. You can see for yourself. She'll need care, good and constant care from someone you trust.' He looks at me. 'You sat with your cousin last time. It seemed to do her good.'

'This is no job for a man,' Jin says. 'I'll take care of Anyi.'

'You can't stay here,' Max objects. 'Master Feng won't allow it.'

'I can come after serving dinner and sleep on the floor until

172

the morning. Master Feng will never know,' Jin says, her chin thrust out.

'What about the amah?' I ask loudly.

I point at Nian slumped in her chair. She struggles to sit upright.

'This is her job, let her work!'

'No,' Kang says. 'I think my sister will feel better if she's nursed by a friend.' Turning to the doctor, he continues, 'I'll stay with Anyi during the day. Jin can watch over her at night. Between the two of us, we'll make her better.'

## Kang

As soon as the doctor left, Kang reached for the telephone.

'Who are you calling at this time of night?' Max asked.

'The police. I'll wake them up. I want the inspector himself! Every policeman in Shanghai must hunt the person who did this.'

'Hush!' Jin hissed. 'She's finally asleep.'

They crowded into the kitchen: Kang and Max and Cho. They tried to keep their voices down but Kang couldn't be stilled. Max put his arms around him. 'Let it out. Cry or scream or laugh, if it will help. Then think straight and think hard. Do it now.'

Kang shook Max off. 'Just give me the telephone!'

'No!' Cho shouted. 'Reporting this won't help. The police won't even pretend to investigate.'

Kang stared as if he had never seen his cousin before.

'Women are raped every day in Shanghai. It's a fact of life here. Max, tell him it's true.'

'But we have to do something,' Kang cried. 'How can you give up like this?'

Cho bristled. 'I'm not giving up. I want to protect Anyi, just as much as you do.'

'To do that we have to catch the criminal.'

'We never will,' Cho said.

Kang wavered, his hands locking and unlocking. Cho seemed very certain and Max, his shoulders sagging, did not argue.

'Listen to me, Cousin,' Cho said. 'I know what you're thinking. That even if the police don't find this criminal, they could at least try and who knows, maybe they'll get lucky? But there are policemen who sell stories to the newspapers and Anyi is famous. There isn't a journalist in town who wouldn't pay a fortune for a story like this.'

Kang's rage suddenly melted into guilt. This never should have happened. He should have known, somehow, to avoid it. But it *did* happen and his one and only thought now was to avenge her.

Cho broke in, his voice low and intense. 'You know how proud Anyi is. If this gets out, the shame will kill her.'

Shame! What was shame compared with her suffering? Yet Cho knew his sister better than anyone. He had been right about taking her away from his parents' home. He knew that the dancing would do her good. He knew, just as Kang did, that pride was her greatest flaw. Kang bowed his head, convinced at last.

*Nian*

Finally, they left: the brother and the cousin and the tall barbarian with his slave girl just as dawn began to light the sky. The brother would be back as soon as he could collect his belongings. Better to rest now while she could. But the wounds on the backs of her legs had opened so first she hurried into the bathroom to wash and bind them. In the kitchen, she made a pot of tea and drank it, her hands shaking.

'Nian,' a voice called.

The amah almost dropped the teacup. She ran down the hallway to find the Lady staring at the ceiling.

'Did you call me, Lady?'

'Of course it was me,' she replied in a weak voice. 'You always said you don't believe in ghosts.'

174

The Lady grimaced as she moved herself into a sitting position. 'I heard the kettle whistle. Bring me some tea and a clean nightdress.'

'Can I bring you something to eat? A small bowl of congee?'

The Lady's face blanched. She rolled to the side of the bed and retched but despite the noise, precious little came out. Pale and drawn, she rolled back. The amah was ready with a cold cloth.

'No food, Nian. Please, just tea and some clean clothes.'

As soon as the Lady dropped off to sleep, Nian lay down too. Piles of clothing surrounded her, trampled by the family treading through the room. A teacup had been left under the Lady's bed next to her notebook. Jin had seen the mess on her way out the door and had frowned her disapproval at Nian.

'Get this room clean before I come back tonight,' she whispered to the amah.

'Don't tell me how to take care of my own Lady!' Nian snapped back.

'Quiet! If you did your job properly, I wouldn't have to tell you what Anyi needs.'

How dare Jin interfere? And to call the Lady by her name when Jin was a servant herself!

Nian retrieved the notebook and replaced it on the nightstand. The teacup could wait for another time. Then she sorted the clothes the way the Lady had taught her: clothes to be washed, clothes to be ironed, clothes to be returned to their proper owner or burned. There was quite a large pile of socks and ties, a dinner jacket, even one leather shoe. The amah had already tried them all on, just in case, but these were not the things she coveted.

Nian wanted the silver that winked at her from the back of the Lady's wardrobe. There were hundreds of coins, more Mex dollars than she could ever have imagined. They were all over the house too, under the sofa cushions and inside the Lady's shoeboxes. Just a handful of coins could make the difference between life and death for her and her child. Dare she take some now?

She peeked at the Lady: still asleep. Could she risk a trip to the market for a fresh chicken? The broth would do them both some good. Maybe she could add some chicken blood as well. It was worth the trouble. The amah took out her long latchkey and turned the lock. Now the Lady was safe inside.

The neighbours found Nian at the market. 'Your mistress is screaming. Can't you do something?'

She ran home then but by the time she arrived, the Lady was no longer in distress,

'Nian?'

'Yes, Lady.'

'Did you tell anyone about Cho?'

The amah went to the kitchen. There she hid, fussing with chopsticks and spoons while she tried out different answers. When she returned to the Lady with a tray of food, she asked, 'Should I have said something?'

'No,' the Lady said.

'Is there anything else you would like, Lady?'

She stared into the distance. Did she hear or not? The amah picked up the tray and was already out the room when the Lady called her back.

'Was Cho here this morning when the doctor arrived?'

'Yes, Lady.'

Her mistress shuddered.

'Are you cold?' Nian asked.

'No.'

The amah shifted from one foot to the other. The tray was heavy. She wouldn't be able to hold on much longer.

'Nian?'

'Yes, Lady.'

'Don't let Cho into this house. Ever again.'

'Yes, Lady.'

*Kang*

Jin said, 'She's dreaming again. She talks in her sleep. She says that she sees ghosts.'

'The man who attacked her?' Kang asked.

'Your mother and father,' was Jin's reply.

Why didn't his parents come to visit him, Kang wondered. Not once had they appeared to wish him well or whisper wise words in his ear. Had he been such a disappointment to them that, even in death, they still held a grudge?

Anyi was so pale. Kang stood over her bed, watching her restless sleep. He wanted to hold her hand but was afraid of waking her, startling her into screaming again. He wanted to do something, anything, that would turn her into her old self, the girl he remembered from Soochow, the girl who had once adored her older brother.

So long ago, Kang thought. When he and Anyi played hide and seek in the orchards, was that the last time they were all happy? Kang couldn't remember a time when he hadn't hated his father and his father hadn't despised his son. Anyi would have made a fine son. She would have been the apple of their father's eye and their mother's too. Kang would have been far happier being the second son, the extra one, who did not count unless the eldest son died or failed to produce sons of his own. Kang would have been delighted to be extraneous.

Anyi opened her eyes. 'When did you get here?'

'I haven't been here long.'

'What were you thinking about just now? You looked so sad.'

'Nothing,' Kang said. 'I wasn't sad at all.'

He leaned down to pick up his satchel and pulled out a tightly rolled newspaper. He opened it and scanned the headlines. 'Shall I read you something? A German airship has exploded over New Jersey. It has a funny name. Hindenburg. Would you like to hear about that?' he asked, his eyes fixed on the print in front of his face.

Anyi sounded tired when she replied, 'Read whatever you like, as long as it's about home.'

# Chapter Twenty

# A Key

*Nian*

The brother brought a man with him. Together they attached bars to all the windows, even those that couldn't be reached from the street. The iron was thick and sturdy and immovable. The man bored a peephole into the wooden fastness of the door. When the man had finished his work, the brother looked through the peephole from inside and out. He shook the iron bars so hard that his teeth chattered. When the brother was convinced that no intruder could ever get inside the apartment, he paid the man and let him go.

Then the brother said, 'I want to sleep in Anyi's room.'

But with Nian, and now Jin too, there was no space. So he took the dining alcove for his own. He placed a cot against the long side of the room and a desk next to it, cobbled together with side tables from the sitting room. He dragged an armchair from the sitting room and angled it so that, when he sat there to read his newspaper, he would have a clear view of the Lady in her bed.

He brought his agenda and his calling cards and a stack of stationery and arranged them neatly at his new desk. He set up his typewriter so that he could write business letters but he didn't dare to use it for fear that the clatter of the keys would keep the Lady awake. Instead, the brother sat in the armchair and read every night until Jin arrived.

It was impossible to predict what time she would walk in the door. One night, Jin didn't show up until close to dawn. Nian grumbled, 'How can I sleep when a visitor might arrive at any hour?'

'Give her a key,' the Lady said.

The brother had a key made and gave it to Jin. She looked dumbstruck, as if Kang had offered her entry into the old Forbidden City.

'It's easier for all of us and more convenient for you,' he said.

Nian could see how much he looked forward to Jin's arrival. As soon as she walked in the door, the brother asked her about the Lady's aches and pains, the nightmares and the blood that still seeped out. Nian could have told him all he needed to know if only he had turned to her instead.

The brother and Jin stood in the hallway, whispering. Nian crept closer, a feather duster in one hand, pretending to sweep away the cobwebs in the hall.

He said to Jin, 'You're the only one I trust now.'

Once Jin had answered all of Kang's questions, they would sit down to eat. Nian's cooking was no longer good enough for the Lady and her guests. Jin brought food with her every night to cook or, like now, already prepared in a heavy iron pot. It was a stew with mutton sliced so thin Nian could see right through it, swimming in a broth thick with spices.

'Will this be too much for her stomach?' the brother asked.

Jin smiled at him. She did that these days, as if she and he were friends. 'She needs meat,' Jin reminded him. 'To replenish the blood.'

'And the spices?' the Lady asked.

'You can taste it?' Jin smiled. 'Your appetite must be coming back. Dry fire is good for you.'

Then the Lady noticed that Jin wasn't eating.

'I'll eat later in the kitchen, together with Nian,' Jin said.

'No, you should eat with us,' the Lady replied. 'You're a

180

member of the family now, isn't she, Kang? You've certainly earned your place.'

Later, alone in the kitchen, Nian sat on her haunches and ate from the pot. The stew had turned rancid, it seemed to her, and so she took it outside and poured it on the street. Dogs licked at the congealing mass while Nian lugged the pot back inside, as heavy now as it had been when full.

*Anyi*

'I don't want a massage tonight,' I tell Jin.

'The doctor said we should start,' she replies.

Her hands are so strong. She cries when she sees the bruises she leaves on my skin. She'll learn eventually, if not delicacy then at least restraint. When I can't bear any more, Jin crawls off the bed and kneels on the floor. She lays out her bedroll alongside Nian's to prepare for sleep.

'Come sleep in my bed, Jin. There's plenty of room,' I tell her.

'My place is here at your feet,' she says.

She takes out her knife from some pocket hidden on her person and from another produces an orange. With each deft stroke the rind falls away and then the pith too. Jin rises now and stands beside the bed. Her hands are still moving. She doesn't even need to look at her knife to know what it does. A single gleaming segment of fruit falls into my waiting mouth.

The next night, she massages my feet. She sits on one end of the bed and I sit propped up against pillows on the other. I've never seen this look on her face before. She strokes the instep and the arched sole. Tenderly, she rubs each toe between her fingers.

'Your feet have been bound,' I guess.

Jin nods.

'Show them to me,' I say.

Jin takes off her shoes. Each foot is wrapped in a white strip

181

of cloth. She talks as she works, slowly at first, then her words gather steam as the long white cloth unravels.

'I was four or five years old,' Jin says. 'Old enough to feel proud of the attention I got, too young to understand why. My mother came to me every morning. She bathed my feet in scented water. She wrapped pretty wet linen bindings around my feet, crisscrossing from heel to toe and back.'

Her hands move in the air, swallows in autumn, swooping and diving, then suddenly still.

'When the bindings dried, they tightened. I couldn't walk. My toes were folded into my foot and the skin around them grew taut and finally burst. The blood and the lymph poured out. I tried to untie the bindings but my fingers were too weak. And when my mother saw what I'd tried to do, she tied my hands behind me.'

Jin's face is drawn. I should never have started this conversation but now it seems, she can't stop.

'The toes fell off, one by one, until I had only the big toe on each foot. I thought it was over then. That I had endured all that was necessary. My mother made a special meal for me that night, a reward for all my suffering. She brought it to me herself on a large tray. Beside the dishes of food and the white gleaming rice, lay a long box covered in green silk and embossed with grey flowers. I got excited then. I thought it was a gift.'

Jin places her foot alongside mine. Her skin is brown and puckered while mine is smooth and white.

'My mother picked up the box and knelt before me, balancing its length across her knees. She placed the heel of my right foot in her palm and reached out with her thumb to pull the front of my foot to meet the heel. Then she opened the box and pulled out a knife.'

Jin places her hand inside her tunic and pulls out her knife. The flame of the candle reflects in the steel, turning it to gold. She holds the knife against my foot, across the high instep, and presses. I wait for the blood to gush out but nothing happens. Jin has used the back of her knife. Now her voice hardens.

'She was supposed to cut me, through bone and sinew and flesh. She was supposed to break my foot in two so that I would have a lily foot no more than three inches long. But she couldn't do it. The knife clattered to the cold tile floor and my mother fled the room. It was the last time she ever came to my room.'

I lean over now and touch the blackened ridge of Jin's foot where her toes once were. Jin cries out.

'Does it still hurt?' I ask.

Jin shakes her head wildly.

'What's wrong then?'

'No one's ever touched me in that place.'

We talk long into the night about mothers and knives, pain and reward.

'If I were normal,' Jin says, 'I could marry. Any man would be proud to have a wife with bound feet. But now, not even a peasant would take me when I'm neither fish nor flesh.'

'Is that why you give yourself to a barbarian?' I ask.

To that, Jin has no answer.

*Nian*

Jin came now at all times of the day and night. Today, she was laden with food and spices and newly harvested rice.

'We have rice already,' Nian pointed.

Outside the kitchen door, a large canvas bag sagged against the wall. Jin stuck her hand inside and pulled out a handful of grains. She pushed her hand under Nian's nose. 'Rice weevils,' she said. 'Throw it all away.'

Nian took the bag downstairs and hid it under some shrubs. What kind of a cook wastes food? Nian would sell the rice tomorrow at the market. What difference could a few insects make to a strong constitution?

Each time Jin came, she carried her bedroll on her back. Rolled inside must have been everything she owned: a comb, an old dress of the Lady's, the kitchen cleaver she refused to leave unguarded at Master Feng. Nian liked to finger the blade while Jin was busy with the Lady. She thought of how much money the cleaver would bring at the market but Nian knew better than to take something so valuable from someone as fierce as Jin.

Every night, now, Jin climbed onto the Lady's bed to massage her. The Lady would fall asleep but not Jin. She watched the Lady and Nian watched Jin until the sun seeped through the window blinds and then all of them would sleep for an hour or two.

But the Lady didn't like having so many eyes on her, Jin and Nian in the bedroom and the brother hovering in the dark hallway outside. So Nian would leave the apartment. She roamed the streets close to the market, hoping still to find her lover, but no matter how long she waited or how far she strayed, he was nowhere to be seen.

Nian told herself it was no more than she deserved. She was a servant, uneducated, not even slightly pretty and utterly expendable. Her father had said so. There would be no father for the child growing in her belly. She would have to fend for herself and the child too.

*Kang*

The doctor came everyday. He would ask Nian what Anyi had eaten that day, did she keep it all down, what was the colour and consistency of her stools? Always, it was Jin who answered. The doctor then leaned down and smelt Anyi's breath.

'I'm surprised,' the doctor said to Kang after the first week. 'The Lady is healing much faster this time. With a few more days rest, she'll be as good as new.'

Kang didn't understand how the doctor could say such a thing. Anyi slept all day, waking only at night when Jin arrived.

Anyi, Jin and Kang would speak briefly, then Jin would close the bedroom door and he would be left to amuse himself as best he could.

He tried to read his old schoolbooks and when he tired of those, he took up the newspaper. But the news was dark and troubling to him. Why would the Germans drop bombs on Guernica? Would he and Helen ever visit the new Golden State Bridge? Eventually he would nod off.

Then Anyi would cry out in her sleep and Kang would startle awake. In the dark, he stumbled over the bedrolls in his haste to get to her side. Angrily, he asked Jin, 'Why is it so crowded in here?'

Jin said nothing, merely glanced in Nian's direction.

'Nian,' he said. 'From now on, you sleep in the kitchen.'

The amah pulled her bedroll out from under his feet and swiftly left the room. Kang closed his hand around Anyi's thin wrist, searching for her pulse.

Gently, Jin peeled away his hand and said, 'Stop worrying. Go back to sleep.'


At the end of the second week, Kang became impatient. At a woman's sickbed, a man can do only so much. Work was piling up. Customers were impatient to see samples. His supplier in America was unhappy. How much money had they lost while Kang sat at his sister's side?

He started visiting customers again. He spent more and more time at his office but he returned each night for dinner and Jin's latest report.

Max called one night. 'Jin says your sister's much better now. Is it true? When are you coming home?'

It was week three by now. Kang had done all he could. He told his sister, 'I'll go back to Max's and leave you in peace.'

Anyi didn't reply. She gazed at him for a few moments then turned her face to the wall.

*Anyi*

No dreams interrupt my rest. No ghosts come to visit. Yet when I wake, I am as tired as ever. It takes every ounce of my strength to open my eyes, even more to focus my gaze.

Jin sits in a chair beside my bed. She's got her knife out again, this time to whittle a piece of wood.

'Where did you learn to do that?' I ask.

'My first master taught me.'

'What was he like?'

'An old man, a widower for many years. He thought a virgin would revive his yang.'

'Did it?'

Jin shrugs.

'Was he kind to you?'

Jin opens her palms. A wooden cat emerges, asleep with its head on its paws, its tail curled along the side.

'He taught me to use my hands,' Jin says. 'I call that a kindness.'

When I wake again, Jin is still here. She brings a stone jug into the room. Whatever is inside sloshes lazily from side to side. She pours a glass with liquid so clear that it could have come straight from the sky. One drop slithers down the side of the glass and Jin catches it with her fingertip. But rather than lick the drop off, she carefully dabs her finger dry with a rag that she then throws on the floor.

'You're drugging me,' I say.

Jin doesn't deny it. She raises my head so that she can tilt the glass against my lips and pour the liquid down my throat.

'You need the sleep,' she says.

I clench my teeth and harden my lips. The potion drips down my chin. Jin stares at me with reproach in her eyes.

'Don't give me any more of that,' I say. 'I want to feel alive.'

That night, Baba and Mama come to visit. They're shy with me. It has been so long since we last met. They stand in the shadow of the wall but I can still see enough.

The skin on Mama's face is loose now. A piece shears off and falls to the floor. Her hair is still long and thick but has become streaked with grey. 'Mama, are you worried?' She won't answer. She only moans, softly, so that Jin cannot hear.

Baba is braver. He takes one step forward, out of the dark. He hasn't been dead as long as Mama, but his body too is rotting. He grips his hands together so tightly that his heavy jade ring rubs off his bony finger. It falls to the floor with a heavy thud and rolls under the bed.

I pat the side of my bed as invitingly as I can but they won't cross the room. Jin is lying in the way.

'Visit me later,' I say to them. 'When I'm alone.'

They nod at me and walk backwards until they melt into the wall.

# Chapter Twenty-One

## You Need a Whip

*Tanizaki*

The Japanese Legation was a sprawling complex. The white house served as the official residence of the Envoy to Shanghai with a tiny jewel-like garden tucked into one side for special guests. Around the back, out of plain sight, stood the barracks where Tanizaki's men were housed, men loyal to Tanizaki first and the emperor second.

Those soldiers now swarmed inside the small parade ground that stood in the centre of the complex. It was Tanizaki's birthday and the mood was festive. The Envoy had insisted on hanging garlands of flowers along the fancy wrought iron fence with its golden tips that separated the Legation from the street. But here, where Tanizaki and his men lived and worked, nothing adorned the plain wooden fence. He could think of no better gift to himself than to give pleasure to his men and so he had organised a wrestling match.

The men shouted. They waved their fists in the air. They yelled encouragement to their favourite or cursed his opponent. They did not, for one moment, look away from the two wrestlers circling each other in the ring two steps below.

Neither wrestler wore a shirt. Their chests were speckled by the shadow of the mulberry tree. Skin that had once been slick with chicken fat now bore a crust of salt and blood.

The taller one lunged. He missed and crashed into the wooden fence that did not even shudder, tall and stout as it was. It had been built to keep the Chinese out, allowing in only the coolies needed for the heavy labour.

The crowd jeered as the big man slumped to the ground, his legs spread wide. His smaller, more agile, opponent disappeared into the crowd only to return running at full speed. He leaped, twisting his body in the air so that both feet landed squarely on the chest of his foe. A loud crack was followed by a simple sigh from the now broken body of the fighter. The crowd cheered wildly while the coolies ran up to drag away the loser's body.

Tanizaki was pleased. He loved all forms of blood sport but right now this was beside the point. It was his men who mattered, their morale kept high by this show of favour, their bloodlust keen at the sight of a dying man. Tanizaki fanned himself languidly, careful to turn his face away from the yard so that he wouldn't see the money changing hands in violation of the ban on gambling. Tanizaki was a man of principle but not when the rules were senseless. These men needed an outlet. Better to spend their money on each other than on Chinese whores or watered-down alcohol.

He gazed coldly at the Legation office workers mingling under the low eaves of the building. No one had invited them. They had turned out to watch the fight when they should have been inside writing reports and manning the telephone, controlling the flow of information in and out of the Legation. They wore starched white shirts and loose grey pants. Most of them would be useless in a fight. Tanizaki turned away with a sneer on his handsome face.

His soldiers stood in the glaring sun, their shoulders thrown back, their faces proud. Tanizaki's heart swelled at the sight, every one of them willing and eager to die for the fatherland. He almost smiled. There were days when he wished he could be one of them. The camaraderie of men. The simple ties of loyalty. But that fate was not his. He was an officer, born from a long line of officers, a hand-picked servant of the emperor. He would never be one of them.

Behind him, the porch door squeaked open. A pale thin man approached. He was a recent arrival from Tokyo, yet another member of the diplomatic corps come to swell the ranks. The man introduced himself but the name did not register. He would be either a nuisance or a threat. Tanizaki had no allies in this place other than Kokoro and both of them reported directly to the ambassador in Peking. Spies swarmed around them like flies on dung.

'Please excuse me,' the man said, bowing deeply. 'The Envoy would like you to know that your birthday celebration is about to begin. You and your men must be hungry by now.'

Tanizaki bowed curtly, dismissing the man with one swift move of his hand. Of course he knew the time but his men could go for days without food if need be. He had tested them often enough. A day might come when sacrifices would have to be made. He wanted them ready. But the Envoy wasn't concerned about that. He wanted the typists back at work and the cooks into the kitchen to prepare his meal. The Envoy thought that a diplomat's job was to write and eat, eat and write. Tanizaki imagined that when the Envoy squatted in the latrines, the cesspool filled with words.

'Come forward!' Tanizaki shouted at the man who had won.

He waited at the top of the steps, legs planted firmly on the wooden porch while a servant rushed to his side carrying a black silk bag. The winner moved carefully through the crowd to kneel before Tanizaki in the dirt.

'Come closer,' Tanizaki said kindly.

The fighter rose. His smile was bright as he took the silk bag. It was a generous prize, one that Tanizaki had paid from his own pocket. He smiled to himself, glad of this opportunity to show his generosity. The message would certainly not be lost on Cho waiting in the shadows.

The match over, Tanizaki did not go inside to meet the Envoy. Instead he motioned Cho toward the garden where a

190

wrought-iron table stood nestled among leafy trees. Maids and bodyguards swarmed around the two men. When Cho began to speak, Tanizaki struck him hard across the side of his head.

Cho rose from his seat, his fists balled. The guards rushed forward, bayonets lowered.

Tanizaki said lazily, 'My friend, try to exercise what little self-control you have or these men will skewer you before you blink twice.'

Cho sat. The two men waited until the tea was poured and the guards had moved discreetly out of hearing distance. Even then, Tanizaki held his tongue. The silence between them became painful but he was pleased to see that Cho learned quickly.

More quickly than my son, Tanizaki thought, whom he had beaten over and over until the mere sight of his father terrified the boy. It was the only way. His son must learn to obey before he could begin to lead. Then he would become a brave soldier, like his father and his fathers before him.

But what a price to pay. Never to cup his hand around the child's soft cheek or breathe in the warm smell of his hair. Gods, listen to me, Tanizaki prayed. Send me home to where the crows gather darkly on the rooftops. Give me one more child whom I can love for a little while.

Tanizaki sighed. Prayers were useless. The gods no longer listened, not even to the emperor himself.

Or so it seemed, based on the orders flowing from Tokyo. One week, all military and diplomatic personnel were told that the emperor desired peace between China and Japan. The next week, the troops were ordered into a state of readiness for war. The army in the north was restive, eager to prove its mettle. No one doubted that China would fall within a matter of months or even weeks.

Yet as much as Tanizaki detested diplomats and their mealy-mouthed ways, he preferred the peaceful solution. War was a waste of good men. And for the first time in years, the Chinese government seemed stable enough for talks, real talks that could lead to an easy alliance between their two nations to create a new East Asia order. Then Japan would take its rightful place at the head of all Asian nations.

But the emperor was growing impatient. The ambassador had said so when he called Tanizaki that morning. Kokoro had brought him the telephone, the one that only they used, much earlier than normal and for a moment Tanizaki was vain enough to think that the ambassador was calling to wish him long life. Instead, his superior launched his complaints.

'You tell me you have new leads, Tanizaki, and that I need to have patience. No more! The emperor's advisers all want war. It was all I could do to stop them from issuing a war declaration then and there. If you have an alternative, offer it now.'

'I need a few more weeks,' Tanizaki had replied, hating the seeds of panic in his voice. 'I want to be very sure I've found the right man.'

'You and your preparations! War is no flower-arranging exercise. Find your Chinese allies now or prepare to lead your troops into battle.'

The line had gone dead then, leaving Tanizaki in doubt. He was a soldier and battle was a soldier's duty. The thought of thrusting his sword hilt deep into another man's body warmed him. It would be a pleasure to kill and have his chance of glory.

But no, he would not give in to this temptation. He would pursue peace, however distasteful the means. He turned to the sullen Chinaman with the opium stained fingers, waiting impatiently for Tanizaki to speak.

'I'm pleased to see you here,' Tanizaki said heartily.

'That's not what it felt like,' Cho responded, his hand gingerly covering the welt on his face.

'I told you before. There are certain rules I must follow here. You mustn't take offence. None of this is aimed at you.'

Cho lowered his hand slowly. Beneath the white glow of his cuff, Tanizaki could see a bandage tightly wound around the Chinaman's wrist.

'What happened to you?' he asked, laughing. 'Were you bitten by a wild cat?'

A dull red crept over Cho's collar. Tanizaki had been studying the Chinaman for weeks and had hoped he would show up on the Legation doorstep in need of help. But his appearance today was earlier than expected. He wondered what the Chinaman wanted.

Tanizaki watched as Cho cradled his wrist. If he had injured himself in a barroom brawl, he would be bragging about it, his opponent no doubt in far worse condition. Instead there was a lost look behind that arrogant gaze and something that could be shame.

Then Tanizaki remembered his visit to the Metropole earlier in the week. He was looking for Anyi and when he couldn't find her, he sent Kokoro to search.

'She's holed up inside her apartment,' Kokoro had reported. 'I only saw her walking outdoors once, leaning heavily on her amah's arm.'

Could it possibly be that Cho had taken Tanizaki's advice? The thought was deeply stirring.

'Wild cats are cunning,' he said to Cho. 'You can't tame them with kindness. The whip is all they understand.'

*Cho*

Is it true, what Tanizaki says? That the only way to get Anyi back is through force? It didn't work the last time. Why would it work now?

I should have gone back while Kang was still there. He would have let me in. He trusts me still. But I waited too long, a month, afraid that the police might knock on my door and of the shame that would follow. I hid in the house so long Mama started to fret, trying to soothe me with soup or a visit to the acupuncturist. Blossom hovered too though she didn't want to hear about Anyi. Neither of them understands how much I love her.

193

Three days ago I went to her apartment, bearing all the white tulips I could find. I knocked gently on the door but there was no answer. I peered through the blinds and saw shadows moving inside. I knocked again, this time louder, and called out for Nian. She came to the window and grinned at me.

I pounded my fist on the window bars, shook the doorknob as hard as I could. A peephole opened that wasn't there before and I hadn't even noticed. An eye blinked calmly at me.

'What do you want, Young Master?' Nian asked through the door.

'I want you to open this!'

'The Lady says you're not welcome any more.'

The peephole closed and the blinds too. I pounded and yelled until a neighbour poked his head out his window.

'Hey, not you again? If you don't stop making a racket, I'll call the police. They'll sort you out quick enough.'

I dropped the tulips then and ran.

Last night, I went to the Metropole. I waited for her to show and when she didn't, I hunted down Manager Lin.

'Did you fire her?' I asked.

'Of course not,' he said.

'Where is she, then?'

'She's sick, didn't you know? I got her note today.'

Lin stared at me then, curiosity burning in his eyes. To avert his questions I said, 'You must be getting soft, Manager Lin. Another hostess would have been thrown out by now.'

'She's popular, your cousin,' Lin said softly. 'Why would I cut down my money tree?'

But tonight she's here. I follow her on to the dance floor. She looks straight through me as if I've become another of her ghosts. I give her my ticket and the smile on her face grows calm. We dance. She's as graceful as ever and as hard as glass. Only once does her facade crack, when I try to say I'm sorry. Then the old fire leaps back into her eyes and she claws my face.

194

I don't know what to do now. Confusion turns into despair, despair into something black and ugly. A whip, Tanizaki says, is what I need.

*Anyi*

Jin can't leave Del Monte House tonight because there's a feast for the barbarians. So it's Nian who bathes me. Her voice sounds high and a little breathless, as if her breast cloth has been tied too tight. Her washcloth is rougher than ever. It grates against my nipples and when I cry out in anger, Nian points at them.

'How long have they been like that?' she asks.

I stare at my breasts, one by one. 'Like what?'

'They're bigger than they used to be, your nipples too,' Nian says.

'Maybe two months? I can't remember,' I say.

'Has it ever happened before?'

'This is the first time.'

Nian drops the washcloth on the floor. She helps me climb out of the bathtub and dries me off. She looks wary. It's not until I'm in bed that she speaks again. 'Lady, I think you're pregnant.'

I lie in bed and try to count. I never knew all their names and long ago their faces blurred in my mind. It could be any of those men and yet I know in my heart that the child belongs to Cho.

I can't think of it as a child. It's a worm. It feeds on my heart. It sucks the warmth from my bones. It travels up my spine and enters my brain. I feel it creeping behind the shell of my ear. It has a mind of its own. It has a will of its own. It knows that I want it to die but it wants to live and if necessary it will eat me alive to do so. It will hollow me out until I am nothing more than a husk, a vessel to bring this thing, bloody and alive, into the world.

I wait tonight for Auntie Wen. I stand at the top of the steps and count the stars that hover over the Metropole Gardens.

She doesn't come until three o'clock in the morning, struggling up the marble staircase. When she reaches the top, she clings to the bannister, panting.

'I didn't think you'd be here,' she gasps.

'Where is the customer?' I ask.

'There isn't one. I need to know first whether you're strong enough. Let me look at you,' she says.

She chuckles at her own joke. The silver scars on her eyelids flash in the lamplight and her breath stinks of betel nuts. She feels every part of me, out there in the street, searching for open wounds and when she finds them, she clucks under her breath.

'You're not ready yet,' she says.

'There must be men who'll take me as I am now.'

'You're trembling,' Auntie Wen says. 'You can hardly stand on your own. Am I right that there's blood now on your dress where that pubic bone of yours sticks out so much?'

'I don't care. Send me men!'

'You're worth far more money when you're strong but I understand your heart. You need those men, don't you?'

The worm squirms. It slithers among the grey folds of my brain. It flicks its tongue and when it does, a flash of pain lights up the sky.

Auntie Wen says, 'That Japanese official is still inquiring about you. I think the two of you would get along well.'

I grab Auntie Wen around the shoulders. I shake her as hard as I can but the blind masseuse is too strong for me. She pushes me away with one hand.

'I won't lie down with an Eastern devil,' I cry.

Auntie Wen remains calm. She makes her way back down the stairs, step by careful step.

'You'll accept any man I send to you,' she calls over her shoulder. 'Nothing can stop you, Anyi. You can't help yourself any more.'

# Chapter Twenty-Two

# Green and White

*Cho*

There's hardly anyone in this place tonight, just the usual gamblers nursing their drinks and diminishing piles of chips. When a party of Brits arrives at the front door, Eve Arnold smiles for the first time.

They're new to the Carlton Café and eager to try their luck. They crowd the cashier's cage, shouting for chips and offering credit in exchange. But I know better.

'Cash,' is what the old man will croak. 'Only cash for chips.'

They huddle then, turning out their pockets, patting down their shiny jackets, whispering among themselves.

Then one of them cries out, 'Look smart!'

He has a small beaded purse in his hands that he tosses among his pals. It sounds heavy as it passes from hand to hand. He slams it on the cashier's counter and the purse spills open. Silver Mex dollars and copper Chinese coins clatter on to the counter.

'We'll have those chips now. Be quick about it!' the Brit demands.

I've seen that purse before and start to climb down from my stool but Beauregard has already sidled alongside the young Englishmen. They're too busy counting the piles of chips to notice the huge black man leaning over them, counting too.

'Where'd you get that purse?' Beauregard asks.

197

At the sight of Beauregard, the young Brits turn heel, scattering chips all over the floor. There's a scramble with us regulars diving for the chips while the Brits look on haplessly.

'That's robbery!' they complain.

But good old Beauregard ignores their whining. Instead he lifts one of them by the lapels of his dinner jacket.

'You didn't answer my question,' he growls. 'Where did you get that purse?'

'Annie,' the Englishman stammers. 'She gave it to us. She said it was okay.' He points to a settee pushed into the corner where the other Brits have fled.

'I don't see anyone who would answer to that name.'

'She's sitting down. You can see her high-heeled shoes.'

Beauregard drops the Englishman and strides to the corner. The Brits scatter, leaving Anyi alone in her seat. Her hair is mussed and a long purple streak stains her ch'i p'ao.

'I haven't seen you in a while,' Beauregard says.

'Get me some wine,' she orders.

'You sure that's what you want right now?'

Eve Arnold snaps her fingers. Waiters bring Anyi seven glasses and a bottle of red wine.

'Bring another bottle,' Anyi says. 'One's not enough.'

I've never seen her drink like this before. She was always so clever, tipping the wine only far enough to wet her lips, nursing a single glass to last a whole night. Now the wine splashes her chin, her neck, her dress. She drinks glass after glass and still her thirst seems unquenchable.

The Brits have abandoned her to the wine. They crowd around the roulette table shouting numbers, 'Red, no black!'

I creep towards Anyi. Get down on my knees. Clutch at her limp hands. 'Anyi,' I whisper. 'Won't you let me come home?'

She doesn't seem to hear me. Her eyes roll back in her head and her tongue lolls thick in her mouth. She doesn't speak until it's time for Beauregard to throw her out.

'She hates me, doesn't she?' Anyi says, as he lifts her from

198

the settee. She cranes her neck over his wide back to stare at the crowd. 'It's because Eve Arnold is ugly and I'm not!' She bucks and squirms in Beauregard's arms. He has to throw her over his shoulder to get a firm grip.

Reluctantly, the Brits tear themselves away from the roulette wheel. 'Lady Luck is leaving! Time for the next stop, lads.'

We watch them leave, Eve Arnold and me. Then we sit down once more, she in her booth at the back and me at my blackjack table, alone.

'Hit me,' I say to the dealer. 'Give me all the luck you have tonight.'

*Anyi*

I don't remember the days. Nian says I sleep. I can no longer bear the light in my eyes or the heat of the sun on my skin.

I don't remember the nights either. Oh, there are flashes but I can't be sure any more what's a dream and what has become my life. I see Cho's face staring at me everywhere I go. His head pokes out of the crowd that gathers around the roulette table. His body, that beautiful body, leans against the brick wall outside my apartment. But when I finally summon the courage to meet him, Mama and Baba and the soldiers block my way.

Auntie Wen can only deliver a client once or twice a week.

'I'll take anyone,' I tell her. 'There are no more rules. They can do whatever they like.'

And whenever I meet Beauregard, he says, 'I don't like to see you like this. You and I both know how this will end. Don't you even want to get better?'

Mama and Baba say this is how it must be. They sit on my bed, one on each side. They don't wear clothes any more. They have no flesh left to hide. Mama strokes my hair with her bony hands.

'In a little while you'll be free of this body,' Mama whispers. 'Soon you'll be with us again.'

199

Last night was the roughest ever. He was a big man from the Great Northeast.

Auntie Wen had warned me. She said, 'The men up north have turned into savages, living as they must among animals and the Japanese. Are you sure you can take what he'll hand out?'

It's what I want. It's been too long. To be savaged once more, like that very first time.

I met the man at the agreed place and time. The soldiers came too. They jostled each other, eager to get in line once more, but the man got to me first. The soldiers watched as the man beat me until I lost consciousness.

Was he the one who put me into a rickshaw and sent me home? All I remember is Jin lifting me out of the back seat with her strong arms, carrying me upstairs and into my bed, singing something soft and sweet until I finally slept.

Now Nian is in the room. 'Hurry,' she squawks. 'You'll be late again! And then what will Manager Lin say?'

He's waiting for me on the front steps of the Metropole Garden when the rickshaw pulls up at the curb. He waits for me to climb the stairs, his eyes narrow slits of concentration. He takes my chin between his fingers and turns my face into the light of the marquee. My left eye begins to leak tears.

'You can't work like this,' he says. 'Your face is a mess and your eye is swollen shut. You've got a nerve showing up in this condition!'

I try to push past him. Where else will I go if not here? But he won't have it.

'Go home,' he orders. 'Don't come back until you're presentable.'

'The men who want me don't care how I look. It's what they can do to me that counts.'

'That's your business, yours and Auntie Wen's.'

'It's your business too, Manager Lin.'

200

'Not any more. You disgust me!'

I make a dash for the door but he catches me before I can slip inside. 'We have a contract,' I remind him. 'You have to let me in.'

'I don't have to do anything. You're fired, Song Anyi. Leave this place before I get the dogs to take care of you.'

*Kang*

He had been knocking on the door for some time before he remembered that he had his own key. He knew she was home because she had just phoned him, asking him to come by. He pushed open the door.

'Where are you?' he called. 'Why is it so dark in here?'

Anyi was curled into the corner of the sofa. She had a book in one hand and a blanket thrown over her legs.

'The light hurts my eyes. I think I have an infection.'

Kang came closer, his fears for Anyi awakened once more. 'Did you see the doctor? What did he say?'

He tried to peer into her face but she pushed him away.

'It's nothing,' she grumbled. 'Jin says I just need to wash them with salt water.'

At the sound of Jin's name, Kang calmed down. Jin's judgment was excellent and her nerves strong. She was faithful too, still coming every night to sleep at Anyi's feet even though they had all agreed that Anyi was recovered now.

He sat down in the armchair across from Anyi and waited for her to speak. She had said she had news. But she turned back to her book so he pulled out his newspaper. He was already immersed in the news of the German elections when her voice broke into his thoughts.

'I've resigned from the Metropole Gardens,' Anyi announced flatly.

'Hurrah!' he shouted. 'Now we can go home. To America!'

Anyi fell back into the sofa as if he had slapped her across the face.

201

'What's wrong?' he asked. 'You wanted to dance and now that's finished. What could possibly keep you here?'

Anyi stood then and turned on the light. Kang could see the bruises across her face, the angry welts on her arms.

'What happened to you?' he cried in horror.

She moved soundlessly toward him, her body as rigid as a corpse.

'I need pain,' she said.

What did she mean? Kang struggled to understand. He tried to find meaning in the expression on her face but he couldn't bear to look for long. Her eyes were dilated and her breathing harsh. She's insane, Kang thought. She doesn't know what she's saying. The attack must have affected her mind. She needs more care, much more than Jin and I thought, far too much to take her home to Helen.

'We'll stay,' he said hastily. 'Until the end of the year, just like we agreed. You've nothing to worry about, Anyi.'

All the air came rushing out of her then. It sounded like a death rattle to him. He caught her in his arms, rocking her back and forth, trying not to let his tears fall on her.

'Oh, Anyi, why did we ever come to Shanghai?'

## Cho

The white house is large: three stories tall and four windows wide. The ornamentation is sober, nothing to break the white surface but black lintels and a heavy wooden door. The flower garlands are gone. The wrought iron fence is bare. Now the Legation looks as it should, a serious place for serious matters, just the right spot for my friend Tanizaki.

I mount the steps. The door opens before I've even had a chance to knock. It's the maid Kokoro again. She bows deeply and in one graceful gesture takes my coat and hat. I can find my way by now but she accompanies me anyway into the small, book-lined office overlooking the canal. She motions me to be seated in one of the deep leather armchairs. I smile to thank her.

We have learned to communicate this way, neither of us able to speak the other's language. Of all the diplomats sent to this post, Tanizaki is the only one to have mastered the Wu dialect. In Tokyo, don't they know that Mandarin is useless in Shanghai?

Bowing, the maid exits the room backwards. Within moments she returns with a steaming pot of green tea and a lacquered dish of delicate candies. It's hard not to be impressed.

Footsteps, slow and purposeful, cross the hallway. Tanizaki is freshly shaven and barbered. He greets me warmly, like the friend he's become. My hope grows stronger. The maid instantly appears with a second pot of tea and an intricately woven basket filled with pastries still warm from the oven.

'Arigato, Kokoro,' Tanizaki says quietly. Her reply is musical and soft. She retreats, silently closing the door.

We drink our tea. Tanizaki bows his head, indicating that I have permission to speak.

'Thank you for meeting me at such short notice. It is an honour to be here.'

Tanizaki says, 'You've been here before. You're my friend, after all.'

'I've often wondered but never dared to ask. Why have you chosen me as your friend?'

He sits back. 'It is odd, I admit. At home, you and I would not meet. But then again, what would a Chinese gambler be doing in Kyoto?'

He laughs heartily at his own joke before turning serious. His mouth grows mobile, as if tasting his thought for the first time. 'I suppose,' he says slowly, 'because you're different from anyone I know, here or at home. And for that reason, I can trust you.'

'Trust? No one's come up with that reason before.' We both laugh.

'It's true, though,' Tanizaki says earnestly. 'I'm alone in this place. My greatest fear is to die in China. To be parted forever from everyone I love by the unfathomable sea.'

203

'You won't die here,' I say warmly. 'Your men would never allow it. And surely your fellow diplomats will protect you?'

Tanizaki smiles. His upper lip curls to the right. The result of a childhood accident, he told me once. Yet to me it looks like a sneer.

'The diplomats are not my friends. They would happily watch me bleed to death in the dirt. They don't share my values.'

'And I do?' I ask with widened eyes.

'You're right. You have no values at all.' He pauses. 'But you had a reason for coming. What is it?'

'I need a loan.'

'I thought you were rich.'

'It's my father who's wealthy although he says he has no more money to give me. He's lying, of course, but in the meantime I need a loan to tide me over.'

Bookie, tailor, opium vendor: none will extend me credit any more on the mere strength of Baba's name. His business is failing. Pirates, he says. He rages at fate and the lawlessness of the seas. Then he turns on me.

'It's high time you earned your keep,' Baba says. When Mama wails, Baba turns his rage on her. 'He's a man and a useless one,' he shouts. 'If he will spare me a little of his sinew and sweat, I'll allow him to stay in this house. Why can't our son work if his cousins can? Did we raise our boy to be a leech?'

My head aches with their screaming. I had to get away, stop the ringing in my ears, master the trembling of my fingers. This morning I traded a heavy signet ring for a sticky ball of opium no bigger than my fingernail. The smoke was harsh but sweet. I'll need more, soon. Tanizaki is the only way now.

His eyes are closed. Two long fingers form a bridge around his fleshy nose. He seems to be thinking or praying, although I've never known him to do either. Then his eyes flash open and he laughs. This is the Tanizaki I know.

He claps his hands. Kokoro reappears, bearing a small bamboo basket. She removes the cover to reveal a tray of mochi, the sweet glutinous rice cakes that Tanizaki loves. An iron teapot appears too, filled with a grassy-smelling tea.

He's going to make me wait. I might even have to beg. I'm ready to weep from frustration. Yet as soon as Kokoro leaves, Tanizaki lifts the pastry tray to reveal another below it covered in silver coins.

'A token of my affection,' he says.

I bow my head repeatedly, my fists clasped in salute, almost knocking my forehead on the coins. 'So generous, so kind! If there's ever anything I can do for you, just ask!'

Tanizaki brushes away my thanks. We eat his pastries and drink his tea, though I'm longing to be out of this house and into the nearest opium den.

Finally, he lets me go. Kokoro escorts me to the door while Tanizaki leans back into the shadows. I'm on the street now, still bowing, this time from the waist. I see a pedicab coming my way and raise my hand to hail it.

'Could you wait one moment?' Tanizaki is leaning against the doorpost. 'I've thought of a favour you can do for me.'

# Chapter Twenty-Three

# The Price of Favours

*Kang*

It was his idea to meet at the Park Hotel. Kang loved the place. He arrived early so he could choose the table, one on the west side of the rooftop terrace with the large leather armchairs that swivelled at the slightest touch. By the time Cho arrived, Kang had turned himself about in every direction and could now identify all the buildings in the vicinity.

'Look, Cousin, there's your family's house, on the other side of Soochow Creek.'

Cho's body sank into the cushions of his armchair. He had gained weight and his face was full and sallow. Kang found it hard to believe that this man was once his idol, when Kang first came to Shanghai and Anyi was still a girl in pigtails playing in the garden at home.

The thought of home led inevitably to other, less pleasant memories. It happened often these days. The sight of Anyi in an old shapeless gown reminded Kang of the dresses their mother used to wear. And now here was Cho with his belly protruding through the buttons of his shirt, looking every day more like Kang's father. The idea disturbed Kang so much that he forced himself to talk about business.

'I had more Japanese visitors today. They sounded quite interested. I've shown them all my machines and wired America to have them send me blueprints of the latest design. I think they're going to buy.'

Cho suddenly sat up straight in his chair, but not to look at Kang. He stared instead at the dimly lit tables on the other side of the restaurant. Kang turned to look but Cho caught hold his armrest.

He asked, 'If they decide to buy, what happens next?'

'The home office would have to ship the right parts for me to assemble here. Or ship the whole machine intact. That might take four to six weeks.'

Cho nodded, 'And then?'

Surprised at his cousin's interest, Kang warmed to his topic. 'The machines might require recalibration on account of the transport. I can do that myself. Then we install and test at a site selected by the customer. If all goes well, then the customer pays me and I'll have enough money to buy tickets for Anyi and me to go home.'

Cho's eyes widened. Kang had never seen them so bloodshot and now that the lamps were lit, he saw that Cho's hand trembled each time he reached out to pick up his glass. Cho had refused to order food and emptied glass after glass of wine, leaving Kang to eat alone.

'Is money all that's keeping you and Anyi in Shanghai?' he asked in a ragged voice. 'I thought the two of you were going to stay longer.'

Kang ignored the reproach in Cho's voice. 'If this Japanese company can decide soon, Anyi and I will be gone before the summer.'

As if Cho hadn't heard a word, he said, 'There's a show at the Moon Palace tonight. Shall we go?'

'I'm going to a meeting tonight.'

'What kind?'

Kang was happy to discuss his newest hobby. 'It's a group of artists, painters mostly, trained in Japan and France. They want to modernise China through their art. They've already asked me to write an article for their house magazine about developments in the United States.'

'What do you want with this crowd?'

'Don't you feel any obligation to contribute? To get involved? It seems as if our government has no other priority than to root out communists. In the meantime, our people suffer and our standing in the world diminishes. Shouldn't we, the privileged class, do something about it?'

'That's stupid. The people don't care whether it's an emperor or Chiang Kai-Shek who rules. They'll be miserable either way. And what possible difference could you or I make in all this mess? The best thing I can do is to enjoy myself for as long as possible. It cheers me up wonderfully.'

Kang couldn't help but laugh.

'All right,' he said. 'I give up. There's no talking politics with you. But you won't destroy my good mood. I'm going to stop by Anyi's on my way to the meeting. Why don't you come along?'

Cho's mood suddenly changed. He shook his head and when Kang left, he stayed at the table, drinking.

*Tanizaki*

Cho came every day now, close to sunset, when the carnival of Shanghai was about to begin. He was surprisingly accurate in his recounting of all his conversations with his cousin Kang though he remained baffled by Tanizaki's interest.

'He's a returned student, sure. He got an engineering degree in the US. He worked for a year at an American steel mill in Ohio. Who cares?' Cho had shouted.

Kokoro shadowed Song Kang on three separate occasions when he attended leftist gatherings but as far as she could determine, Kang was not yet a member of any group. His cousin described Kang as hostile to the ruling Nationalist party. A promising subject, Tanizaki thought.

But when it came to the reason why Kang had returned to

China, the story grew muddied. Cho had admitted that Kang came for Anyi but he had uncharacteristically refused to elaborate further. Tanizaki turned to Kokoro for more details but even she was unable to tell him any more than he already knew.

He stared down at Anyi's dossier. *Dance hostess at the Metropole Gardens. Prostitute specialising in violence. Considered to be mentally unstable. Recommendation: do not pursue.*

That was Kokoro's conclusion after observing Anyi for seven consecutive days and nights. She had included meticulous notes on the customers who visited Anyi in her own home, including sketches of their faces and any peculiar physical traits. She had even included an estimate of Anyi's fee, an amount that had taken Tanizaki's breath away.

'I know you're interested in her.' Kokoro's black eyes were particularly steely though her hands were folded calmly on her lap. 'But she has nothing to do with our mission. There are others under surveillance who look more promising.'

She pushed forward another file and left. The folder that now lay open on Tanizaki's desk was about Max Lazerich. A resident of Shanghai for the past eight years, the American had risen through the ranks of the Maritime Custom Office and was rumoured to be fluent in Chinese, written and spoken, a very unusual ability for one of his kind.

Yet Tanizaki had met Lazerich and was not impressed. The occasion had been the funeral of an insignificant American woman whose death had been deeply embarrassing for the Japanese Legation.

'It was one of our snipers,' the ambassador had explained to Tanizaki. 'And during a ceasefire too. Someone must go to the funeral to show remorse on behalf of the government.'

'Do you mean apologise?' Tanizaki had asked, incredulous.

'Of course not,' the ambassador huffed. 'Just show some humility. Can you manage that, Tanizaki?'

The memory of the old man's sneer still burned. The shame

of his role had fused with his recollection of the funeral and all who had attended, including the damn American. Tanizaki was tired of charades, tired of China and the interfering foreigners, tired of this interminable mission.

Disgusted, his eyes fell on the tangled pile of papers on his desk. Song Kang, Max Lazerich, Cho and Anyi, their reports had become jumbled together, Anyi's recommendation now inside her brother's dossier. He swept the papers into one pile. He was ready to shove the entire stack into his safe and relieve his weariness with a good long round of sword practice when he saw the address.

The American and Song Kang lived in the same house, a place where both Cho and Anyi had been regularly sighted! But Cho had never mentioned his relationship with the American, even though he had been ordered to tell all.

It made no difference to Tanizaki whether Cho had made an omission of intent or neglect. If he did not yet understand blind obedience, then he must be taught.


*Blossom*

The family had just sat down to dinner. For a few moments at least, Blossom was at leisure. She dawdled in the kitchen but Cook paid her no attention.

'Where's Driver Zhang?' she asked.

'Shouldn't you get the door?' he said in reply.

Blossom heard the knocking now, a rhythmic thump that made the front windows vibrate.

'I'm coming,' she shouted irritably.

A well-dressed young man stood outside. Blossom thought he was quite handsome with his military bearing. 'Yes?' she asked, smiling.

The man slapped her across the face, the welt of his five fingers burning red on her plump cheek, knocking her to the floor. Blossom cried out but when the man raised his hand to strike her once more, she grew quiet.

'Song Cho lives here?' he asked.

Blossom nodded, her eyes bright with tears.

'Get him.'

Blossom hesitated. She knew the rules. No one was to disturb the family during mealtime. Any servant who did would be dismissed on the spot. But the man at the door was a more immediate threat.

Before Blossom could get to her feet, one of the dogs strayed into the courtyard. She was a new bitch, a Hungarian Pointer purchased only that week by the Young Master together with her litter of nine pups. The Young Master had named her Caramel because of the colour of her beautiful fur.

The man at the door pulled out his pistol and fired once. The bullet hit the dog between her eyes and the bitch sank on to her forelegs.

'Get Song Cho now!'

Blossom ran screaming into the house, 'He shot the dog! He killed the new bitch! There's a man here who's killed the Young Master's dog.'

By the time the Young Master arrived at the front door, Blossom quaking in his wake, three dogs lay at the door. Two were dead. The third was still twitching. His front paws beat the air as if to ward off some unseen enemy. At the sound of a familiar voice, the dog's tail beat out a final welcome before his body shuddered to still.

The Young Master stared at the widening pool of blood and then at the man who had wreaked such havoc.

'Who the fuck do you think you are?' he screamed.

The stranger pushed his pistol into the Young Master's face. Blossom couldn't bear to watch. She clapped her hands over her ears to block out the shot.

Instead, the stranger laughed. Blossom raised her eyes then, just as the stranger handed over an envelope containing a single sheet of rice paper. Once the man had seen that his message had been read, he turned on his heel and marched out the gate.

211

The Young Master stood for a long moment. Then he knelt and bowed to each of his dead dogs. 'I'm sorry,' he whispered. The Young Master rose once more and shouted, 'Driver Zhang!'

The driver emerged from the garage with straw covering his stubbly head, his eyes glued to the ground as he pulled the rickshaw into the yard. He tried desperately not to look at the poor animals or to drag any of the wheels through the blood. The Young Master got in.

'Where to?' the driver asked.

'The Japanese Legation,' the Young Master said, as if Zhang should have known.


*Cho*

A manservant answers the door this time. He doesn't usher me into the cosy little sitting room by the canal but marches me through a long hallway and down a short flight of stairs. He stops abruptly in front of a closed door, raps twice, then leaves.

The door opens. It's Kokoro, the maid, and I'm so relieved to see a friendly face that I could piss myself. I want to grasp her hand, show her how pleased I am to see her, but she pulls away to reveal Tanizaki seated at a tiny wooden desk.

'You've never been properly introduced,' he says.

I look around the room but there's no one here but him and me.

'Sagano Kokoro, servant of the emperor,' Tanizaki says.

The maid moves forward and bows stiffly, not in the correct way for a woman but as one equal to another. She stands so still, so unsmiling, that it takes me a while to realise what's wrong. She's not wearing her usual kimono but a dark-coloured blouse over dark pants.

'Where are your manners, Cho? Why don't you bow back?'

The sibilant whisper of cloth is my only warning. Kokoro's arm is pinned against my windpipe. I struggle to free myself, the woman's grip impossibly strong. Just as I think I've finally succeeded, a knife appears. As thin as a needle, Kokoro points it at my left eye. The cold tip kisses my eyelid and immediately blood floods my eye.

'Stop!' I scream.

The stiletto is gone. No, there it is in Kokoro's hand. Is that my blood I see staining the steel?

Tanizaki chuckles. 'The cruelty of men is nothing compared to that of a woman. Not even your own mother would recognise you if Kokoro ever got hold of you.'

'What do you want?' My voice is girlish with fear.

'The truth,' he replies.

'I've never lied to you,' I squeal like a pig on its way to the slaughterhouse.

'Maybe that's true. But you haven't yet told me all you know. Sit down. You're making Kokoro unhappy.'

She flicks the blade. It leaps into the air landing with a thud on the desk before me. I sit. Tanizaki sits with his arms crossed while Kokoro writes, her ink brush whipping up and down the page.

'Yes, the Americans paid for Kang to study. Didn't I tell you before? I don't know his friends, other than Max. He's a big shot, a very influential person. He directs the research of the Custom House. He knows them all: the American ambassador in Peking, the members of the Shanghai Municipal Council, every businessman in town. They all want to know what Max knows, the price of grain or the tonnage of steel imports.'

Kokoro asks me to recite the names of the members of the Municipal Council but I don't know them except by sight.

'I'm Chinese remember? I don't live in the International Settlement but Max does. Kang shares a house with him. Did I tell you that? Of course, I know the address. Do you have a pen and paper?'

My hands are shaking. Tanizaki asks if I need a drink.

'Yes, that would be nice. Something tall and cold, please. It's awfully close in this room. You'd think a basement would be cooler.'

Kokoro disappears and returns dressed once more as a maid, bearing a tray of drinks and snacks.

'Ah, that's very refreshing, thank you, Kokoro. Listen, Tanizaki, I think we've talked enough. I've told you all I know.'

She pulls the stiletto out of her obi. Now she holds it at my throat, the steel cold against my skin.

'I'm sorry. That was rude of me. I'm happy to talk. I have all the time in the world. Just tell me what else you want to know. Yes, anything.'

The blade returns to its hiding place. Pen and paper appear in its place. I'm not stupid. I write what they want to know and more.

When I finish, Kokoro brings the opium tray. 'Shall I light the pipe for you, Master Song?' she asks sweetly.

*Tanizaki*
He could hear the rain, even down in the basement. He imagined the windows upstairs shedding long tears. He wanted to be outdoors, away from the opium fumes and the stink of a traitor, out of this rabbit's warren of interrogation rooms but he had to wait until Cho had finished his opium and could find his feet again.

Kokoro had already left to check and cross-reference Cho's information against what they had on file. She didn't need to know about what would happen next.

'Cho,' he said. 'Introduce me to Anyi. Make it for tonight at the Palace Hotel.'

*Cho*
Nothing I say will change his mind. 'Why Anyi? When there are so many other, more beautiful women in this town?'

'Do I tell you what to eat?' Tanizaki retorts. 'You should prefer this fish to that one?'

'Is that what she is to you? Something to consume?'

Tanizaki is frowning now, his mind sending out tentacles. I

214

feel their delicate touch. I cannot fail Anyi. Not again. I wear my shiniest smile, let loose my gayest laugh. 'You're so generous to me. No man could ask for more! But I'm speaking to you as your friend, with only your interests at heart. Forget about Anyi. Let me find someone else for you, someone better. In all honesty, she's not all that she's cracked up to be. You can believe me.'

The frown is gone now. In its place is a look of interest, a mild curiosity. 'She doesn't satisfy you any more?'

I try to laugh but the sound seems thin. 'No, no, no! I hear that she's ill. It could be anything, even something contagious. Better not to waste your time. You may well be disappointed.'

Tanizaki's words roll out slowly. 'Your cousin has certain talents that might appeal to me. That's what I hear. I want to know if it's true. I need to find out for myself.'

'Ask me to do something else for you,' I beg. 'Anything at all. Just leave Anyi alone.' I offer him Max. I offer Kang. I even offer to betray my own father to the Japanese.

'Do not disrespect your father,' Tanizaki replies. 'It's wrong. That part I won't agree to.' Then he relents. 'Because we're friends, I'll compromise. Let me have Anyi for just a little while. When I'm done, I'll give her back. How about that, my friend?'

# Chapter Twenty-Four

# An Invitation

*Nian*

The Young Master appeared out of the blue. It had been weeks since his last visit but this time he didn't even knock. He pushed an envelope under the door and walked away. Nian picked it up and took it to the Lady.

The Lady was asleep even though the Bell Tower had just struck midday. She slept all the time now and when she wasn't sleeping, she drank. The red jar containing Auntie Wen's sleeping potion was almost empty. Auntie Wen had refused to refill it on her last visit.

She had screamed, 'If you think you can get customers behind my back, then from now on you can take care of yourself.'

The Lady had just sat there, her eyes closed, while Auntie Wen walked in circles around her armchair. Nian had stayed in the kitchen, unwilling to draw the old woman's wrath on to her own head. But Jin had no such qualms. She browbeat the blind masseuse until Auntie Wen finally fled.

That night and every night since, Jin slept in the Lady's bed.

But there was no Jin now to intervene between an amah and her mistress. Nian tugged on the Lady's arm to wake her. As soon as she opened her eyes, Nian thrust the envelope into her hand. 'The Young Master was here. He left this under the door.'

The Lady said, 'Open it.'

Nian reached down for the knife the Lady kept in her

mattress. She was tired of pretending that the knife didn't exist, though after placing a finger on its blade, she was surprised by its sharpness. The envelope fell open with one slice.

Inside was a calling card, a name embossed on heavy paper in shiny black characters. The amah gave the card to the Lady who traced the characters with her forefinger, stroke by stroke.

'What's it say on the back?' Nian asked.

'Jin Jiang Club, six o'clock, tonight.'

'That's all?'

'He says Kang is in danger. He says I must meet him to save Kang.'

'Is it some kind of a joke?'

The Lady was quiet for such a long time that Nian wondered if she had drifted back to sleep. Perhaps the Lady's child was sapping her energy just as Nian's was.

The amah curled up most afternoons now on the sofa like a cat. Yet no matter how well Nian took care of herself and the child, there could be no comparison with the Lady. *Her* son would get attention and an education. *Her* daughter would be taught to keep her hands soft and her skin white. She would be cherished.

And what would become of Nian's child? A boy might grow up to be a boatman like her father and all her brothers, if he didn't drown or starve or become afflicted by one of the thousand diseases that hung like a miasma around her people. But if it were a girl, well, Nian might as well drown her at birth. A girl's life was worth nothing without money to protect her.

The Lady's eyes opened and she began to speak, but not to Nian. The ghosts were back, keeping the Lady awake. Nian moved away from the bed, tired of waiting.

'Stop,' the Lady called. 'Help me get dressed.'

*Cho*

Here at the Palace Hotel, the waiters wear stiff red jackets that exactly match the colour of the upholstery. They're angry that

I've turned up so early, before any of the other guests, before even the cook has arrived. They can't joke around while I'm here. They've got to be stiff and formal and carry everything about on large silver trays: the candles and the wine glasses and the silver forks and knives.

One of the waiters approaches. He sneers ever so slightly as he removes my overfull ashtray and replaces it with another.

'That one's dirty,' I say, pointing at the grey rim around the crystal dish.

The waiter takes away both ashtrays. I know that when he returns, if he returns, he'll bring an even dirtier one so I let my cigarette ash drop on the fine linen tablecloth. By the time the waiter comes back, tiny burnt holes have ruined the cloth and with it his wages for the night. I smile as the waiter leads me away to a better table, where I can see the view of the city, where Shanghai can still take my breath away.

When she finally arrives, I see the girl from Soochow as she once was: young, fresh, in thrall only to me. My head is light with the smell of jasmine blossoms. I rise from my chair to take her arm from the waiter who escorts her to this table.

'Sit,' I say to her. 'Sit close by me.'

'Kang,' she says. 'You said Kang was in danger. What is it?'

'Let's get married, Anyi, this week, next week, whenever you like. We can have a family together if that's what you want. Let's go away. Right now.'

'What about Kang?'

'Your brother wants to go back to America. Let him go!'

'You've asked me here to tell me to abandon my brother? You don't know me, Cho. You never did.'

*Anyi*

The table glitters with forks, knives, all those empty glasses. I peer into my own glass, empty but for a smear of red at the base. I stick in my tongue but the bottom is too far away. Hold the glass upside down over my waiting mouth. The candlelight

218

dances, the flames elongate, twin and embrace. The last drop
of wine falls into my lap so I wave my glass in front of Cho's
nose. But he doesn't understand that I need another drink. That
I would rather die than leave Kang behind.

'Look at the view,' he says. 'Isn't it pretty?'

He takes my chin in his hand and turns it toward the window.
But all I can see is the reflection in the glass: me and Cho,
Mama and Baba, and the back of the waiter leaving the table.

'I want another drink,' I say.

'You're drunk already,' Cho replies.

And so I am. I can smell my own breath: sour and hot. If
Cho won't help me then I'll have to help myself. I stand, raise
one hand, lose my balance and slide into Cho's arms. He's drunk
too, but in a different way. He's talking to me, his mouth opening
and shutting. I hear the sounds but the words make no sense.

'What, my love? You say that you want me? Well, who
doesn't in this town? It's time for a drink. Where did that
waiter go?'

My ankles wobble. Have my shoes grown? I try to find the
waiter. I lurch from table to table. Cho comes after me and
wraps his arms around my waist, feeling oh so good. He carries
me back to our table. He's warm and strong and all mine.

He says, 'You look lovely tonight, Anyi.'

Or was it the man now seated at our table? His hair gleams
darkly in the soft lamplight. One hand rests elegantly on the
white linen. The other is draped over his knee. My eyes focus,
one at a time, on his smooth face. Then I recognise him and
my mind is wondrously clear.

'I know who you are. You're that Eastern devil.'

The man smiles at me. His teeth are white and even, strangely
small in such a broad mouth. He devours my body with his
eyes.

I say to the man, 'You're the one they call the Crow.'

The man laughs like a schoolgirl. A high-pitched giggle.
Hardly the laugh of a man of his status.

'Honourable Tanizaki, it is my pleasure to introduce you to the famous dancing star and my cousin, Song Anyi.' Cho turns to me. 'Cousin, this is the political attaché of the Japanese Legation in Shanghai, the Honourable Tanizaki Haruki.'

The Eastern devil holds my hand as delicately as if it were a rare bloom and plants a kiss. His lips are dry and his tongue pointed.

When he speaks, his words are slow and measured – Chinese words that are still awkward in his Japanese mouth.

'I am most honoured and gratified to make your acquaintance, Miss Song. I told you we would meet again. Do you remember?'

*Tanizaki*

Normally he hid the amulet under layers of clean cotton not wanting to call attention to his sentimentality, this lapse in personal discipline. His wife had given it to him, a parting gift the day he left Kyoto.

'So that you won't forget home,' she had said.

'How could I do that?' he had chided. He took both hands and cupped her round face. 'How could I forget you and our child?'

'Children,' she murmured, taking one of his hands and placing it on her belly. 'When you come home again, your second child will be waiting for you, another small son or perhaps a daughter for you to spoil.'

His throat grew tight then, from the happiness that streamed from her eyes into his heart. There were times, here in Shanghai, when he could summon up that joy simply by rubbing his thumb over the smooth soapstone.

'What is it?' Anyi asked.

She had gone with him willingly, straight from the Palace Hotel to the Japanese Legation. They entered through a side gate with well-oiled hinges set in the heavy wooden fence that backed the compound, a door hidden among the jacaranda trees. He led the way through the dark garden, his ears pricked for the presence of witnesses or the sound of Anyi turning to flee.

But she didn't even try. She followed him up the wooden stairs and down the long narrow passage to his private quarters. She said nothing as he sent the maid away nor did she make any sound at all when he took her, quickly and savagely, without bothering to undress her.

He washed himself carefully before lying down on the bed. She lay naked by his side, confident in the beauty of her bare skin. She stretched out her hand to cover his. It surprised him so much, this intimacy from a whore, that he released the amulet into her grasp.

She rubbed the black surface with her thumb. 'Is it a cat?'

'Inari,' he said. 'A fox. The servant of the god of rice.'

She laughed then, a sound he was not prepared for. She looked almost happy and very young with her hair tumbling into her face.

'My brother calls me his fox spirit because I cause so much mischief.'

'In the Shinto faith, we believe that the inari are messengers, that they can intercede on our behalf with the gods.'

'So you are a messenger of the gods?' she asked, tugging lightly on the leather thong.

In her eyes, Tanizaki caught a glimpse of a rare intelligence. 'Do you know what I miss the most from home?' he blurted out. 'It's the sound of crows. A most distinctive caw, don't you think? They're everywhere in Japan but not here. Why is that?'

'I don't know,' she said. 'Maybe in the countryside? You could send someone to catch a crow for you. Bring it back to Shanghai and keep it as a pet.'

'No,' he said, lifting himself on one elbow. 'To cage a crow is to kill its spirit. I could never be so cruel.'

He threw his legs over the side of the bed. Turning to look at her, still lying on her back, he asked, 'Are you ready?'

She nodded and rose from the bed.

221

'Where should I stand?' she asked.

'There.'

He placed her in the centre of the large room. He measured with his eyes the distance to the wall. He calculated speed, trajectory and flight. He clenched his fist and drove it hard into the middle of her chest.

She was lighter than he thought and the blow sent her crashing against the wall. For a moment, she lay crumpled on the floor and Tanizaki wondered if she might be dead but no. Dazed and pale, she struggled to her feet and walked punch-drunk back to her position.

Again he struck her, this time with his open palm, a crack against her rounded belly like the sound of a whip. She fell on her back, her mouth gaping for air like a fish that doesn't yet know there's a hook sunk deep in its throat.

Once more she stood. A thin ribbon of blood trickled from the side of her mouth. Her tongue darted out to taste it.

'Come here!' Tanizaki screamed and Anyi obeyed. He liked that in her. He liked it very much.

# Part Five: The Pockmarked Moon

# Chapter Twenty-Five

# Yin, Awake

*Tanizaki*

She came to the Japanese Legation every night. For her sake as much as his, they delayed her arrival until well after midnight. She would come to the wooden gate, instructed not to knock, required to wait until a servant was at leisure to let her in.

Most nights, it was Kokoro. Tanizaki knew they didn't speak from Kokoro's stiff stance when she ushered Anyi into his rooms.

'If it's so much trouble, I can find someone else to take care of Anyi,' he had suggested to Kokoro one night.

'It's not the inconvenience,' she had replied. 'It's the risk you're taking. And you know it. Why else have you added extra sentries to the schedule? But even they can do nothing once you are alone with her in this room.'

So Kokoro remained vigilant. Every night, she undressed Anyi and slipped a sleeping kimono around her thin frame. She took away the clothes ostensibly to fold but in fact to search for weapons, a shuriken or a vial of poison. So far, Kokoro had found nothing but that did not lessen her distrust.

Tonight was no different. The women performed their silent ritual while Tanizaki pretended to read the newspaper. As soon as the shoji door slid closed behind Kokoro, Anyi smiled at him.

'Look at me,' she said softly. She crossed the floor in a perfect imitation of Kokoro's mincing steps. When she reached Tanizaki's armchair, she knelt on the floor and, in Kokoro's soft Kyoto accent, said, 'Good evening, Master Crow.'

Tanizaki had never encountered a whore like this one. Anyi made him laugh.

She pinched the end of his nose, pulling hard on his fleshy beak. 'Is this why they call you the Crow?'

His hand instinctively rose to slap her. She stared at it with calm welcome. That was something else he liked. So he tucked behind one ear a tendril of hair that teased her chin.

'My father gave me the nickname,' he said. 'Because I have the memory of a crow.'

'What does a crow need to remember other than where the best grain is?'

'That's more difficult than you'd think. Farmers harvest the grain as soon as it's ripe and put it inside barns until they can sell at the market. That's why there are so many crows in Japanese cities. They follow the grain.'

'You don't need a memory for that, just a good pair of eyes.'

'Crows can see farther than any man, it's true. But did you know that they can see the difference between you and me?'

Anyi rose to remove her robe. Her nakedness did not shame her despite the scars that covered her body. She poured water out of the pitcher Kokoro had left for them and began to wash. Tanizaki sat up to watch.

'What do crows see when they look at us?' she asked with her back still to him.

'A crow knows the difference between friend and foe. And they communicate that fact to each other so that once you've been marked as an enemy by one crow, the whole murder remembers. They'll descend upon you, shrieking and scolding. If you're weak, they'll pick out your eyes.'

The sponge fell from Anyi's hand. She stared at Tanizaki, a

crooked smile curling from the corner of her mouth. 'You never forget an enemy. That's why they call you the Crow,' she said.

Tanizaki clapped. The shoji door immediately opened to reveal Kokoro with a knife in her hand.

'I wasn't calling you, Kokoro. I was applauding our guest here for her swift wit.'

The screen door closed. Tanizaki pointed to a spot in the middle of the floor, the one where she always stood.

'Come here, Anyi,' he said. 'Are you ready?'

*Anyi*

He'll use whatever is within reach: an ashtray, a burning candle, his own belt. But what he likes best is to beat me with his own hands. I goad him on, each time a little farther. The bloodlust glitters in his eyes. His breath grows ragged as he chokes all the air out of my body. I arch my back hoping that he will pull the knife that's strapped to his shin and slit me open from neck to navel.

When he has spent himself, he rolls away quickly, as if my skin burns his. He calls in the maid to towel him off. I wave her away. I want the sweat and blood on my skin to chill in the cool evening air.

His breath has a surprisingly delicate scent. He's particular about his food, hovering with his long-tapered chopsticks over the many small dishes on his tray. He takes a pickle, two pieces of fish, all of the cold spinach. He watches as I clear my plate and then his. He never questions my hunger or comments on my lack of manners. He smiles, his upper lip curled to the right, almost hiding the moles that indent either side of his mouth.

'Come at noon tomorrow,' he says. 'There's something I want you to see.'

Nine soldiers stand in the courtyard, their eyes straight ahead, each one wearing an identical blue uniform. Tanizaki strolls among them, commenting on the shine of their bayonets. Nine more soldiers jog into the courtyard and stand to attention along the fence. They look just like the others, but they wear khaki instead.

Suddenly, Tanizaki shouts, 'Shuriken!'

The blue soldiers move so fast, I don't see their feet touch the ground. They've formed a circle around Tanizaki, so tightly that I can hardly see his face. The circle turns, the bayonets splay and suddenly the soldiers have become a wheel of death. The wheel spins across the courtyard, headed straight for the fence and the soldiers who are standing in front of it.

Then another order emerges from deep inside the blue wheel. The khaki soldiers attack. From all sides, they try to penetrate the circle, to crack the wheel to reach the prize inside. Sixteen times the khaki soldiers attack and fail.

A final order is given from inside the wheel and the blue circle breaks apart. The soldiers now stand in even rows, all eighteen of them, each one's face without expression though I can see their chests heaving.

Tanizaki dismisses his men. He mounts the stairs, his eyes bright with excitement, to the landing where I sit. 'It's a new manoeuvre I've just designed,' he explains. 'To mimic the way a shuriken works.'

'What is a shuriken?'

He pulls a thin metal disc from his breast pocket. It could have been a coin from the olden days, burnished from constant use, a starfish from a metallic sea. Each edge has been filed to the sharpness of a razor and as I finger one, it shreds my flesh. A drop of bright blood leaps on to its copper skin.

Tanizaki laughs. 'A shuriken is a woman's weapon. It requires no strength, just excellent nerves. You would be good at it. The name means sword hidden in hand. Some call them throwing stars.'

'Can you kill someone with it?'

Tanizaki shakes his head. 'The shuriken is a defensive device, to distract the attacker, until the real weapon is ready to be revealed.'

'You?' I ask.

Tanizaki smiles and bows his head.

*Cho*

The days are long, the nights interminable. There are just the three of us at every meal. These days, neither Baba nor Mama goes out. There's no more money for things like that.

Mama calls Cook into the dining room. She wants to know exactly what he paid for fish today. He comes into the house splattered in blood from head to toe.

'What happened to you?' Mama screams.

'I'm slaughtering a cow in the kitchen yard. Blossom said you wanted me?'

'Go away,' Mama urges from behind her lacy handkerchief. 'I cannot bear the smell of blood!'

The day stretches on. There's nothing else to do but sleep. Blossom tries her best to stay out of Mama's way. At least, that's what she says when she crawls into bed beside me just as the day is finally ending.

'What's that smell?' I ask.

She sits up, her bare back gleaming in the last light of day. She sniffs the air and then her own breath.

'I don't smell anything wrong.'

'It's not wrong,' I say. 'It's quite nice actually, a sweet aroma.'

Blossom raises her nose one more time and snorts.

'Jasmine,' she says. 'See the vines outside your window? You always liked those flowers. Shall I fetch some for you?'

I remember a floor strewn with white petals. I remember a bed with Anyi lying on top of it, waiting for me. I see myself as I once was and my stomach turns.

'Close the damned windows!' I shout. 'And get out of my sight.'

When I come down for dinner, there's an envelope waiting for me, the kind of stationery that only rich people and governments use. I tear open the envelope while Mama and Baba stare.

'Is it good news?' Mama asks.

'Is it work?' Baba hopes.

It's been weeks since that nightmarish dinner at the Jin Jiang Club. Turned away from Anyi's home, now Tanizaki too refuses to take my calls and I know I cannot push my way past Kokoro.

I beam at my parents. 'My friend Tanizaki wants to see me. I should leave right away. This is good news.'

Tanizaki is waiting for me in the garden, seated at the same wrought iron table where we once talked. There must be a bathhouse somewhere on the grounds since he's wearing a short yukata robe. His legs are bare and surprisingly hairy.

He tugs at the collar of the light cotton robe. 'I hate the summer here. Well, what are you waiting for? Sit down!'

I wait until the maid has poured the tea before I say, 'I thought you were displeased with me.'

'I've been busy. I'm not always at leisure to entertain, you see.'

'Why have you sent for me?'

'I need your help.'

I choke on the green liquid. Never have I heard Tanizaki speak in such direct terms. My shock makes Tanizaki laugh.

'Yes, the words sound strange to me too. Such an unmanly way of communicating, don't you think? Yet those are the exact words I heard an American use the other day. What a childlike people they are!'

My stomach churns. He wants me to do something. Does it have to do with Max? Oh, please, don't ask me to hurt my friend.

'Do you still dance?' Tanizaki asks.

Dance tickets, horse races, new linen suits: these are all luxuries of the past. Mama's fist has grown so tight I can barely squeeze out enough for an occasional opium pipe.

'Not much these days,' I say.

'Too bad.' Tanizaki finishes his tea with one swallow. He rises to leave, pausing first to tighten the belt on his yukata.

'How is Anyi?' I burst out.

Tanizaki grins. He claps me on the back of my shoulder, calling out to Kokoro for another pot of tea.

'You're right. I should have thanked you at the start. I am most satisfied,' he says.

The heat in my face now spreads down my neck and through my chest.

'Does she ask about me?'

'Of course not!' Tanizaki booms. 'Why would she when she has a man like me?' He claps himself loudly on his barrelled chest.

'What more do you want from me?' I ask through clenched teeth.

Tanizaki lunges forward, his large hand around my throat. 'Jealousy is an unbecoming emotion in a man,' he mutters. His hand squeezes and the world turns black. I try to push him away but his grip is too tight. Is this how it ends?

Suddenly he releases me. I catch myself on the edge of the wrought iron table. My ears are ringing. It takes a long time before I can take in what he's saying. He's going on about dancing, hostesses and ballrooms.

'What was the name of that little man, the one who ran the dance floor where Anyi worked?' he asks.

'Manager Lin.'

'And he used to keep a little black notebook on him?'

'Yes.'

The blow to my face knocks me to the ground. When I can see straight again, it's Tanizaki's two legs straddling my body. Behind him are two solders, bayonets lowered, waiting for the order to kill.

He says, 'You've become awfully stupid since we last met. Do I really need to spell it all out? Manager Lin has something that could be of value to me. Bring it!'

# Chapter Twenty-Six

# A Little Black Book

*Cho*

The dancers twirl across the ballroom floor, the skirts of their pastel dresses rising and falling with every beat. Manager Lin's head nods in sync as he watches from his customary place beside the bandstand. One set has just started. If I'm lucky, Lin will stay put and I can get in and out before the next round of dancing begins. I open the door that leads backstage.

I don't remember my way through this warren of dressing rooms. The first door I open contains scattered costumes and Anyi's old mirror turned to face the wall. The next door is locked but from inside I hear sobbing. I move on quickly. Whoever she is, she's not my problem.

Now I remember. Lin's office is at the end of the hallway. It's his custom to sit at the open door with his pocket watch in his hand, timing the hostesses as they emerge from their dressing rooms to enter the dance floor.

There's a commotion behind one of the closed dressing room doors. I've just enough time to press myself behind a dusty harp case before a man comes strutting out, his shoulders bristling with military insignia. I suppose Manager Lin's rule against visitors backstage doesn't apply to high-ranking officers: the Japanese admirals and the German advisers to Chiang Kai-shek and even this little Italian puppet of a general whose medals glint on his chest like paste diamonds.

I have to wait until he's gone, him and his whore. How many songs has the band played now? I've forgotten to keep count. I rush to Lin's office. Of course his door is locked but Kokoro has given me a tool that will open it.

Inside, there's a bed tucked into one corner of his room, the cover rumpled and the smell of a woman still sharp in the damp cloth. There's a desk too stuffed with business papers but if Rosa's information is true, that's not where I should look.

I reach under the bed and find the cubbyhole cunningly set into the heavy wooden frame. Inside is the Western style safe Rosa described. She didn't know the combination so I take out the thin stick of dynamite Tanizaki was happy to supply.

Three, four, five strikes of the match: finally the fuse starts to burn. I hear the band crescendo, a sure sign that the set is almost over. What did Tanizaki say, a two minute fuse?

'Knock a hole in the safe. The dial to the combination lock is usually its weakest point. Push the dynamite in as deep as you can get it. And don't forget to keep your distance. This stick packs more power than you'd think.'

*Tanizaki*

Kokoro had strict instructions. Tanizaki said, 'Bring the Chinaman to the bathhouse. Make sure he undresses completely and wash him well before allowing him to sink his body into one of the baths. Then remove whatever he's brought and bring it to my room. Lock it in my safe.'

'What shall I do with his clothes?'

'Burn them. The Chinaman won't need them. He'll be staying in the Legation from now on.'

But when the Chinaman arrived, he refused to hand over his prize. Tanizaki was already deep inside one of the cedar baths, his mind wiped clean of his daily troubles, when he heard the Chinaman's voice.

'The package is for Tanizaki,' Cho was repeating excitedly. 'I want to give it to him myself.'

From the commotion outside, it sounded as if Kokoro was manhandling Cho yet that too Tanizaki had foreseen. She was not to kill or injure him severely. But a few cuts and bruises could do no harm. Tanizaki smiled.

Then the door flew open and there stood Cho, grinning like a lunatic, his shoes muddying the otherwise pristine floor. Kokoro soon followed, her hair in disarray, one fist raised to slam into Cho's neck.

Tanizaki rose like a sea god out of the water to tower over them both.

'How dare you come in here like that?'

Cho's face fell. Behind him lay a trail of dirt that began at the wide open door to the bathhouse and continued through the small tiled room lined with wooden buckets and long-handled brushes. A civilised person would have stopped there, disrobed and scrubbed himself clean before entering the inner sanctum.

'Clean him up,' he ordered Kokoro.

She grappled Cho from behind and dragged him backwards into the wash area, slamming the inner door shut with her foot. When Cho returned, he was naked, long red welts displaying Kokoro's fury. She held a package bound in cloth. Bowing deeply, she offered it to Tanizaki with both hands.

Tanizaki emerged from the water and took a towel from the bench to dry his hands carefully before taking the parcel.

'You've read it?' he asked Cho.

'I tried but it's written in some sort of code.'

Tanizaki schooled himself to keep his face impassive. He unwrapped the cloth to find a slim black notebook inside, not much larger than the fan Tanizaki now used to cool his face. Casually, he placed the book on the bench and returned to the steaming bath.

'You get in too,' he said to Cho, gesturing at the opposite corner of the bath.

Cho scrambled in, carefully stepping around Tanizaki's legs.

233

They lay there in silence. It was torment for Tanizaki to ignore the notebook but he waited patiently, concentrating on the steam curling across the water, until Cho finally grew so drowsy from the heat that he had to be helped out of the bath and into bed.

Then Tanizaki quickly dressed and, with his treasure in his hands, barricaded himself inside his room. It was better not to involve the decoders who worked in the basement of the Legation until he knew exactly what he had. But there was no need. The code was child's work. Tanizaki wrote out the contents himself.

What a disappointment. The world of a dance floor manager was a petty one: gambling debts, squabbles among the dance hostesses, records of injections for venereal disease. He regretted having given Cho all those silver dollars though he had learned much from the look on his face. The father was ruined and with him many other merchants in Shanghai. Economic collapse would lead to political chaos. The conditions would soon be ripe for any initiative the emperor decided to launch. Would he choose wisely?

Tanizaki lit a small fire in his office. He threw incense on the wood to cover the smell of burning paper. Angry at the time and energy wasted, he gave the notebook a hard shake and another smaller notebook fell out. The writing inside was microscopic, more fitting for an ivory carving than a bundle of folded rice paper. Tanizaki took a magnifying glass from his writing desk. Here was a far more sophisticated code.

He worked through the night to finish the task, even absenting himself from a reception in honour of the Japanese ambassador, newly arrived from Peking. He had hoped for a silver bullet, some secret so deadly it would solve all of Tanizaki's woes. Instead, the notebook contained a litany of names, hundreds of them, with dates and times. What did it mean?

Tanizaki now sat in the entry hall downstairs waiting for the ambassador to receive him. The door to the reception room opened and the Envoy emerged, smiling smugly. Tanizaki bowed stiffly, his nerves alert for danger. Once inside the room, Tanizaki barely had time to arrange his kimono around his kneeling body before the ambassador spoke.

'How long have you been here, Tanizaki? Close to two years and still your mission remains unfulfilled? How do you account for this failure?'

Tanizaki remained calm, his face bland and his manners impeccable, but the word *failure* hung heavily in the air.

'You have seen all my reports, Ambassador. I too am disappointed by the fecklessness of the Chinese. They agree to the logic of a union between Japan and China but none of these politicians will commit to any action, not even to speak in public.'

The ambassador grunted. It had been their joint mission to cultivate contacts among the Chinese ruling classes, to co-opt persons of influence into opening the door to Japanese rule. Of course Tanizaki would take the blame for their collective failure. The only question was what punishment the ambassador would deem fit for such a defeat.

Tanizaki waited on his hands and knees, allowing himself only to shift his weight slightly to his feet. As he did so, he could feel the slight pull of fabric around the knife still strapped to his shin. It was a terrible risk, an executable offence. How would his men react to his failure and his inevitable punishment? They were outside now in the harsh sun, diligently practising their bayonet work. He could imagine the sun on his own skin, the initial resistance of the burlap sack before the needle-sharp blade penetrated its skin.

'I hear that you have engaged the services of a whore, a Chinese bitch who bleeds but does not die.'

Tanizaki almost lost his balance and cursed under his breath that he had given away his weakness. He knew there were spies inside the Legation. Who had betrayed him? The Envoy hated him. A servant might be willing to sell information for filthy lucre. Even Kokoro was capable of it. He forced himself to push away the rage and concentrate on the danger immediately before him.

'It is true,' Tanizaki said. His voice was flat and it pleased him that he could so quickly regain control.

'Your wife knows?'

Tanizaki looked up in surprise.

'I'm not referring to the insignificant person but your predilections,' the ambassador murmured.

How dare the ambassador inquire into Tanizaki's personal affairs? Tanizaki wasn't ashamed of his sexual preferences and neither was his wife. She honoured him for the love and respect Tanizaki bore for his father and the rest she accepted, as a good wife should.

His father had taught Tanizaki to hunt. That first time, they went to the forest outside Kyoto and lay in the wet grass until a pheasant stalked into view. Tanizaki remembered it all: the heaviness of his father's arm as he guided Tanizaki's young hand to the trigger; the explosion of blood and feathers when metal met flesh; the warm wet release he felt inside, the smell of blood and ejaculation forever fused in his mind. Yes, his wife knew it all and when his need grew too great, she would send him off to the port cities of Osaka or Kobe or Uno to find women who could satisfy him.

It troubled him greatly to speak of his wife to the ambassador. Tanizaki shifted once more on his knees, this time to obtain easier access to the knife. The ambassador leaned forward, placing his own hands within one mat length from Tanizaki.

'It is no concern of mine,' he said. 'I mean no offence. You and I have known each other for many years. As a friend, I offer a word of advice. You are a man of obsessions. It is your greatest strength and your only weakness. Do not let this woman become a trap.'

Tanizaki saw the gaping jaws of a bear trap and its hungry metal teeth. He heard the bone-snapping clang as he finally understood. Lin was identifying the dance hostesses and their guests, the men who came to the Metropole to speak quietly under the flash and bang of the band, the Americans and the Brits and the Nationalists and, yes, the Japanese too, whispering secrets to each other while Manager Lin recorded it all.

Anyi and her brother, her brother and his American friend, the American and the head of the Shanghai Municipal Council: the myriad revelations were so clear that Tanizaki had to blink. It would be his way out of this hell. He could go home at last.

But he knew better than to voice his thoughts. First he must verify his facts, then work out his plan: rehearse it, test it and only then reveal it to the ambassador.

'You are kind to share your wisdom with me,' Tanizaki murmured. The ambassador droned on, while Tanizaki was busy sifting information, laying plans, smiling to himself.

Now, he and Anyi met only at her apartment. He needed complete privacy, more space to move around without damaging thin walls or paper screens, no witnesses.

That first time, the attractive neatness of her place surprised him. There was a large blood-coloured vase in the entry hall filled with dry rushes and a climbing jasmine plant that covered the large picture window, giving the room a cool green air.

When Anyi appeared, her face was puffy and there were deep lines in her cheeks, as if she had just woken up.

Tanizaki said, 'Send the servant away.'

'I can't cook,' Anyi said. 'There will be no snacks for us when we are done.'

'I didn't come to eat.'

He had come to test himself. Those other women, the ones who had died, had been weak, undernourished and sickly. Anyi was strong and her desire white-hot. He could sense the violence she held inside, a tight hard ball of self-hatred that was the very core of her being. He wanted her to unleash that violence, to fight back, to match him blow for blow. His dreams were filled with images of her, wild and furious.

All his life, Tanizaki had been in control. Now he wanted to dance along the razor's edge. He wanted to peer into the abyss of death and smell its reeking breath. And he knew he could do that with Anyi. She was a woman of passion, cunning and unpredictability. She should have been a warrior or a leader of men but instead here she was, lying on the floor, her heart throbbing as his fingers closed around her throat.

# Chapter Twenty-Seven

# Two Worms

*Kang*

He thought he was dreaming when she opened the door. She wore a loose sheath like the ones they both had as children. 'You look like a kid again,' Kang said.

'It's hot,' Anyi replied.

She went into the sitting room and he followed. He could see now how tightly the silk bunched around her hips.

'Have you gained weight?' he asked.

She sunk heavily into an armchair. The room was sweltering, despite all the curtains and windows being shut tight against the summer heat. An assortment of newspapers and magazines lay scattered across the low salon table and the floor below. Kang bent down to straighten the pile.

'Stop fussing,' she said. 'If you want to do housework, go to your own home.'

She fell back into her chair, her face red and shiny.

'Are you still sharing a house with that barbarian?' she asked.

'Don't call him that! Soon you'll be living in his country. You won't be so patronising then.'

He got down on his hands and knees and groped under the radiator. He pulled out a book, two magazines, one slipper and a cigarette lighter. He tossed them onto the sofa, then sat down, causing them to slide back to the floor. He gave up then, moving to unbutton his shirt, conscious of the sweat spreading under his armpits.

'That amah of yours is terrible,' he continued. 'Why don't you get her to clean this place up?'

Anyi had shifted in her chair so that now her head lay on one armrest while her legs dangled over the other.

'Which foot do you think is uglier?' she asked.

'Where is Nian?'

'The big toe on my right foot is crooked but the one on my left is as fat as a ginger root.'

'Did she leave? She didn't say anything to me.'

'Because I told her not to,' Anyi snapped. 'She went to visit her family this weekend, all right? Now stop worrying.'

He bit his tongue but his eyes remained fixed on Anyi. A fat fly circled overhead. It buzzed angrily through the apartment, unable to find a way out. Kang rolled up a newspaper but the fly was too smart. It stayed just out of his reach, up by the ceiling where the cobwebs had collected.

Then it buzzed out of sight and for a blessed moment, the room was silent. But when it returned, it was louder than ever. Green and glistening, it landed on Anyi's foot. She shrieked. Kang swung. Unharmed, the fly flew away but the lamp beside Anyi's chair tottered and leaned into the plant that had taken over the windowsill. The jasmine pot crashed to the floor, spilling earth across the carpet. The lamp landed on top, the light bulbs exploding. Kang and Anyi looked at each other and burst out laughing.

She jumped out of her chair to fetch the broom and dustpan from the kitchen. He hauled a trash bin inside. Brother and sister chattered.

He said, 'When I was in college, we would bring our records to the cafeteria. Someone would fetch a phonograph from the dormitory while the rest of us pushed the tables and chairs against the walls. We danced all night long. It wasn't the Paramount Ballroom but we had fun.'

She was on her knees, fishing out the shards of the broken flowerpot. She smiled at him. 'I can see you sailing around the room. Do you think this plant can be saved?'

He swept around the edges of the carpet, whistling, careful not to step on any of the broken glass.

'I don't recognise that song,' she said. 'What is it?'

'I took a trip once into the mountains to see the autumn leaves change colour. There were seven of us piled into an old sedan. We sang songs the whole way. Helen was the best. She knew them all by heart. That's what I was whistling, one of her songs.'

He stood the lamp upright. The lampshade was dented though still functional. Carefully, he turned the shade so that the dent faced the wall. He replaced the light bulbs. He took his time and when he was done, he stood up straight and looked at her.

'We've set the date for our marriage, Helen and I. All the arrangements have been made. You and I will leave Shanghai on the first of September.'

Anyi said nothing. She seemed intent on crushing the jasmine plant into a tiny ball. Her dress was covered in soil and one of her hands was bleeding. Blood welled out of the wound.

'Anyi, did you hear me?'

'How can you dishonour Baba like this?'

'He never loved me. You were the one he loved. You were the son he never had and I was the son he didn't want. I don't give a damn about Baba. Let him rot in hell!'

She pushed herself to standing then. A bloody handprint marked the carpet. She headed into the hallway.

'Where are you going?' he yelled.

'I need to wash.'

'Anyi!'

Her back shuddered, as if he had thrust a knife and wedged it between her narrow shoulder blades. She turned to face him.

'You gave me your word. We would stay in Shanghai for one year. It's not time yet.'

'You have no job any more, no reason to stay. And I have my whole life waiting for me in America. Why do you make me suffer like this?'

'What about the money?'

'Why won't you answer my question?'

She turned away from him and walked down the dark hallway. He stormed after her but she had already locked herself in the bathroom.

'Get ready to leave, Anyi!' he shouted through the door.

The bath water was running and it was hard to hear, so he couldn't be sure Anyi was crying in there.


*Nian*

The man claimed to be a physician. She didn't believe him, but what choice did she have at this point? Nian gave him the knotted handkerchief that held all the coins she had been able to pilfer. She didn't think of it as stealing, rather as her well-earned wages.

The man took his time counting each one. When he was satisfied that the price had been paid in full, he pushed the potion toward Nian. She grabbed the bottle and shook it. Muddy sediment clung to the glass bottom.

'Should I eat anything beforehand?' she asked.

The man shook his head.

'Tea, water?'

The vendor shrugged.

'Don't you have any advice at all?'

The man looked into her face. His eyes grazed the front of her body, stopping for a long moment on her belly. The skin around her navel felt strangely warm, as if the man's eyes were burning a hole in her.

'Drink the bottle empty before you go to bed at night. In the morning, it'll be over. You'll want a bucket of water close by,' he said.

The cramps began around midnight, when the Drum Tower

242

sounded the last warning that the city gates would close for the night. Nian was confused. Was she at home with her mother and father on the family boat? Or with the Lady whose child grew every day while her own seemed to shrivel.

It was the blood in Nian's urine that had made up her mind. The child had no chance of surviving. Without a father, what child could? Better then to rid herself of this burden, this new life sucking all the energy from her body, weakening her with every hour. Better to come to this place deep inside the walled city where other women sought release.

The first time she vomited, she was afraid that the potion she had swallowed with such effort now lay in a dark pool at her feet. The heavy tar smell was overwhelming. She'd have to buy another bottle but how could she steal enough money from the Lady? How much longer would the Lady live?

Nian couldn't worry about that now. She was so tired. She put her head back down, as far away as possible from the tar pool. Maybe if she slept, she'd feel better.

When she woke, her face was smeared in black vomit and she was on all fours, dry retching. There was an intense pain in her back that spread to her loins. Then the cramps began in earnest.

In the morning, it was all over, just like the man had said. Nian washed herself: the vomit from her face, the dregs from between her thighs, all that was left of that sweet boy she once knew. What was his name? It didn't matter any more. When she was as clean as she could manage, she threw the bucket of water over the floor to wash the rest away.

*Anyi*
Tanizaki leaves no marks, not a bruise or a scratch, nothing to show for all the violence he metes out but for an ache deep inside. He won't empty himself inside me. Instead he sprays my face with his seed, a dog marking his territory.

I know he spoke to Auntie Wen. Jin told me the blind woman

left Shanghai in a hurry, not even stopping to collect the money I owe her.

'Was that your doing?' I ask Tanizaki.

He's begun to ignore me, to come to my apartment and treat it like his home, reading the newspapers Kang leaves behind even though he says they're trash. 'It's all lies,' he mutters.

'Where did you send her?' I try again.

His eyes flash. 'What do you care? It's done. Now, what about Jin?'

He told me last week to get rid of her but I can't do it. 'What harm does she do?' I plead.

'I don't like witnesses.'

'Nian's here every night. I'd rather get rid of the amah and let Jin stay.'

Tanizaki smiles. 'Your amah doesn't love you. She wouldn't lift a finger to save you if I decided to kill you one night.'

He teases me like that, taunts me with the final release he could so easily grant. I beg him to dispatch me, in any way he likes, but he refuses. 'You please me very much, Song Anyi. I'm not ready to let you go yet.'

'Soon?'

He doesn't reply.


Tonight, I lie awake waiting for Jin to come to me. I hear the front door creak open then her syncopated tread, foot — cane — foot. The lights are out but Jin can see in the dark.

She massages me now. I sit on a low rattan stool and she stands behind me, rubbing the oil into my skin.

I obey Tanizaki. I say to Jin, 'Don't come here any more.'

'Why?'

She comes around to kneel at my feet, her shiny palms splayed open, as in prayer. 'Are you angry with me? Have I displeased you in some way?'

'I'm not angry,' I assure her. 'You've given me enough of your time and I'm ready to sleep alone again.'

244

She doesn't believe me. She knows so much, this cook of whores. She hears stories about me at the Del Monte House but her eyes see more. They read the truth written on my skin.

'I'll tell your Aunt and Uncle what you're doing.'

I laugh, 'They don't care what happens to me. In fact, I think they'd prefer me dead.'

'I'll tell your brother,' Jin says, her voice rising.

'No!' I scream. I turn on her, rising from the stool to shake her by the shoulders. She cowers in front of me, her face between her knees.

'Let my brother go to his grave knowing nothing of my life. Let him at least have that peace. There's nothing he can do, nothing he can say to change my fate.'

I get down on my hands and knees. I lie prostrate on the floor in front of her. I hold out my hands, palm up, to beseech her, 'If you love me, you'll say nothing to Kang. Please. I cannot bear the shame.'

It takes me all night to convince her. Then she sleeps fitfully in my arms.

When she wakes, she asks, 'Where will I go? Master Feng has sold my place in the kitchen yard to another servant.'

I hadn't thought about that, the perfidy of a pimp. Then I see it: the perfect solution. I say, 'Go and live with the American. He'll be happy to have you. My brother will enjoy your company too.'

# Chapter Twenty-Eight

## Sea of Glass

*Kang*

His days had never been so full, not since he left America: train times, shipping lines, exchange rates. A flurry of telegrams crossed the Pacific Ocean: *Helen, I'm coming, wait for me.* His plans were laid with an engineer's precision and he told no one what he was doing.

'You look happy,' Jin said. 'Change must be in the air.'

These days they often sat together in the sitting room, Max and Jin on the sofa, holding hands beneath an abandoned newspaper, while Kang pretended to read in his armchair.

'Since you're in such a good mood,' Jin continued, 'now's a good time to visit your sister. I think she needs cheering up.'

Kang drew a picture for Anyi. It was a bridge with an impossible span with the two of them crossing it on foot. Their boxes and sea trunks floated behind, propelled forward by an unseen force. One end of the bridge was embedded in China, its steps muddy and uneven and high. The other end could not be seen, so dazzling was the sun reflected a thousand times in the windows of the skyscrapers on that far side. He drew them disappearing into the light so that only their backs were visible, Kang with his fedora set at a jaunty angle and Anyi with two long braids down her back.

He rolled out the drawing on Anyi's low table.

'Why did you draw me with long braids?' she asked.

He was still smiling at his bridge, warm from the glow of so many suns, and her question glanced off him. Finally he drew his eyes away to smile at her.

'You always wear your hair that way,' he murmured.

'Look at me, Kang.'

Her voice was strained. Did he hear tears behind the words? 'What do you see?'

'I see you, of course. Is this some kind of riddle?'

She stood, turned her back to him and said, 'Tell me what you see, Kang.'

He tried to humour her. Anyi's temper was so frayed these days, the slightest thing could set her off, like that poor flower girl at the end of the street who had tried to sell her a handful of jasmine blossoms.

'I have the flowers you like so much, you and the man who always buys them for you. I haven't seen him in a while. Where is he?'

Anyi had tried to gouge out the girl's eyes with her fingernails.

Kang took a good look at Anyi before saying, 'I see that you're wearing blue again. It's a very becoming colour, my favourite. Is it new? Is that what you're getting at?'

When Anyi turned around again, her face was stark.

'What is it?' he asked.

She sank slowly into her chair. She was crying and when she bent her head, the tears fell on her bare knees.

'I cut my hair a year ago,' she whispered.

Kang's eyes moved to the blunt line of her bob. He saw how heavily her hair swung against her jaw. He saw the blue veins that protruded down the length of her slender throat and he thought he saw a darker spot under the collar of her dress. Her skin was so pale that Kang could see the muscles moving, especially the one that jumped in her jaw.

'You're right!' he said cheerfully. 'How stupid of me. I've drawn you as if you were still a young girl in Soochow. I can change it. The likeness wasn't very good to begin with.'

Already, he was rooting around in his satchel, looking for the right pen and some ink. Then he heard the bedroom door close and the lock click shut. He stood outside the locked door, his head against the wood.

'Are you tired?' he called softly.

'You don't see me any more.'

'Of course not, the door's closed.'

'Go away, Kang. Let me sleep.'

He packed his things: the brushes and the ink stones, the maps and the tickets. The drawing of his bridge he rolled up tightly and took with him too. He crept quietly back to Anyi's door and pressed his ear against its wooden fastness.

'I'm leaving now,' he said. 'Anyi, I've bought the tickets. I'll hold them for safe keeping but mark the date in your calendar. The first of September is when we board ship to leave China forever.'


*Anyi*

'Nian!' I scream.

She leaves the apartment now whenever she likes. She doesn't say where she's going or when she'll be back. She abandons me in this place with only my thoughts for company, all those voices in my head.

Where is the wine? Has Nian hidden it all? I search the apartment, under the sofa and inside the potted plants. The bottles I find are all empty, lined up in the kitchen, rows of brown and green glass glinting in the sun. A sea of glass.

I search the cupboards for Auntie Wen's jars. They're gone too. If I want to drink, I'll have to go out.

I fetch my purse but at the door, Kang's voice pulls me back, insistent, disapproving, dictating what I must and mustn't do.

'A lady doesn't drive a car.'

'A lady doesn't go out without stockings.'

'A lady never drinks alone. She drinks only to please her host.'

Kang loves to pontificate. Wouldn't he have made a wonderful minister, all puffed up with importance, nearer to God than me?

Now it's Beauregard who mutters in my ear, 'You shouldn't make fun of the Lord,' he chides. 'He might forgive you but he sure won't forget. And when the time comes to ask for His help, well, you might be sorry.'

So the Christian god holds grudges. Our gods are more sensible – too busy with their own concerns to care about ours.

Tanizaki holds grudges. A snub at the Shanghai Race Track is like a blade in his back. His skin grows thinner every day. Just last week, a man talked to me at the Carlton Café. He's dead now. Tanizaki went after him with a bamboo cane and by the time Beauregard pulled the man away, the skin from his face lay in strips on the floor. We were all there that night: me and Eve Arnold and the young Brits who used to sit at my table at the Metropole. They're careful to lower their eyes when I pass by. No one dares look at me when Tanizaki is around.

Are you here too, Tanizaki? I know how much you hate the smell of alcohol on my breath. For weeks now, I've gone without wine but right now I have other needs to take care of.

I saw Cho in the street today. He and Tanizaki were drinking coffee in a Viennese pastry shop. I went inside but he didn't talk to me. He had eyes only for Tanizaki. Cho, what's happened to you, my love?

Do you know about the worm that is growing in me? It's as strong as you are. No amount of alcohol can kill it. Believe me, I've tried. But the worm and I have merged and now, to kill the one, I must kill us both.

Am I ready to die? I stand before my wardrobe, surveying the life I've lived. There are hats for the winter, hats for Racing Days, hats to keep the sun out, hats to lure. Is this all I have achieved?

Mama fingers the stiff ruffles of a taffeta dress, her bony digits bleached white against the vibrant cloth. Baba peers into the darkness of the wardrobe.

What do you want this time, Baba?

He points. I follow the wavering tip of bone into the back of the wardrobe where I find the wine bottles. I drink until the wine and my parents and the walls of this house fade away.

I'm in a woodland glade. They're coming for me. I can hear them creeping through the brittle leaves. A hand reaches out, heavy on my shoulder. I open my mouth to scream but another hand reaches round to muffle the noise.

'It's me,' Jin says.

She holds me tight, her arms crossed over my breasts, my back warm against her belly. I could sit like this forever but she lifts me in her arms and lays me on my bed. Somehow my clothes have become torn and stained so she removes them from my sweating body. She washes me with a hand cloth, firm circular movements like the doctor said or was that Auntie Wen?

Jin's face softens as she touches my belly. Could it be that she longs for a child? No barbarian would be foolish enough to leave his seed inside a Chinese girl. Who, then, will transform my friend into a mother?

I sit up and push Jin and her cloth away. 'Jin,' I shout. 'Do you love me?'

'You know that I do.'

'Then you must help me, I need it now, more than ever.'

'Tell me.'

'I want you to take care of my brother for as long as he needs you.'

'What's wrong with Kang? He doesn't need me.'

'He will. Things are going to change, Jin. I don't know exactly when or how but Kang could get hurt or lost. He doesn't understand the world like you and I do. Will you help him, Jin?'

'Of course I will. Max will too.'

'I can't rely on Max,' I tell her firmly. 'He's a barbarian. He'll leave China some day as all barbarians do. And then what will become of you?'

'What are you saying?' Jin cries. 'Have you heard something? Tell me what it is! Is Max going to America and leaving me behind?'

Jin sinks to her haunches. She balls her fist and strikes herself, on the thighs, the chest, her face. She's so strong she'll hurt herself.

'I've heard nothing, Jin!'

She stops pounding for a moment to look me in the eye.

'I swear, it's the truth. But that day will come. You know it too. Learn to love Kang and, in time, he'll love you too.'

## Tanizaki

His ink brush flew across the paper, his strokes careless. It was only a draft, he told himself, his thoughts tumbling over one another so quickly that he could hardly grasp them long enough to commit anything to paper.

Song Kang was a member of the Storm Society, a leftist organisation of painters and sculptors and, most dangerous of all, writers. This group headed the list of cells to be watched by the Chinese secret police. Some of its members had already been arrested, tortured and executed.

His friend, the American, was intimately acquainted with the head of the Shanghai Municipal Council. Tanizaki had seen evidence of their friendship with his own eyes. Lazerich knew all the members of the diplomatic corps. He was even rumoured to have acted on their behalf to quash disputes that might otherwise have erupted into full-blown diplomatic incidents.

Song Kang and Max Lazerich had access to the men Tanizaki wanted for the Japanese cause. Song and Lazerich were the key to his plan.

He wrote: *I have over the past few weeks turned my focus*

*to the business class. Money and politics, the underworld and the government: it is all the same thing here in Shanghai. These men of business may be more receptive to a vision of long-term prosperity than any government official.*

But Tanizaki needed to be cautious. Too often he had promised results only to offer excuses. Time was running out. The ambassador had already talked of a reassignment.

'It won't be a place as civilised as Shanghai,' he had warned. 'We need good men in Manchukuo and Formosa and Burma too. You'll have to go back to using the military brothels, hey Tanizaki?'

If Tanizaki had to be exiled from Japan, then let it be here. The occupation would start soon. Shanghai would need a collaborationist government, preferably one led by the Chinese themselves. Should Tanizaki apply to be their puppet master? Relinquish any chance of honour on the battlefield for the sake of a mere whore?

He took up his brush once more and wrote: *The Song family is our best option.*

He tore up that sheet and tossed it on the growing pile of discarded paper. He would burn it all later. First he must get his thoughts straight.

'Keep Anyi out of the report,' he muttered to himself. 'Focus on the men.'

Finally, his brush strokes were steady and firm. He wrote: *I request permission to convert the subjects Song Kang and Max Lazerich to our cause. For reasons of security, I cannot reveal my methods until we next meet in person. I can confirm, however, that the leverage needed to put pressure on both subjects is already in my possession.*

# Chapter Twenty-Nine

# The Summons

*Cho*

It was supposed to be a visit, Tanizaki had promised. 'Just a few days to get to know each other a little better. Wouldn't you like that? We'll share our meals and go out at night.'

'And during the day?'

'You can lie here on the veranda and smoke all the opium you want!'

That was four days ago and I don't like it here any more. I'm not supposed to leave the compound alone: no horse races or cockfights or visiting the casinos. And Tanizaki never has time for me.

'Go to sword practice if you're bored,' he shouts. 'Don't come to my office uninvited!'

Grudgingly, his men widen their circle enough to let me squeeze in. With all the thrusts and parries not one of them will cross swords with me, not until Kokoro orders them to fight.

She follows me everywhere: on to the parade grounds bristling with heavily armoured men and even into the bathhouse where she sits fully clothed at the side of my bath, sweat streaming down her face.

Today when the opium tray arrives, I push it away. The opium is tasteless and it brings troubled dreams: Anyi hurt, trapped, waiting for me to come.

The spirit lamp flickers out. I turn my gaze to the yard. Something's happened. Men rush in and out of the white house without a glance in my direction at my table on the veranda. Even Kokoro runs past me in her white tabi socks and high geta shoes, the wooden shoes clack-clacking up the stairs. Then the yard is silent. Now is my chance.

The gate by the bathhouse is unguarded. A heavy rock from the garden should do the trick but someone's saved me the trouble. I slip out and quietly push the gate shut, the latch falling neatly into place.

I'm free! The air in the street smells fresher and my muscles feel looser. I've got money in my pocket and no one to please but myself.

Then the noises of the street crowd in on me: the cars and the trams and the plangent cries of the hot water vendor. I turn back to look at the stout wooden fence, so safe and now locked tight. How can I get back in without raising the alarm? Where do I go? What do I do now?

*Blossom*
Soldiers came to the house today looking for the Young Master.

'What do you want?' Mistress Song shouted. 'My son's with Tanizaki!'

They searched the house anyway and when the soldiers found nothing, they got angry. But this time they didn't shoot anybody or anything.

When they left, Mistress Song sent Driver Zhang to comb the streets and when he returned empty-handed, she drove the Old Master out into the night to search. They grew old, the master and mistress, in the span of a few days. Then Mistress Song turned practical.

'You're fired,' she said to Blossom. 'My son found you amusing but with him gone, you're a useless mouth.'

The mistress sent Blossom to collect her things. She was to

leave immediately: no lunch, no customary gift of money, no thanks at all. Stunned, she walked through the kitchen yard to her corrugated tin shed. She strung her bedroll across her back and returned to the house, now with a plan.

The phonograph was playing so Mistress Song must be upstairs. The Old Master would be in his study, hiding from his creditors. A steady thud from the kitchen told her Cook was at work and Driver Zhang was probably asleep under the rickshaw. Blossom decided to risk it. She opened the door to the dining room and stepped inside.

When she left the house, her bundle jingled. She walked aimlessly, crossing the Soochow Creek into the International Settlement, but shied away from the roar of motorcars. She walked on until she found a pawnshop and spilled the contents of her bundle on the counter.

The owner laughed at her. 'What do I want with a pair of candlesticks? They're not even silver!' The pawnbroker chipped the surface with one long yellow fingernail. Bits of paint fell on the counter.

'You'd have to pay me to take a worthless thing like that. But you, little girl, are a different matter. Why don't you come live with me? I'll treat you well, I promise.'

Blossom lifted a candlestick and cracked it against the man's head. Blood spurted out and she panicked. Had she killed the old pervert? Would the police come and cut off her head? She ran out the door, thinking to flee one corpse, only to find another, face down in the gutter.

She screamed. Disgusting as the body was, she saw something familiar in its curve. This was no Eastern devil, even if he did wear a Japanese style robe. When she stooped to take a closer look, the man lifted his face and groaned.

'Young Master!' Blossom cried. She pulled his head on her lap and tried to stroke his matted hair. He protested but his hands were too weak to push her away. She wept then. She kissed his hollow cheeks. She kissed his slack mouth and when he didn't respond, her blood turned cold.

'I just kissed a dead man,' she screamed. 'His spirit has flown into my mouth! He's inside me, eating my intestines.'

A crowd formed round the hysterical girl, some gawping at her, others more interested in the man who lay limply in her arms. Then the pawnbroker came out, a wet rag clutched to his head.

He yelled at Blossom, 'Still here, are you? I'll give you something to bawl about.'

She ran away, her bundle jingling all the way back to the Song family house. Perhaps they would take her in again once they heard her news.

'I found him! I know where the Young Master is!' she cried.

Old Master Song himself came to the door. 'Where?'

When Blossom told him, he slapped her across the face. 'Silence!' he roared. 'Go with Driver Zhang and show him. Don't tell anyone what you saw.'

To Driver Zhang, the old master said, 'Bring my son home, in whatever condition he may be.'

By the time they returned to the pawnbroker, the crowd had grown.

'He's been lying here for hours,' the pawnbroker complained.

'Is he alive?' the driver asked.

'We think so,' the bamboo vendor said.

'Because he doesn't stink,' the tofu maker explained.

'Who is he?' they all wanted to know.

Slowly, Zhang climbed down from the rickshaw. 'Are you sure this is him?' he asked the maid. 'Is he alive?'

She felt brave now. She placed her warm cheek against his mouth. The crowd hushed. She nodded to the driver who fetched the white sheet to wrap him, not like a corpse whose dying stare had to be hidden, but as an invalid who needed comfort and warmth. The driver lifted the Young Master into the back of the rickshaw and pedalled off.

Now that he knew the Young Master was alive, Driver Zhang relaxed. 'Where will you go?' he asked the maid.

'I don't know. What kind of work can a girl like me do?'

'Be a maid in another household?'

'Never!'

'What about that dance manager who said you could work for him?'

'Manager Lin?' Blossom hadn't given him a thought since the Young Mistress had left. She remembered the dresses and the heavy curtains and the brilliant chandeliers. She liked the idea of gliding across a shiny dance floor in the arms of a handsome man.

'I don't know how to dance,' she said.

A quiet moaning interrupted them. The driver turned round.

'I've seen him look better,' he remarked.

'He used to be handsome. He made me so happy.'

'That's what you could do,' the driver said.

'What?'

'Make men happy. You'd be good at that.'

Blossom smiled. Of course. If Auntie Wen were still in town, she would have said the same. 'Take me to the Bridge of the Eight Immortals,' Blossom said.

When Blossom had first arrived in Shanghai, Auntie Wen brought her here to watch the street performers. It was like going to the circus. There were also plenty of pleasure houses in this part of town.

'Why don't you come with me?' she asked the driver. 'Since you'll be fired too, sooner rather than later.'

The driver shrugged.

She jumped from the rickshaw before he had a chance to stop. She didn't wave goodbye nor did she hear his words.

'No need to rush.'

*Tanizaki*

The apartment was dark when he arrived.

'Where's Cho?' Anyi asked when she opened the door.

'I don't know. Do you?'

'I already told your men I don't. How could you let him slip away?'

He hit her then. He was beside himself with despair and rage at the loss of his valuable pawn, the incompetence of his men, and now the ridicule in Anyi's voice. He hit her again and again and when he stopped to catch his breath, he saw the amah peering at him from the kitchen. She seemed to be smiling.

His skin tingled, like a wave moving from the base of his spine towards his brain. By the time it reached his fingertips, he was ready to kill.

Anyi rolled out of reach and jumped lightly to her feet. She stood there with her fists on her hips, jeering at him. 'You're getting old. And soft.'

He leaped. His body hit hers midriff. When they hit the ground together, he landed on top, knocking the air out of her lungs. For a moment, she lay there stunned, her limbs splayed. He wanted her to fight back. He struck her with his open hand, breaking her skin, then with his fist until she was unconscious.

When she woke, he was sitting in the armchair, smoking a cigarette. 'I have some questions for you,' he said.

Slowly she pushed herself to standing and stumbled to the sofa. 'Why should I answer? Will it help Cho?'

'Maybe.'

'What do you want to know?'

He asked about Soochow, how she had been raised, whether her brother had gone to school.

'Why do you want to know about Kang?' she asked.

'I think he could help me.'

'How?'

Tanizaki did not answer. She watched him, tapping one fingernail against her front teeth.

'If Kang were useful to you, what would you do with him?'

'Keep him by my side.'

She told him then that her father had sent Kang to boarding school. About the friends he had made there. 'Some of them became important men in the Kuomintang. Others joined the communists,' she said.

'Do you have names?'

She wrote them down, as many as she could remember. Nian brought in a tray of cold tea and salted nuts, setting it on the table in front of Tanizaki. She poured his tea while Anyi blew gently on the paper to dry the ink.

'So you'll take care of Kang? Better than you have of Cho?'

'Oh yes,' Tanizaki said. 'I guarantee it.'


*Cho*

Mama cries when the soldiers come for me. She keeps asking, 'Why must you go so soon?'

I can't hide the truth from myself any more.

Tanizaki says, 'I must punish you for running away.'

I ask, 'What kind of a friend are you?'

He unleashes Kokoro. She uses no weapon, just her bare hands, punches to the belly, over and over, until whatever was once inside me liquefies and drains. Lying in a pool of my own excrement, I tell her everything. Then she beats me again and I remember no more.

But here's Tanizaki, as jolly as ever, seated across from me in his cosy front room. My hair has been washed and my clothes changed. A neat tie is knotted through the starched collar of my shirt but my feet are bare.

He says, 'You don't look well, my friend. Have something to eat.'

'Give me the sweet smoke. Please.'

259

I inhale deeply, holding the opium for as long as I can. It trickles out of my nose like incense from a burner.

Tanizaki laughs. 'Take as much as you like. There's plenty here.'

He opens a small silver box. It's filled with the shiny sticky balls that populate my dreams. My hand reaches out to caress the box, to finger each and every one of those precious orbs. Tanizaki snaps it shut.

'I saw your cousin last night,' he says.

My stomach turns.

'She's very amusing. I wish I could keep her forever but then I would be breaking my promise. I said I would return her to you, didn't I?'

'When?' I ask.

'Soon,' he says. 'First I need you to perform a small service for me.'

He calls for a pen and paper. He tells me what to write. I try but my hand shakes so much that the ink splatters.

'Wait. Let the opium do its work,' I plead.

His face flushes, but he waits all the same.

I write: *Please meet me this Saturday at noon at the White Crane. I have a favour of great importance to ask.*

Kokoro arrives and I try not to cringe. She stands silently in the corner, waiting for her instructions.

'Tell her where to go,' Tanizaki says.

I write the address. 'Whose name should I put on the envelope? They live in the same house, you know.'

'Invite them both.'

Kokoro takes the envelope and secretes it in the long sleeve of her kimono. She leaves. Tanizaki laughs.

'Don't worry. I just want to speak to them. You are going to introduce us.'

'Why do you need me? You're the powerful Japanese attaché. You could invite Kang and Max here any time you like.'

'I want us to be friends. You must convince them to help me.'

260

'And then I get Anyi?'

'Then you may have Anyi.'

*Kang*

The invitation came as a surprise, written as it was on the stationery of the Japanese Legation and delivered by a soft-spoken woman who waited until she had his reply.

Kang had never been inside a shoyu. There had been first class pleasure houses in Soochow but his father hadn't approved of them and Kang was always too shy to venture in on his own.

Cho was waiting for them in a private room. He rose from his cushion and crossed the tatami mats quickly to shake their hands.

'Thank you for coming! Please come inside.'

Kang lingered in the doorway while Cho ushered Max to a cushion near his own. Cho was limping and when he sat down again, he winced. But nothing dampened his enthusiasm.

'Tanizaki found the place,' Cho said proudly. 'It's the nicest I've ever seen. Even my father would be impressed, don't you think, Kang?'

Kang didn't answer. He fingered the wall hangings. His thumb brushed the spray of azalea that stood in a niche by the window. Its petals were tissue-thin and throbbing with colour.

'It's real,' he murmured.

'Of course it's real,' Cho chided loudly. 'Now, what will you have? Or should I ask, who?'

Kang blushed and turned away, while Max merely laughed, waving away the offer.

'Little Sister,' Cho called out.

A maid rushed in, her feet light on the rush mats. Cho pointed at the spirit lamp and she rushed to prepare the long opium pipe.

'Won't you join me?' he asked.

Max leaned forward, his face now close to Cho's. 'Have you been in a fight, old man? You look awfully stiff today.'

'I'm fine! Come on, Max, enjoy yourself.'

But Max asked quietly, 'What's this all about, Cho?'

He spoke the words mechanically, as if learnt by heart. 'Tanizaki Haruki is my friend. He's Japanese and that might feel uncomfortable. I want you to meet him anyway and hear what he has to say. As a personal favour to me.'

Max was worried. Kang knew it by the way he rubbed his fleshy nose.

'Why the elaborate introduction?' Max asked. 'I know the Japanese like their formalities but this is a bit extreme. I've met the man before, for God's sake.'

'He thought you would say no,' Cho blurted out. 'He thought you would snub him for being Japanese. But I set him straight, and about you too, Cousin. I promised him that you were both broad-minded.'

A thread of panic ran through Cho's voice, one that Kang had never heard before. Now that he was closer, Kang could see the cloud of bruises on his cousin's left cheek.

'What happened to you?' Kang asked.

'Nothing!' Cho shouted.

He gave them a date and a time. He said it was important. All they had to do was listen to what Tanizaki had to say. They could decide for themselves what to do next.

Max and Kang exchanged looks. Both had been suspicious when the invitation had arrived. Now they knew for certain. Something was very wrong. Max lifted one eyebrow and Kang nodded.

'We'll come, if that's what you want,' Max said.

'Will you be there too?' Kang asked.

'If Tanizaki asks me, then I will.'

'Are you in trouble, Cousin?'

'Do you need money?' Max asked.

Cho looked at the pipe. The spirit lamp still burned but the opium was gone. 'Don't worry about me,' he said. 'My luck is turning again.'

They passed the maid on her way in. She seemed surprised to see them leaving.

'Get him some more opium,' Kang ordered. 'Charge it to Tanizaki.'

# Chapter Thirty

## Second Chances

*Tanizaki*

As soon as he arrived at the Legation, he went to the bathhouse. The stench of opium, the sand in his sandals, the oiliness on his tongue: he had to wash it all away. The bath brushes weren't enough. Their handles shattered under the violence of his scrubbing, leaving him with wooden shards to rake his skin. When he finally allowed himself to sink into the steaming water, clean at last, the heat seared the wounds shut.

Finally, he grew calm. He made his way back to his rooms. Once there, he bolted the doors and shoved cabinets against the outer walls to stop intruders entering that way. Only then could he concentrate on the task ahead.

The killing dagger lay before him on a low rosewood table. Beside it was a sheaf of paper, the last letters he would ever write. They weren't all finished. He sat cross-legged before the table and tried to concentrate but the flowered pattern of his robe distracted him.

If only he could have worn his white kimono. He had left it at home, in Kyoto, never dreaming that a day might come when he would need such a robe in Shanghai. He had never contemplated failure. He scowled at the tatami mat. The Legation would have to replace the floor at tremendous cost once he had finished but there was no other way.

His wrist ached from the strain of writing. He needed more

sword practice. He had become as weak as a clerk. But his orders were almost complete, the most important one written as soon as he had returned from his assignation with Song Kang and his American friend.

Tanizaki flushed with rage. It took all his willpower not to grasp the dagger and sink it deep into his belly. He had never understood before the desire to be hurt, to be beaten like Anyi. Now the revelation thundered in his ears. The release would be exquisite. The pain could be no more than just. Tanizaki would relieve the ambassador of a useless servant and wash clean his family's name with his own blood.

He should have listened to Anyi. She had told him how proud her brother was. 'If you can get him alone, to flatter and cajole, he'll do what you want. But if you offend his pride, he'll balk,' she had warned.

Instead, he had allowed Cho to arrange it all: choose the location and even travel there alone ahead of time. 'I'll make sure all the preparations are right,' Cho had promised.

By the time Tanizaki had arrived, Cho had already passed out in a haze of opium fumes, utterly useless. That was Tanizaki's first mistake.

Then he surveyed the place. It was filthy and stank of noxious fumes from the open sewage canal. Tanizaki began to perspire uncontrollably. He dismissed it as a sign of weakness, ordering his men into that foul place.

They hustled the customers off their opium beds and out of the door, all of them, except for Cho. They held the proprietor and his whimpering wife at gunpoint. His men imposed order in that disorderly place and then they silently waited. And so Tanizaki had pushed forward. He would not retreat, regroup or rethink his plan. That was his second error.

In that opium den, he had turned to Kang. 'Help me form a government, here in Shanghai. You will be among like minds, open and modern, the leaders of all Asia.'

265

To the American, Tanizaki had said, 'Your countrymen will listen to you. Tell them to leave us alone. Let Asians solve the problems of Asia.'

To these offers of glory, the two men had laughed.

'He thinks I'm a spy,' the American guffawed. 'Do you suppose the US ambassador would pay attention to a guy like me?'

'Me, a leader of men?' Kang smiled. 'A visionary fit to rule all of China. You should bow to me!'

The American was laughing so hard that he could hardly catch his breath. He leaned heavily into Kang, one hand pressed into his side. When his breath finally quieted, the American put one large hand on Tanizaki's shoulder.

'Who's been telling you these fibs?' he asked. 'Has Cho been winding you up?'

They looked at Cho, sprawled on his low rush bed in the middle of the room, his mouth slack, a pool of saliva forming below.

Tanizaki had no choice then but to smile. He managed a small chuckle, finally breaking the tension in the room. The innkeeper offered a timid smile. Gathering his strength, Tanizaki released a belly laugh, long and hard. Then his men laughed too. The servants laughed. Song Kang and the American were still laughing.

It was his third mistake and one Tanizaki would never live down.

For the last time, he checked his letter to the ambassador. It read: *Song and Lazerich are not suitable for our purpose. I have been duped and our mission possibly compromised. I accept all blame. I will take the appropriate actions to relieve you of any responsibility.*

He picked up the house telephone and dialled. Within seconds, Kokoro knocked quietly at the door. Her eyes widened at the sight of the furniture piled high, but she took his letter without a word. She would encrypt the message herself and telegraph the code to Peking. She would understand its meaning. Should he ask her to join him in committing ritual suicide? No, Tanizaki decided, the woman was a good agent. The ambassador might still have uses for her.

The letter to his wife contained his last instructions, nothing so inconsequential as burial or memorials, but what she should say to their family. *Tell our son and daughter that I died in battle. There is no reason to burden them at their tender age. But tell my father the truth. Spare him no detail. If he orders you to kill yourself and our children, obey him. I will arrange to have my killing dagger returned to Kyoto for that purpose.*

One last order remained. Tanizaki was pleased to note that his hand was now steady. The brush flowed smoothly down the page, the characters clear and bold. *Raze the opium den to the ground. Kill the innkeeper and his wife. Spike their heads on the back fence of the Legation so that when my spirit rises from my body, I can spit in their faces. Do the same for every soldier who accompanied me to the opium den, every one of them who laughed at me.*

At long last, his duties were done. He stripped off his sweat-stained clothing and left it on the floor to be burnt. If he couldn't be clad in the correct white kimono, he might as well die naked.

His senses were acutely alive: the particular hue of the sky, the tap-tap of the typewriters downstairs, the faint scent of the wisteria branch in his alcove. He leaned forward and felt with his fingers the richly carved hilt of the dagger. He stared at it. Nothing could surpass its beauty, unless it were the blade itself, emerging like a needle from the hilt, glinting in the sun.

Tanizaki turned the blade toward his belly. He closed his eyes and tried to purify his mind: to banish all thoughts of the opium addict Cho, to forget Anyi and her thin white skin, to deny the laughter and the rage and the sorrow he felt at leaving this life behind.

The doorknob rattled violently. Kokoro called his name.

'New orders from the ambassador!' she screamed. 'Seppuku is forbidden. Find Song Kang and the American. Take them at any cost. The ambassador wants them alive.'

*Anyi*

The soldiers bring me to the riverside to wait for Tanizaki. One soldier is tall and thin, the other short with eyeglasses. My Japanese is good enough to ask them simple questions but they don't respond. They seem nervous. Why?

My ankles swell in the heat of this summer's day. There's nowhere to sit on this rickety wooden jetty. I could squat like a child, hiking my dress high above the hips. Would that make these toy soldiers smile? I giggle.

The short guard flinches, raising his bayonet high enough to pierce my eye. The other soldier barks and the bayonet lowers. He points at the gunboat rounding the bend of the river. The engines whine loudly as the boat pauses at the pier. The soldiers march me double time over the gangplank and into Tanizaki's cabin.

Tanizaki hasn't bathed in days. The grey stubble makes him look old. He hurls a bottle of cognac at my head, half-full and still heavy, easy to dodge.

'What's wrong with you?' I cry.

Clothing, papers, kerosene lamps are scattered all over the cabin. The bed is a jumble of glass shards and wine stains. Tanizaki tries to topple the closet, but it's bolted to the floor of this ship.

I laugh. 'You've lost control!'

He lunges at me. His hands are as strong as ever. They close around my neck and squeeze my breath. My ears fill with a buzzing noise. My brain cleaves in two.

Then he lets go. I fall to the floor, my throat raw from the effort of breathing. I scramble away but he doesn't pursue me. Instead, he weeps.

I understand now. 'They won't help you.'

He shakes his head from side to side before pounding it against the cabin wall. I run to him, wrap my arms around his head to cushion the blows. Finally he stops and we sink together to the floor.

'Did you tell the ambassador?'

Tanizaki nods.

'Tell me everything.'

As Tanizaki talks, my mind clears and I know what to do. 'You must use Cho once more as your emissary.'

Tanizaki pushes me away. 'Song Cho is a fool,' he spits. 'I won't trust him again.'

'You shouldn't have trusted him in the first place,' I say calmly. 'I warned you.'

'He fed me lies and so did you.'

'You just said, the ambassador wants Kang and the American alive. You cannot disobey.'

'Your brother and the American told me they're not spies!'

'And I tell you they are. Would I lie to you?'

He leans against the wall, his legs crooked, his arms limp by his side.

'Give Kang and his American one more chance. Give them a deadline and, if you want, a reason to cooperate.'

'What kind of reason?'

'The only kind they'll listen to.'

Tanizaki is quick to make up his mind. He bathes and orders food. The houseboy arrives with a heavy tray. Tanizaki finishes the dishes and calls for more. He gives the sake bottle back to the houseboy.

'No more alcohol,' he says. 'Never again, not even if I beg.'

The houseboy bows. I watch him leave, certain that no one on this ship would ever refuse Tanizaki anything.

'Why are you so eager to help?' he asks.

'Teach me some more Japanese.'

'Like what?'

'Something you would say. Give me an order.'

Tanizaki laughs long and hard. 'Take off your dress.'

'That's not an order you would give to a guard.'

'Very well, halt or I'll shoot,' he says in a lazy drawl.

'Who could be afraid of someone who talks like that?'

Now Tanizaki is standing, his feet placed wide apart and his erection visible, though not complete. He takes a deep breath and bellows, 'Halt or I'll shoot!'

I open my mouth and echo his words, in a voice louder and deeper than his own. He gapes at me then laughs uproariously. 'Do it again! That was magnificent. Wait. Let me try something else.'

Tanizaki roars, 'The prisoner is escaping. Shoot her!'

I repeat his words exactly while pounding on the wall behind me. The door flies open and three guards storm in, their bayonets at the ready. Two of them rush to Tanizaki and station themselves on each side, their bayonets bristling. The third guard throws me to the floor and pins me down with the length of his body. His knife is drawn and ready to thrust deep into my throat.

Tanizaki's erection is full now. With a nod of his head, he dismisses the guards. I'm still on the floor, panting. Tanizaki gets down on his knees and enters me in one thrust. His hands grind into my belly, pushing him deeper inside.

'You please me greatly, Song Anyi,' he says.

# Chapter Thirty-One

# The Jute Bag

*Tanizaki*

He took Cho to see the heads. Kokoro had personally dispatched each traitor, severing the heads from the bodies, spiking each head on to the teeth of the stout wooden fence. Eleven heads in a row. The Chinaman's face was expressionless until Tanizaki pulled his sword out of its sheath. Then he fell to the ground and wailed like a child.

Tanizaki charged the fence. With his sword held high, he sliced the head of his lieutenant in two. The two halves tumbled to the ground, grapefruit sliced and ripe for the birds to pick. He leaped once more. Tanizaki grew ever more frenzied as the heap of skull shards grew. When he'd finished, Cho was hysterical, crying for Anyi, his mother, anyone who could save him.

'Shut up,' Tanizaki said.

Cho froze. Tanizaki smiled. Finally, the subject was pliant, just as Anyi had predicted. He considered toying with Cho a little longer but the angry buzzing of flies at the fence reminded him that time was running out.

'Sit up,' he said to Cho in a voice as thin as a needle. 'I have new instructions for you.'

Cho knelt in the dust, his body shaking.

'Your friends have declined my offer. They have offended my honour and deserve to die like those fools.'

Tanizaki spat on the pile of heads.

'But I am generous. I will give them a week to reconsider. You must find the arguments that will persuade them to agree. Don't worry, my friend, I will help you. Sometimes a message is most effective when there are fewer words.'

Tanizaki turned to Kokoro and gave the order: 'Deliver him to the home of Song Kang and the American in a manner that will impress upon them the seriousness of the situation. Just make sure he can still talk.'

### Cho

The houseboy finds the jute bag waiting on the doorstep. He finds me inside and almost pisses himself. I would laugh except they've gagged me and bound me and the blood from my wounds has dried so that now my bindings and my skin and the threads of this jute bag have become one and the same.

Max comes rushing outside. Kang runs too. They carry me into the sitting room where there's light enough to see. Kang rushes through the house carrying bandages, hot water and blankets. Max is calmer, in control.

'Let's get you comfortable first,' he says as he cuts away my clothes, trying to sound cheerful. 'No use saving any of this. You'll never be able to get the stains out. You can wear my clothes. Take your pick.'

Kang moans. He sits behind a bowl of steaming water and rinses the bloody sponge.

Max's voice grows sharp. 'If you're going to be sick, go outside.'

Kang runs. I hear him retching in the garden. When he comes back, tight-lipped, they try to straighten my legs. I scream.

When I wake again, Kang and Max are watching me. They look exhausted and afraid. I lie at their feet on a makeshift bed. I don't remember being moved. I don't remember anything except the words Kokoro told me to say.

'Tanizaki will kill us if you don't do as he asks. Anyi and Jin will be the first to die.'

'How much time do we have?' Max asks. He's making plans, picking dates, taming the chaos Tanizaki has unleashed.

'Go to the ticket office,' Max says to Kang. 'Buy whatever's available for the five of us.'

'For Cho too?' Kang asks, casting a terrified look in my direction.

Max doesn't wait to hear my answer. He's got his hat on and his face is set. 'I'm going to call in some favours.'

They leave the house without answering Tanizaki's question or bothering to wait for my reply.

'No,' I say. 'I won't go with you. My life is here.'

The houseboy stares at me from the hallway, his black eyes hostile. I have to leave, right now. If Kang won't save his sister, then I must.

I sit up. My wounds crack and ooze. The bandages have stiffened and start to smell. I peel them off as best I can, leaving the brown gauze curled on the floor.

It takes three tries to rise from my makeshift litter. More to find the silk purse Kokoro threw into the jute bag before the soldiers sealed it.

'Get me a rickshaw,' I order the houseboy.

He obeys but he won't lift a finger to help me in. Instead, he wants to know, 'Where are you going?'

'Home.'

'Where's that?' the driver asks. The rickshaw sways from side to side and stars of pain explode behind my eyes.

'Slowly, please,' I gasp.

'I'll move as slowly as a funeral procession if you'll tell me where to go.'

'To the Japanese Legation.'

*Anyi*
Kang's note is full of plans: a time, a date, a place. His writing is forceful. He no longer uses a brush, preferring instead a

273

new-fangled ballpoint pen. He keeps a row of them gleaming in the breast pocket of his suit. But he hasn't yet mastered the art of the steel nib, the effortless flow of ink. I raise the note once more to the light. Tiny cuts shine through the paper.

I knew what Tanizaki had done as soon as the note arrived. Now, would the American play his part? They're all the same, aren't they? Barbarians think they own the world and all the women in it.

I send Nian to get Jin. I roll the dice.

Jin arrives, panting. 'Has something happened? Are you all right?'

I pull her on to my bed. I lace her hand inside mine. Tell her the news the way I want her to hear it. The shock on her face reveals all. The American has said nothing to her about Tanizaki or ships or leaving China. Maybe he'll ask her but by then he'll be too late.

'He doesn't love you,' I tell the weeping Jin. 'Didn't I warn you? All barbarians leave sooner or later. China cannot be home to them.'

'Max was distracted this morning and on the telephone all last night. He said he would explain later, when there was time again to breathe.'

'What is there to explain? You belong here and he belongs in America.'

'But you said the tickets are for you and Kang too. You're all going to abandon me!'

'I won't go, if you don't,' I swear. 'But only if you promise to take care of Kang.'

'He'll stay too?'

'Do you promise?'

'Yes,' Jin whispers.

I seal her promise with a kiss. I hold her in my arms until her sobbing subsides. I murmur in her ear the things she must do and the things she must not say.

'Don't tell the American we've spoken. Share nothing I've

said with him. Swear on your life and the lives of all your children to come that you will never tell Kang what I've asked you to do.'

## Nian

The Lady was restless last night. She was up and down, rustling deep inside her closet, dragging something heavy across the bedroom floor. In the morning, she was waiting for Nian outside the kitchen door.

'Get up,' she said. 'We have work to do.'

The lockbox was so heavy. Nian could hardly budge it from its place. No rickshaw driver would be able to manage the weight. Nian went out into the street to hail a taxi.

The cab driver grumbled about coming inside, but when she showed him the silver dollar held tightly in her fist, he relented. Together they wrangled the lockbox down the steps and into the trunk of the cab. The Lady sat calmly in the backseat, hatted and dressed as if she were a glamorous dance hostess again.

'Get in,' she told Nian.

The cabbie drove them to the Carlton Café, a place Nian had heard of but never seen. The Lady, however, seemed to know her way around. She walked through the gate and into the kitchen yard where she rapped sharply on one of the windows. A door flew open and a Negro appeared.

Nian and the cab driver both spat into the dirt.

'I've never seen a black ghost before,' she whispered to him.

'This one is bigger than any I've ever seen,' he responded. He inched his way toward the driver's seat, ready to abandon Nian to her fate, when she clutched him by the front of his shirt.

'There's a lockbox in your trunk,' she reminded him.

The driver sullenly opened the trunk then scurried out of the way as the Negro reached in and lifted the lockbox as if it were a feather pillow.

'Where would suit you?' he asked the Lady.

'Over there,' she pointed. 'Underneath that tree.'

The Negro started digging a hole deep enough for a body. The Lady watched closely, fanning herself and sometimes him too. Nian grew tired and bored. It was taking a long time and soon she fell asleep, warm in the sun on the kitchen porch.

When she woke, the hole was gone and in its place a mound of freshly turned dirt. She thought their business was done but the Lady and the black ghost talked on.

'I need another favour,' the Lady said.

'Tell me,' the black ghost answered.

'I can pay you for your trouble,' she added.

He put both hands on her shoulders and leaned down. 'What kind of a friend do you think I am?'

'Come to the docks. The day after tomorrow. Kang will be there. You'll need to take him away and hide him for a few days. Then help him leave Shanghai for anywhere he wants to go as long as he stays in China.'

'How do you know he'll want to leave?'

'He'll have no choice.'

'He'll be alone?'

'Jin will go with him.'

'And where will you be?'

'I'm not going.'

'What aren't you telling me, Anyi?'

She kissed him then, on the lips. Nian was horrified. The Lady rose and dusted the dirt from her skirt. She walked to the street as Nian found a pedicab and scrambled inside.

'Come on!' she called to the Lady.

But the Lady was still looking at the black ghost, holding his hands right there in the street. Nian flushed at the shame of it all.

'Goodbye, Beauregard. My friend.'

*Anyi*

So many pages left in my journal, blank pages I'll never fill. Do I take my diary or leave it? It's all the same now.

Jin is asleep, her face shiny with tears. She wanted to spend her last night in my bed and I couldn't refuse her. Her greatest fear is being alone while mine is people, all those men whose faces crowd the mirror as I try to comb my hair.

The silk stockings are tight on my swollen legs. Kang told me exactly what kind of clothing a lady should wear on board a ship and I don't want to disappoint him. Not yet. So I'll wear the stockings and the gloves and the hat with its demure net. But the dress is my own choice, a silk the colour of buttercups. I like the way it swirls around my knees. I think it will stand out nicely in a crowd.

The bell tower sounds. The day begins at last.

# Chapter Thirty-Two

# The Yellow Dress

*Cho*

Kokoro points the way into the garden. She takes me down the dark winding path of flagstones that leads to the bathhouse. The air inside is heavy and metallic despite the ceiling fan that rotates slowly overhead.

My fingers shake. I can't get hold of my buttons so I tear the layers off. I stand there naked and vulnerable. I scream when Kokoro touches me but she looks at me with reproach, showing me the soft sponge in her hand. She soaps me tenderly, careful not to open any of my wounds.

Once I'm clean, she guides me to the raised tub. Steam rises from the water's surface. The water is never hot enough for Tanizaki. It kills me. I lower myself — foot, ankle, calf — until finally I'm in.

She pokes a hand through the murky water. 'Don't fall asleep,' she reminds me.

My body steams as I rise out of the tub and step into the blue-tiled foot basin. A bucket of cold water bites into my scalp, my eyelids, my chest. The water clatters into the footbath, only slightly tinged with fresh blood.

She dries me. She dresses my wounds. She says, 'Tanizaki will come to see you soon.'

I sleep. My dreams are frightening. Tanizaki screams at me, firing questions. What did they say? Where are they going?

When do they leave? In my dream, the blows rain down on my face and chest but when I wake, Tanizaki is sitting next to my bed, my smiling friend once more.

'Come along, Cho,' Tanizaki says. 'Let's go for a ride.'

We drive to a hillside overlooking the port of Shanghai. He places me in the shade of a tree. It's a wonderful vantage point, one I know well. I can remember a time, long ago, when Max and I sat under this very tree, chewing long blades of grass and talking of the pleasures of Shanghai. I was his teacher then. Look at me now.

One of the soldiers nudges me, waving his hand into the distance. I'd almost forgotten there was a reason for my being here, that I am the lookout on this farcical mission. As if Tanizaki wouldn't be able to find Anyi just by breathing in the air.

But I oblige. I cast my eyes in all directions, as if it were possible for them to approach the port from the open sea. Tanizaki steps out of the car to stand by my side. We both know exactly where they are.

Far below on the barren plain, they walk in single file. I can't make out their faces but it's easy to spot Anyi. Even when she's struggling across this rocky terrain, she moves with sinuous grace. They stop to let her rest. Jin fans her with her hat. Max moves ahead.

I lower the binoculars and hand them to Tanizaki.

'They're coming.'

*Kang*

They walked under the blazing sun. The land was white all around. The light ricocheted across his eyes. They were crossing the no-man's land that bordered the sea, where no one and nothing lived. Kang had thought it would be safer to enter the docks on foot and from a different direction than that used by most of the passengers.

Max had called him crazy. They would be completely exposed

279

to the heat and the keen-sighted. He had wanted to arrive in a rickshaw but there was no transportation to be found this far away from the inhabited world.

'Kang, you have to slow down,' Max called out. 'Jin can't walk this fast.'

Kang shook his head, finally accepting the truth in Max's warnings. 'We can't wait out here in the open. We'll be safer by the ships. She can rest then.'

Jin carried Anyi's valise in one hand and her own bedroll on her back. She used her walking stick to gain purchase on the rubble-strewn ground. They were hot, all of them.

'What time is it?' Anyi asked. 'Are we close yet?'

'Are you thirsty?' Jin asked, frowning at Anyi's distress. It comforted Kang immensely to know that someone else on this journey would have eyes fixed on Anyi.

'Do you think she should rest?' he asked Jin.

When she nodded, Kang scanned the horizon for somewhere that could offer them comfort. The rocks were useless, chipped into shapes too ragged to sit on. A slight hillock was the only place he could find. There, Jin opened her bedroll on the ground.

'Sit here,' she said to Anyi. 'On my lap.'

Max fidgeted. He wanted to walk on. He called to Jin, 'Come with me. You can lean on my arm if you like.'

Jin refused. She stayed close to Anyi, a squat shadow to Anyi's lithe form.

From far away, the church bells chimed. The city had disappeared behind a haze of heat though still Kang could recognise the copper peal of Moore's Methodist Church. The Shanghai Racetrack, the Custom House, the go-downs where his own office had been: he was leaving it all behind for good. Soon, he would be free.

The caws of seagulls announced that the sea was near. The outline of the docks appeared on the horizon, so many wooden piers jutting out into this elbow of the Whangpoo River. Kang could see the signs announcing the ships, their names and departure times. It had been near impossible to get tickets at such short notice. The best he had managed was a series of ocean passages, starting with a mail boat from Shanghai to Batavia. They would be the only first-class passengers on board.

'There it is,' he said. It was the smallest steamship at the docks with a black funnel and the red, white and blue flag of the Netherlands.

'Let me go ahead,' Max said. 'I'll secure our places on board. Give me the tickets, Kang, so they'll let me up the gangplank.'

Anyi set off after Max, leaving behind her valise. Kang picked up the small bag, calling in vain to his sister. He was about to break into a run when he heard Jin cry out. Kang turned to find her writhing, still on the ground.

'What's the matter?' he asked.

'Water,' she croaked. 'I need something to drink.'

Kang tugged impatiently at the thermos strapped to Anyi's valise. He offered its contents to Jin but she pushed it away. 'You drink first. You must be thirsty too.'

'Stop playing games!' he cried. 'Don't you understand? We have to get on board the ship. Look, Anyi is almost there. Hurry up!'

He tried to pull her to her feet. He tried to carry her on his back. With each attempt, she slid to the ground, her strength leaking into the dust along with her tears.

'Anyi!' Kang yelled. He could no longer see her yellow dress in the crowd milling about the dock.

He had no choice but to leave Jin behind. But before he could, he felt a strange lightness in the back of his leg. He looked down to find his right trouser leg slashed open and his calf streaked in vermilion red. Confused, he looked to Jin for an explanation. She was staring at her hands stained the same colour as his leg.

His leg buckled. His head struck a stone. He knew no more.

*Tanizaki*

The view from the hill was perfect. He could see the dock below, as wide and busy as Nanking Road. He could hear the ships as they knocked and strained against their guy ropes. The American was already on board, one hand shading his eyes. He waved wildly at the others, who were probably still approaching the dock.

He lowered the binoculars and rubbed his eyes with the back of his hand. He had worked frantically, trying to verify the information Cho had brought. Kokoro had confirmed that the American and Kang had abandoned their house. Cho said they were headed to the United States but Tanizaki could find no ships leaving for any American port.

Tanizaki had agonised through the night. He had no facts to rely on other than what Cho had told him. Would the ambassador fault Tanizaki for wasting manpower on such weak intelligence? Or tear him to pieces because Tanizaki had been afraid to act?

He raised the binoculars once more, this time carefully scanning through the rubble of the no-man's land. It was slow tedious work and his eyes burned. The American was accounted for. Where were the rest?

Then he saw them, the brother and the servant. The woman was bent over Kang, who was on the ground for some reason. No matter. They were sitting ducks.

Tanizaki motioned to his men, waiting silently in formation at the base of the hill. He sent two of them to guard Kang.

'Keep your distance,' Tanizaki told them. 'Do nothing until you hear my signal. Then seize the Chinaman. Remember, I want him alive.'

To the other soldiers, he said, 'Come with me.'

*Anyi*

I feel like a child, running like the wind, skipping over stones, hurtling past other travellers, all my burdens left behind. There's nothing to keep me on this earth except for this one last thing I must do.

Kang will be thankful some day. He and Jin will marry and soon there will be children to carry on the Song name. He'll be an ancestor, beloved and revered and thoroughly Chinese.

The boat waits ahead and on it is the American who must be sent away. He waves, beckoning me to his side. I turn my back on him, once and for all. I see a line of black cars hurtling down a nearby hill. The cars pay no heed to the road or anyone on it. They crash through fences, scatter the coolies, cause panic long before anyone recognises the flags that whip from the car bonnet. Tanizaki is here.

I turn to take one last look at my beloved brother, down on the ground just as Jin and I had planned. Beauregard stands over the new couple, as if giving his blessing. He raises one large hand towards the sky.

It's time.


*Kang*

'What did you do?' the Negro shouted.

Kang startled into consciousness. He was on the ground, a cloth wrapped around his head and another on his leg. He blinked but the image of the black man would not go away. Then he heard Jin's voice.

'He was supposed to drink from my thermos. He was supposed to fall asleep.'

She started to scream, hysterical, out of control. The big man leaned down and slapped her hard across the face. 'Get a hold of yourself! Tell me what you did.'

Jin held out her knife. 'I cut a tendon. Like on a chicken to soften the meat.'

The black man fell to his knees in front of Kang. 'You still with us, Kang? Can you hear me? It's Beauregard from the Carlton Café.'

'Anyi.' It was all Kang could manage.

'Yes, I know,' Beauregard said. 'She sent me to help you. Come along now.'

Beauregard hauled Kang up and threw him over his shoulder. They started off, away from the dock, Jin scurrying behind, sending pebbles skittering in all directions.

'Where are we going?' she asked him, panting.

'Some place where we can hide. But first we'll have to deal with them.'

He nodded in the direction of the two Japanese soldiers barring their path.


*Cho*

The cars stop at the foot of the gangplank. Nine soldiers emerge, each with his bayonet drawn. The lieutenant barks and the soldiers fan into a perfect half-circle, their backs to the sea, their guns shining in the harsh sunlight. Now no one can get either on or off the ship. Yet the crowd doesn't move. Why don't they leave while they still can?

I can't. Tanizaki needs no chains for me. He knows I want to be here. Wouldn't miss it for the world.

He rolls down his window. The lieutenant leaves his men and rushes to our car, ready to take his orders.

'How good do you think my lieutenant's aim is?' Tanizaki asks me. 'Do you think he could kill the American with one shot?'

I lean out of my window. I can see Max clearly. If I say no, Tanizaki might decide to prove his point.

'Of course your man could kill Max, if that's what you command.'

Tanizaki frowns. 'You used to have more spunk. I don't like yes men.'

'I'm a gambler, not a fool. I don't like the odds on this bet.'

'Fair enough. Let's make a different wager. Why do you suppose I've brought you here?'

'To keep me out of the way?'

'It would have been easier to shoot you. Two more guesses.'

284

'To make me watch what happens.'

'Wrong again. Last guess.'

I close my eyes. I'm tired of this game. 'I don't know,' I say. 'Get out of the car!'

As soon as Tanizaki steps out, his soldiers move closer to him, left and right, so that we are now one circle of death, heavy and sharp, hinged to his will alone.

'Song Anyi!' Tanizaki bellows.

Slowly, a yellow dress slips through the crowd and comes closer. The skirt whispers around her knees. It says to the crowd: Hush. Now is my time.

Anyi stands on the dock. The crowd trembles behind her and the soldiers stare her down. It hurts to look at her. She's so bright.

She smiles at me, 'Cousin, how nice to see you here.'

The sun burns through the bandages on my head. Something damp trickles down my temple. I wipe my face. There's blood on my hands.

Anyi is laughing. It's a sound I had almost forgotten, a sound I was afraid I would never hear again. It pierces my ear. I cover it with one hand and find more blood.

Anyi and Tanizaki greet each other as if this were a summer day like any other. Then Tanizaki strikes her hard across the face. I run to her side, place my body between his and hers. 'Don't hurt her!'

The sound of my own voice reverberates in my head, sending a pain deep into the base of my neck. Tanizaki's face contorts with rage.

'Get out of the way,' he seethes.

'Please let her go,' I beg.

His fist slams into my face. Colour explodes across my eyes. I spin. With nothing and no one to break my fall, I land face down on the ground. I feel dirt and small stones embedded in my forehead and pain everywhere. But I must get up. I must save Anyi.

The feet of the crowd begin to shuffle and stumble, finally alive to the danger. The dust churns and seeps into my mouth, choking my words.

An order ricochets through the crowd, 'Shuriken!'

The soldiers break formation. Their heavy boots rush to circle Tanizaki, their rifles bristling outward, their backs to him, Tanizaki caught inside the tight circle of men.

He's not happy. He's shouting at them. 'I didn't give the order. Get out of my way. Go back to your positions. Now!'

Then another order barrels out. I can see his face. I can hear the words even though his lips never move. He's staring behind me at something both great and terrible.

It's Anyi. Her mouth opens and his voice rolls out.

'The prisoner is escaping!' she cries. 'Shoot her!'

*Tanizaki*

She had tricked him, manipulated him every step of the way. He stared down at her broken body. The soft indents, where metal had met flesh, were filling with blood. She writhed in agony and Tanizaki could hear the delicate crackle of her ribs. She was still alive, though not for long. Even now, broken as she was, his body ached for hers.

She should have been the bait, the final lever that he could push if Kang and the American refused to do his bidding. But he hadn't been ready to sacrifice her yet so he had brought Cho instead.

Tanizaki walked back to the line of soldiers. The two who should have been guarding Kang had run pell-mell to join their comrades when they heard the order, Shuriken. Fools! He would deal with them later. For now he had more urgent business.

'Give me your bayonet,' he said.

The weapon felt light in his hands. The blade glinted in the sun. He walked slowly and steadily back to Anyi, stopping just outside the pool of blood, unwilling to stain his own clean feet before it was time. He thought of all the pleasure she had given

286

him, the heights to which they still could have gone. She was fading, but the fire in her had not yet gone out. He had so looked forward to snuffing it out himself. What an ungodly release that would be.

Tanizaki lunged. He roared like a beast. He buried the bayonet in her belly, all the way to the hilt. He experienced one last time the ecstasy of blood spraying on his hands, his shoulders and his smiling face.

Cho screamed. He crawled to Anyi's side, through her pooling blood. He used his hands to push away that river of red.

Tanizaki sighed. The Chinaman had lost his mind. He was useless now. Tanizaki dropped the bayonet and unsheathed his sword.

'Sit up,' he said.

The Chinaman struggled upright. He was fouling himself. The stench was extinguishing the sweetness of the blood. Tanizaki lost all patience then.

'Anyi is yours now,' he said.

Tanizaki raised the sword high. Each muscle in his body was perfectly coordinated, the blade and the arm a single mighty weapon. It was a musical sound: the swoop of sharp metal through the air, the vibration of the steel as it passed through flesh and bone. Cho's head a drumroll in the dirt.

# Acknowledgments

There are times when you know you are loved and writing a book is one of them. No words can express my gratitude for all the help I've been given. Yet I must try to give credit where credit is due.

To my very first readers, when this novel was little more than a twinkling in my eye: Geert van der Kolk, Jim Kirkland, Lucia Paz Hernandez and especially Dee Ann Fujioka.

To the members of my critique groups, the Pub Scrawlers and Write Club, intrepid writers and critics, one and all.

To Monica Bremer who held my hand and Lynn Michell editor extraordinaire.

Above all, to the three men in my life who love me and let me love them in return.

Lightning Source UK Ltd.
Milton Keynes UK
UKOW05f2208160317
296779UK00001B/40/P